THE DARKNESS *that* FOLLOWS US

Copyright © 2024 by Lana Vargas

All rights reserved.

No part of this book may be reproduced, distributed, or transmitted in any form or by any means, including photocopying, recording, or other electronic or mechanical methods, without the prior written permission of the publisher, except in the case of brief quotations embodied in reviews and certain other non-commercial uses permitted by copyright law.

Any resemblance to actual events, locales, organizations, or persons living or dead, is entirely coincidental.

First Edition, Paperback. April 2024. United States

ISBN: 979-8-9901048-0-8

Editor: Alexa Thomas

Formattor: Grace Elena

Cover Designer: Silver Grace - Ever After Cover Design

❀ Created with Vellum

"Someone I loved once gave me a box full of darkness. It took me years to understand that this too, was a gift."
Mary Oliver

Playlist

Video Games — Lana Del Rey
I Wanna Be Yours — Arctic Monkeys
Here With Me — D4VD
Angeleyes — ABBA
Hits Different — Taylor Swift
Different Lives — Fly by Midnight
Call It What You Want — Taylor Swift
To Build A Home — Patrick Watson
Heaven — Niall Horan
Till Forever Falls Apart — Ashe, Finneas
Fall in Love with You — Monte Fish
Bad for Business — Sabrina Carpenter
POV — Ariana Grande
Look After You — The Fray
Fix You — Coldplay
I Don't Want To Miss A Thing — Aerosmith

Content Warnings

This book will touch on sensitive subjects such as:
   Coping with mental health issues (Anxiety, Depression, PTSD), grief, mourning, addiction, substance usage (pills), and a *brief* mention of domestic violence. Please only read if you're comfortable.

Disclaimer

While this book can be read as a standalone, it takes place a month after my debut novel, Summer in Phoenix. There are spoilers for that book mentioned in this story. Happy reading!

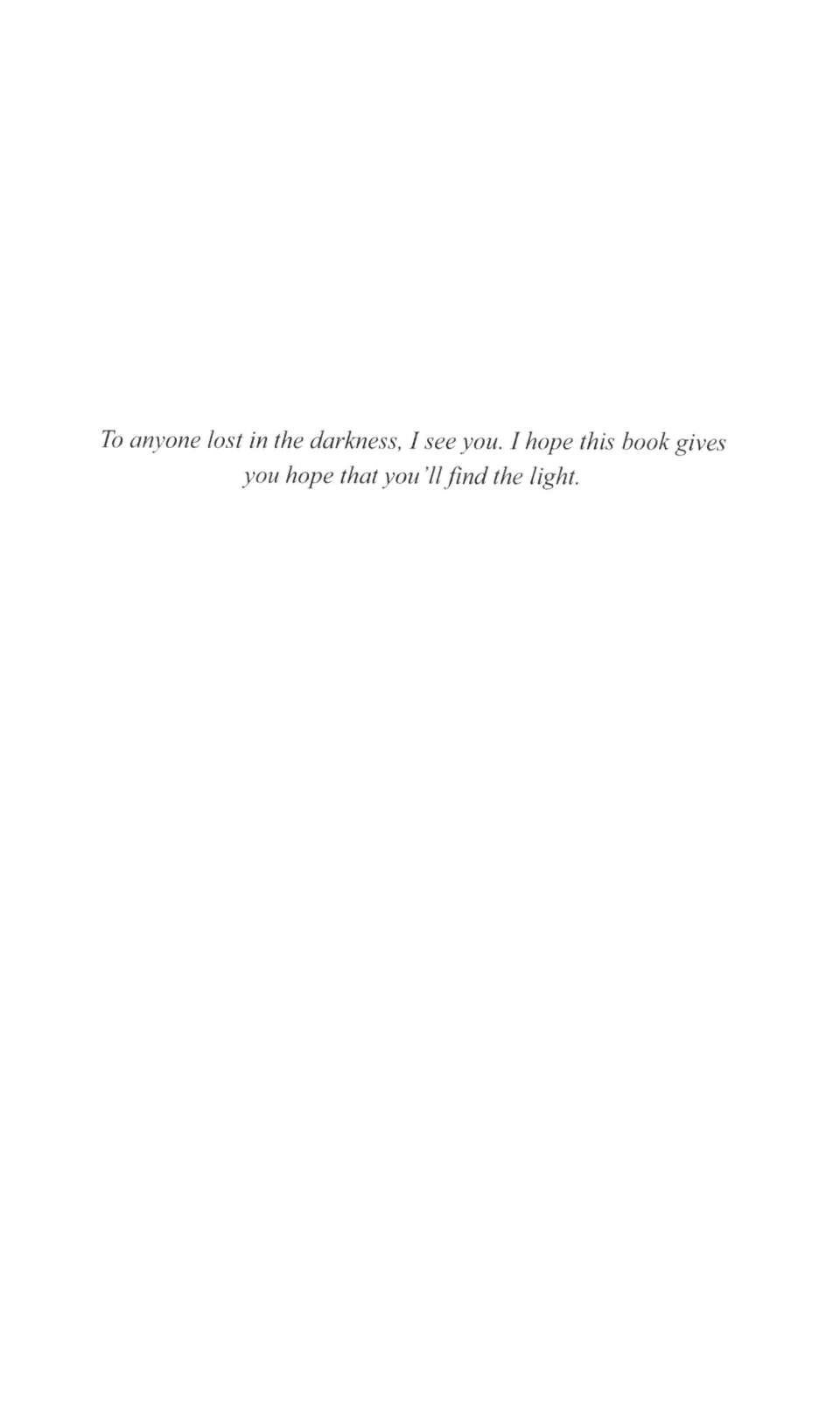

To anyone lost in the darkness, I see you. I hope this book gives you hope that you'll find the light.

Prologue
KAT

Family Line - Conan Gray

7 YEARS AGO

I'VE BECOME WELL ACQUAINTED WITH NOT ONLY THE PITCH-black darkness of my room, but also waking up to the sounds of my parents screaming mindlessly at each other until they're too tired to yell anymore.

Every night, I lie awake, just imagining how different my life would be if I was born into a family that cared about me, not where they're going to get their next fix. I don't pity myself, but having to learn how to administer Narcan at the age of seven after finding my parents passed out isn't a life I would have wished for. I'd be lying if I said that image of them doesn't still haunt me eight years later.

I have to thank them for one thing, though—because of them I know exactly who I *don't* want to be.

"I'm done, Chris!" I can hear Mom shouting from the living room even over the music blaring on my headphones.

Music is the only thing that keeps me sane, but at night,

when all the yelling stops, I bask in the silence. It's comforting to me. It's better than the alternative.

"You say that every time and you always come back." I don't miss the slurring of dads' words as he shouts back. He's either high or drunk, but my money is on both.

I slowly creep out of bed, putting my ear up against the door to listen in on them. I try and be very quiet, because if they find out I'm eavesdropping, I'll be on the receiving end of his wrath too.

"Not this time. You're never putting your hands on me ever again!" Mom shouts it loud enough that I'm sure the neighbors heard. I hate that I'm used to hearing her get slapped around by my dad, but I hate even more that by tomorrow morning, she'll act as if nothing happened. I narrowed it down to two reasons: she's either too high to care, or she's too scared to leave him. My guess is the latter.

"Fine! Then take your worthless daughter with you on your way out." he shouts, disgust in his tone. His hateful descriptions used to hurt, but after hearing them so many times, they just became muff-led words.

Footsteps approaching my door catch my attention. I dart to my bed, hiding under the covers, hoping they don't suspect I've been listening this whole time. My doorknob rattles, and then I hear mom's voice on the other side as she tries to push it open past the chair I keep propped up under the knob.

Her voice sounds weak, which is the only reason I get up to open it. "What's wrong, Mom?" I ask, trying to pull off a groggy voice to make it seem like I just woke up.

I stand in the doorway with my arms folded across my chest defensively, staring at her bloodshot eyes and smeared makeup.

I can't help but resent her in these moments. I resent her for choosing drugs over me, for staying with my dad all this time and dragging us both down in the process. Most of all, though, I resent her for never wanting to get clean.

She was once so beautiful, you couldn't help but look at her, but over time, those features started to fade from the drugs. Her dry blonde hair has knots as if it hasn't been brushed in weeks, her face sunken in and covered in red patches. The only feature that's still hers are the emerald-green eyes that she passed down to me. Right now, though, the bags under those eyes are so dark, they almost hide the fresh black ring forming.

"I'm leaving, Kat," she says, barging past me.

Wait what? Usually after they fight, she locks herself in the room while Dad passes out on the couch, and then everything is back to "normal". Nausea goes straight to my gut. She paces my room, picking at her finger nails frantically before sitting down on my bed.

"What's going on?"

"I can't be here anymore, Kat. I have to leave."

There she goes again with the *I* and not *we. Please don't leave me here with him.* I look at her with pleading eyes, hoping she can somehow read my thoughts. Who am I kidding? She wouldn't know what I was thinking even if I wrote it down for her. *I can't stay here with my dad, I just can't.*

"I can go with you. I have some cash lying around, we can stay at a motel until we find somewhere permanent."

I've saved every dollar I've gotten from babysitting since I was thirteen, hoping that by the time I'm eighteen, it would be enough to get the hell out of here.

"No. I have to go by myself, but once I'm settled, I'll come and get you." I feel the vomit wanting to surge up my throat, but I push it down.

"Please, let me go too." My eyes glisten with tears as I plead with her.

"Three days tops, and you'll be with me." She places a cold, boney hand on my cheek, but it doesn't comfort me in the way that a mom's touch is supposed to.

She gets up from the bed and walks out of my room quickly,

with nothing but a blank stare in my direction. I guess I can survive three days with Dad. I'll just lock myself in my room until I have to go to school or eat. *Three days, and it'll be over.* Maybe now, Mom will have a chance at getting clean, and be the Mom I've always wanted her to be.

I hear her rifling through her room, collecting her things. Dad stays seated in the chair, a baseball game blares in the background. A deadly stare is aimed right at Mom. It send chills up my spine when I catch a glimpse of it.

She takes one last, longing look at me before walking towards the door. Something comes over me as I run after her, forgetting to put shoes on.

She's already loading her stuff into the trunk of a car when I get outside. The cold air hits me like a ton of bricks, but I stay put on the front steps, staring blankly as she tosses her stuff in at lightning speed. I don't recognize the man in the driver's seat, but the devilish smirk he's throwing in my direction makes me want to vomit.

"Three days, Kat, and I'll be back for you," she yells before crawling into the passenger seat of the stranger's car. Why do I have this weird feeling this is the last time I'm going to see her?

Dust flies everywhere as the car peels away, taking my mom with it. "Please, come back," I whisper into the darkness.

September

PRESENT

CHAPTER 1
Andrew

This is Me Trying - Taylor Swift

MOM SCREAMING. ELLIOT'S DISTRAUGHT LOOK. BLOODY KNUCKLES.

I startle awake, drenched in sweat, just like I have every day for the past month. *That fucking night.* It haunts me like a ghost that has attached itself to my soul. I thought that after six years, I wouldn't possibly be able to recall my mom's bloodcurdling screams, or have my little brother's frozen stare still seared into my brain, but it's as if those horrid memories stored themselves in the back of my mind, just waiting for their moment to make an appearance.

That night was nothing but a shitty memory I thought of from time to time—until recently.

According to my doctor, my brother's death might have trigg-ered some past trauma, as if I didn't already have enough shit going on in my head. I miss the person I was a month ago. It feels like the day we buried my brother, a part of me went with him—the good part, at least.

Elliot was the best person I knew. I would have traded places with him in a heartbeat just so the world would get to experience him. He beat cancer when he was fifteen, but it came back with vengeance and took him from us at nineteen. The house feels vacant, all of our voices suddenly echoing in his absence. Some say it's easier to grieve someone when you see it coming, but I say that's bullshit.

I check my phone to find messages from friends, but just as I have every other day, I ignore them. I haven't left the house in weeks. My best friends came to check on me a few times, but being around anyone suddenly feels like a chore. It's as if there's a mask I have to put on now so no one can see how I'm really feeling. If you always look happy, people automatically assume you are, so that's what I pretend to be.

The pills help, I suppose. Two months ago, I was put on Xanax. I used to take them just to sleep, but since Elliot's passing, I find myself reaching for them throughout the day to get through the razor-sharp pain that has become my new normal. I guess my body has built up a tolerance, because in order to get the effect I want, I have to double the recommended dose.

I reach into the top drawer of my desk and find the almost-empty bottle that no one knows exists, but before I can uncap it, a knock on my door sends me into a panicked scatter. I shove it back into its hiding spot before opening the door for my mom.

"What's up?" I ask, slightly out of breath. She looks at me skeptically from the other side of the door, and I'm suddenly aware I'm still covered in sweat.

"Don't say what's up to your mom." She walks in and smacks me playfully on top of my head.

She and I have always had a good relationship. We're not as close as we used to be before Elliot died, but that's all on me. She's still one of my favorite people, though. Her sunny disposition has a way of rubbing off on people, and she's always been able to peel back the bullshit and see the good in people. It's her greatest attribute, but also her biggest flaw.

"Sorry, Ma." I say, rubbing the back of my head with a hint

of a smile. I walk over to stand in front of my desk since she has a habit of snooping.

"I'll let it slide this one time." She grins at me, but it slowly fades into a frown. "I actually came in here because I wanted to talk to you about something." All the air gets sucked up out of the room as I dreadfully wait for her to speak.

"I'm worried about you, mijo. Ever since..." She chokes on the words but continues with a brave face. "Ever since Elliot died, I hardly see you, and when I do, you're a million miles away. I'm not expecting you to be your old self tomorrow..."

I wish.

"I just don't want to see you dig yourself into a hole you can't get out of." I nod my head, but don't say a word as we sit in silence. What she doesn't know is that I avoid my parents because they seem to be handing Elliot's death *a lot* better than me. They went back to work a week after the funeral, and I haven't seen them cry once, while I can't even go a day without taking a pill.

"I'm fine, Ma." I try my best to make her believe me, but the doubtful look on her face says otherwise—like I said, she can see through anyone's bullshit.

"I get it if you don't want to talk to us; I just wish you would talk to *someone*." She runs her long, painted fingernails through my messy hair.

I squeeze her hand and present the fake smile I've mastered over the past month. "Seriously, I'm okay."

"What about the girl who was with Emory at the funeral? You practically stopped breathing every time she walked by." She asks, trying to hide a smile.

"Honestly, I don't know." I say dismissively. I haven't talked to Kat in weeks. She said her condolences to me at the funeral, but that was it. If I wasn't so numb that day, I would have said I'm sorry instead of just *thank you.*

I have a rule when it comes to girls—no second dates. It's a rule that's helped me avoid relationships. Usually, I'm upfront about it to avoid conflict, but when I met Kat, she was different.

So different, I broke my rule.

I started to like being around her, but that scared the shit out of me, so I started avoiding her. I expected her to be mad, but I didn't expect for me to feel remorse. I called her weeks later to try and be friends at least—I even told her about Elliot being sick—but she shot me down.

Because she's Kat, she was there for me when my brother was admitted to the hospital, but since then—silence.

Typically, I'd be relieved if a girl didn't want to speak to me again, but with her, it's oddly unsettling.

"What'd you do?" Mom asks, narrowing her eyes. It must've been a strong gene, because me and my brother got the exact shade of rich brown eyes as her.

"Why do you assume I did something?"

She chuckles and nudges my shoulder. "Because you're my son, and I know how you are." I try to summon a smile, but it comes up short. I know she notices, but like most things nowadays, we don't acknowledge it.

"Anyway, what do you have planned for today?" She gathers my dirty shirts scattered on the floor, which I find off because she hasn't done my laundry since I was a kid.

I have every intention of staying in bed, avoiding the world like I do every day, but if she knew that, she would try to convince me otherwise, so I lie. "Probably see what Chance and Hiro are doing—they've been bugging me to come out."

"Well, be careful. I'm working an extra shift, so fix yourself something for dinner, okay?" She kisses the top of my head before closing the door behind her. It's supposed to be her day off, but she's been picking up extra shifts—same with Dad. As soon as she leaves, her words echo through my head. *Because you're my son and I know how you are.*

I know I'll have to face Kat soon, I just can't yet. I can't face anyone. Besides, her face when she last saw me still burns in my mind. It was a mix of empathy and disappointment, and I don't know which one is worse.

I reach for the bottle again and shake the pills out. They feel like steel weights pulling me to the ground as they rest in my hands. I wish I could be a different person, someone who could go a day with-out a gaping hole in their chest, and didn't need pills to endure that pain, but I'm not.

The sooner I face reality, the better off I am.

CHAPTER 2

Kat

Summer Child - Conan Gray

You don't know hell until you work an eight-hour shift serving drunk people at the local bar. You'd think after three years I still wouldn't dread it, but I do. My body feels like hefty weights are dragging me down as I quietly make my way inside my house, trying not to wake up Grams since it's after one a.m.

The familiar scent of apple and cinnamon fills my nose when I step into the living room that holds all my good memories. Grams likes to leave the lamp on so I can see where I'm stepping when I get in late, so I click it off and go into the kitchen.

Bills scatter across the granite countertop, but I walk past them like they don't exist. I don't have to open them to know that they all say PAST DUE in bold red letters. Money has been tight since Grams had her stroke.

Thankfully, I started a teaching position a few weeks ago, but I also had to keep my job at the bar to keep us afloat. It's been a rough adjustments juggling both jobs, to say the least.

My stomach is rumbling with hunger, but my need for sleep is overpowering my need for food. I have to teach second graders in the morning, so I need every second of shut eye I can get.

As I make my way down the hallway, I peek my head into Gram's room, and let a soft smile cover my face when I see her sound asleep. I start to shut her door, but she startles awake when it creaks loudly.

Her fragile voice calls out to me, "Is that you lovey?"

"Yeah, it's me." I try to hide the exhaustion lacing in my voice.

"Come here so I can see your face. I haven't seen you all day." All I want to do is melt into my bed, but I can never say no to her. She runs her slender fingers across my cheek with a radiant smile when I join her on the bed. Over the years, her hair has grayed and wrinkles have appeared on her delicate face, but her smile has always been the same.

"How was your day?" I ask, finally letting my hair out of the messy ponytail it's been in all day.

"Better now that you're here," she murmurs.

Her ocean blue eyes pierce into mine, and I'm reminded how much I wish I got them over the green ones I share with my mom.

"I missed you too, Grams."

Between both jobs I'm gone the entire day. I was able to hire a nurse who stays with her while I'm gone, but I wish I was able to do that for her.

"You work so hard, lovey. Don't forget to rest." Her nickname for me warms my heart. I'm not even sure what lovey means, but it's what she's called me since I was a kid. I kiss the top of her head and tuck her under the blankets.

"I will. Get some sleep now." She drifts back to sleep seconds after, as if she was waiting for my permission. I worry about her more since we lost my grandpa six months ago—she had her first stroke a week after his funeral. She's all I have, and if tirelessly working two jobs is what I have to do to care for her, then so be it.

I enter my room, and let my body sink into the mattress. I'm in need of a shower, but my body is glued to my bed. I'm startled by my cat, Sage who's now looking at me with waiting eyes.

"How selfish of me to forget your treat," I say, reaching into the jar on my desk. I never pictured myself with a pet, much less a black cat, but I just found him hiding under my car one day. Looking back now, I probably needed him more than he needed me.

I put my headphones in and start to fall asleep to my 80s playlist, just as I do every night. It's almost two a.m., which means I have to be up in four hours to do all of this over again. I'm accustom to my chaotic routine, but every night I lie awake, hoping it won't always be like this.

I guess I'm just waiting for the moment where something comes along and changes everything.

CHAPTER 3
Andrew

Echo - Jason Walker

I STAY PARKED IN FRONT OF THE GYM, FROZEN AND UNABLE TO go inside. I don't want to be here, but with my mom home, I needed any excuse to leave the house so she won't check on me every five minutes.

It's my first time back here in weeks. It used to be my favorite place when I needed a break from everything, but now, it's another place full of people who are going to pity me. It nauseates me that to them, I'm not Andrew anymore: I'm the guy that just lost his brother.

I try to settle my uneasiness by running my hands along the leather steering wheel. I have a love hate relationship with this truck. Elliot worked on it day and night to get it working last summer. It was left to me after he died, and the air in here feels heavy every time I drive. In a weird way, I find it comforting, it reminds me that I'm not completely deprived of emotion.

I look over at my gym bag, my pill bottle laying temptingly on top. There's always a little voice in my head every time I look at it. *One pill won't hurt. The day would be easier to bare.*

Another voice follows. *You don't need it. Don't let it win.* Sometimes, I swear, that voice sounds like Elliot's. I inhale deep breaths through my nose and exhale through my mouth, trying to summon a sliver of good that I think is still in me, until my hand no longer itches to reach for the bottle.

I finally gain the courage to walk inside of the gym, and I'm immediately overwhelmed with the smell of sweat and cologne. Most of the guys here train to box professionally one day, so punching bags and rings for practice matches fill most of the space, the rest taken up by weights and exercise equipment for people who come just to work out.

"Cortes!" Rafael's booming voice calls me over.

He's standing tall, watching closely at the drill going on in the ring, just as he always does to give pointers. He fought pro until a bad fight caused partial blindness in his left eye. This gym was opened shortly after.

We've become close since I started coming here years ago. He came to my football games in high school, my graduation, and even used to keep the gym open after hours in case I needed to blow off steam.

"What's up, Ralphie?" *Act happy*, I repeat in my mind as I approach him.

"What'd I tell you about calling me that? I'll revoke your membership," he threatens me, but I don't take it seriously—he's said that a hundred times before.

"You don't even charge me for a membership."

His smile ripples as he brings me into a tight hug. "Good to see you, kid." My chest constricts when he starts to pull me farther away from people. "Okay, now, don't bullshit me. How are you?" he asks with a tight grip on my shoulder. I tower over him in height, but he still intimidates the hell out of me.

"I'm good. I'm here, aren't I?" He pierces me with his gray eyes, but I don't falter.

"You can pull that crap with other people, but not me, Cortes.

If you don't wanna talk that's fine. Just come to me if you ever do, got it?" he nudges his head in the direction of my friends, and I walk away, but not before taking a final glance back at him.

I catch sight of Chance's dirty blonde hair first, then Hiro's prominent stature. I knew they'd be here because it's Saturday, the only day they both don't work. They look stunned to see me, but also relieved.

"Look who finally decided to show up." I'm greeted by Chance's familiar sarcasm as he wraps tape around his hand, Hiro is too busy putting his bag away to add to the conversation.

I've known them both for six years, since our junior year of high school. I was the new kid when I moved to Phoenix from Los Angeles, so they took me under their wing.

Each of us serves a purpose in our small friend group. Chance is the smart, reliable one you go to for advice because he's not afraid to call you out on your bullshit. He was supposed to go to Harvard like his parents but changed his mind last minute. Everyone judged him for it, but I've always admired his inability to give a shit.

Hiro is the funny, slightly irresponsible friend, the one you go to if you need a good laugh or to do something stupid. He moved here from the Philippines when he was ten, so he always has a story of his life back home.

I used to be a balance of both of their traits, but now, I'm not sure what I bring to the group.

"What'd I miss?" I ask, letting my gym bag fall to the ground.

"Chance has been a human punching bag for Mateo since you've been gone." Hiro says, trying to hide his satisfaction.

Mateo is probably the only one here who could go pro. No one wants to run drills with him, though, because he's well over six foot and two-hundred pounds of muscle, so it feels like you've been hit by a fucking train the next day.

By now, Chance would usually say something sly back at

Hiro, but I notice his grim expression out of the corner of my eye.

"Hey Cortes." One of the gym regulars stops to greet me with awkward body language, as if the words 'I'm sorry for your loss' are on the tip of his tongue. *Don't say it. Don't say it,* I repeat in my head.

The tightening of my chest suddenly greets me, reminding me my anxiety has the control, instead of the other way around. I try to inhale deep breaths, but the air filling my chest is shockingly cold. I ignore the stinging pain and push the words out.

"Hey, Dylan." My skin is crawling, but I swallow the feeling down along with the nausea when he walks away.

"Why are you so quiet?" I ask Chance, whose silence is more eerie than other people's pity.

He tries to hide an angry frown under his furrowed brows.

"I'm not quiet, D." I see right through his unconvincing smirk. He's usually not the type to keep shit in, so whatever it is can't be good. I used to be a good friend, the kind who would try to lift his friends up when they needed it.

Maybe I can try to be *that* guy again.

I nudge toward the heavy punching bags dangling from the ceiling by thick chains. "Hold the bag for me?" I ask.

"Fine, but don't *accidentally* miss the bag. You almost gave me a fucking concussion last time." I try to hide a wide grin: it really was an accident, but that doesn't mean it wasn't enjoyable.

We both take our stances—him holding the bag full of sand with both arms, me in front of it with my gloves on. A fiery sting shoots up my arm at the first impact, but it becomes comforting after the third and fourth hits.

"Are you ready to tell me what's actually wrong?"

"I don't know what you're talking about, D." He's the only person who calls me D. Most people call me Drew, or even by my last name, Cortes. I roll my eyes at his stubbornness and walk over to the other side of the bag. "Switch me."

Maybe by getting his anger out, he'll fess up. I've been a shitty friend lately, but I can still tell when something is up. Neither of them are experts at hiding their true feelings like I am.

Anger lights up his eyes as soon as he starts to hit the bag.

"Cut the shit, Barrett, and tell me what's wrong," I bite out as I try to keep steady. It's natural for me to call him by his last name instead of his first. He stops abruptly, out of breath from his rage fit and gives me a broken look.

"Izzy cheated on me." I don't try to hide my shock. Him and Izzy met sophomore year of high school, and he's been disgustingly in love with her ever since. The concept of relationships is off-putting to me, but I thought for sure if any one would make it, it was them.

I hesitate to ask. "How'd you find out?" His jaw ticks before he answers, as if the words are fighting him to come out.

"The guy texted while she was in the shower. They've been meeting up every week when I thought she was at work." His face is full of rage, but his voice sounds defeated and crushed. I don't know what to say to him; I've never experienced heart break. Giving some-one this much power over your heart sounds fucking miserable.

"What's gonna happen now?"

His tired eyes water as he shakes his head. "All I know is that she's packing all her stuff, and I came here so I didn't have to watch." He walks away to sink onto the nearby bench and throws his gloves to the ground.

"I know you think Izzy is the only girl in the entire world, but she's not, Barrett. This is your opportunity to be free, to do whatever you want." I pat him on the back, but he scoffs at my shitty attempt at a pep talk.

"Not everyone wants to date a new girl every weekend like you, D."

"It beats moping around like a lost goddamn puppy." He fails at holding back laughter. At least I can make someone laugh; I wish I could do that for myself from time to time.

He nudges me on my shoulder, "I can't wait for the day you fall in love so I can throw it in your face."

For the first time in awhile, my chest rattles with laughter. "I wouldn't hold your breath."

Hiro comes rushing towards us, drenched in sweat. "Fuck this. Can we get beers instead?" His face is bright red as he hunches over, trying to catch his breath. It's only been twenty minutes, but you would think he's been working out for hours.

"It's barely noon." I say with distaste.

"So? Our friend is in distress, Drew." He gestures to Chance, who looks like he's actually considering it. A bar is the last place I want to be, so I'm hoping he isn't.

"Fuck it, let's go." His strides have more purpose than before, and Hiro silently celebrates.

"Which bar?" he asks. *Don't say Sam's. Don't say Sam's.*

"We haven't been to Sam's in awhile."

Fuck me. Out of all the bars in Phoenix, they choose the one where Kat works. I almost bail—I've had enough socializing for one day anyway, but someone needs to keep them both in check. Who knows, maybe she's not working today?

"I'll meet you guys there. I need to change." I didn't bring extra clothes since I wasn't planning on going out afterwards.

I take long strides across the lot towards my truck. The more I think of being in a bar, the more the nerves take over my body. It took me weeks to build up the courage to come to the gym, much less a bar where everyone knows me, and also knew my brother. I don't know if I'm ready. Everything is happening too fast. I gave myself too much credit, thinking I was ready to leave the house. *Fuck it.*

There's only one way I'm going to get through it.

I scramble through my bag, thinking of nothing but the bottle that holds the key to my sanity. No one would even notice if I took just one. It'll do the job. I don't feel the full effects unless I take two or more anyway.

Don't do it. The voice that sounds like my brother's echoes in my head again.

"I'm sorry, Elliot." I say, before swallowing the white tablet down dry. I wait for relief to roll through my body, listing off things that'll calm me.

Working on the truck with Elliot. Lake days with him and Mom. Senior year with Chance and Hiro. Long brunette hair. Green eyes.

My eyes spring open at the image of Kat. *What the fuck?* It's not the first time she's invaded my mind, but it's the first time like this. What freaks me out the most isn't the fact that I thought of her—it's that as soon as I did, all the other bullshit disappeared entirely.

CHAPTER 4

Kat

"The new girls can't keep up, Sam." I walk over to my boss and throw my notepad down. I usually don't mind training new hires, but after teaching second graders all day, my patience is thin.

"Is it training the new girls, or the fact that Emory isn't here anymore that's bothering you?" His gray mustache furrows with amusement.

Emory is my best friend—probably my only friend. She and I bonded pretty quickly when she worked at the bar last summer. You could say she's the dark cloud that rains over my sunshine, but we balance each other out. She's in San Diego now, going to college to be a nurse.

She's how I met Andrew, since they're practically family. I remember that day vividly—his ruggedly handsome face and broad frame that demands attention caught my eye the first time I saw him, but I was always too chicken to go up to him.

Then, when I finally met him, he was nice, and nice guys are hard to come by. Obviously, I found out that it's just part of his act.

After he ghosted me, I wondered if it would have been better if we stayed strangers.

"It's both, but seriously, I'm exhausted. Cut me some slack, old man." Since the moment I got hired three years ago, Sam took me under his wing. I think it had to do with the fact that he has a daughter my age who he hardly sees now that she lives out of state. He's more like family now, rather than my boss.

He's your typical country boy who moved to the city for the woman he loved. The bar is his pride and joy. There's a piece of Texas all over this bar with the western theme, not to mention his iron grip on Levi jeans and cowboy boots. My favorite thing in here is the old juke box in the corner that contains every pre-90s song. I think any music made after that is a disservice to your ears, so it's perfect for me.

He sighs in defeat as he sets down a beer glass. "Fine. You don't have to train for a month if you take over Ashley's section so she can go home early."

Her section is the worst to wait on since the tables are near the flat screen. I almost decline, but if one night of suffering equals less workload for a month, I'll take it.

"Fine, but I hate you," I say rolling my eyes playfully.

"What can you do? You'd miss this place if you left." I hate that he's right—luckily for him, I don't see that happening any time soon.

It's only noon, but the place is already packed with people. The tip money here is great, but the downside is waiting on a bunch of men who think you're just a piece of meat. *I'm living the dream.*

"Kat, could you take these to table six for me? I have to help Kelly." One of my coworkers places four cold beers in my hands and walks away with haste.

When I approach the table, there's already a multitude of empty bottles occupying it. I've worked here long enough to know that with this many beers, and only two guys sitting here, one of them is probably going through a serious life crisis.

"Here you guys go. If you need anything else, I'm Kat—try not to need anything else," I smile faintly as I try to slip away.

"Wait...Kat, is it? Can I ask you something?" I hiss when the one with puffy red eyes pulls my attention back. I know a heartbroken guy when I see one. If it wasn't for the sad look in his eyes, the stench of booze would give it away.

"What is it?" *Keep smiling. You could still get a good tip if you play it cool.*

"Have you ever been cheated on?" He reeks of devastation as he brings the bottle to his lips.

"No." I've never even had a serious boyfriend; they were all high school flings that fizzled out just as fast as they came.

"Well, would you forgive them if you were?"

"No." I watch the hope in his eyes die when I say the word sharply. "What if you really love them? I gave her everything, and she goes and cheats on me with some asshole from work." I'm used to drunk people oversharing, but I've never had the urge to help until him. Anyone with a conscience would feel bad for the guy—he's drowning in loneliness.

I let out an exhausted breath as I slide into the booth. Now that I'm getting a good look, the two guys across from me aren't bad looking. The heartbroken one has these mesmerizing blue eyes that are over-shined by dark circles. He might be heartbroken now, but someone classically handsome like him will find someone in no time.

"I get a lot of people who've been cheated on in here, but I also get people who cheat, so I've learned a few things. Guys will typically sleep with anything that breathes with a pair of tits, where women usually cheat emotionally before they cheat physically. She probably cares about the guy, and that's your sign that it's over, no matter how much you love her." I try to be sensitive, but I can't be a therapist all day when I have tables waiting.

"That's what I said! I know I'm the brains of the group, but damn, the answer was obvious. Thank you for your wisdom, Kat—Katherine?" his friend next to him says with a joyous grin before taking a swig of his beer.

I can usually spot the jokester of any friend group, and he's definitely the one. His tan skin is glistening with sweat, making his thick black hair cling to his forehead. His features are softer than his friend, but he's definitely handsome, with one of the best smiles I've ever seen.

"It's just Kat," I say. I almost inform him that my name is actually Katlyn, but I hate that name; the fewer people who know, the better.

"You look like a Katherine." His words are starting to slur, so I see no point in trying to correct him on my name. It's not like I'll be seeing him again.

"On that note, I'm definitely getting shit-faced. Keep the beers coming, Kat." The unnamed Casanova speaks with a perky demeanor now, but I know he's feeling the opposite—it's all in the eyes. He confidently slides a fifty-dollar bill across the table towards me.

"You pay your tab after you close it." He stops me when I try to slide it back.

"That's for your advice and listening to me bitch about my problems." He smiles genuinely at me, moving his dirty blonde hair out of his face. I return the gesture as I slide out of the booth.

"Bye Katherine!" the other friend shouts. As soon as I'm a safe distance away, I can't help but let a smile peak through across my face.

"I NEED YOUR HELP IN THE STORAGE ROOM, KIT-KAT." Sam pleads, peaking his head in the break room where I'm hiding away from the madness.

"I just barely sat down." I whine. He always guilt trips me into helping him stock because of his "bad back", but I call bullshit after seeing how confidently he rode the mechanical bull last week on rodeo day.

"Five minutes, then you can avoid me the rest of the night." I roll my eyes, but still follow him. We both know he's lying, but a girl can dream.

"So, how are the kids at the new job?" he asks, handing me a heavy box of glass bottles.

"They're really cool. It's nice not being around a bunch of drunk people who constantly try to grab my ass."

"Who tries to grab your ass?" He waits for me to answer with fire flashing in his dark brown eyes. There's a strict no touch rule here at the bar. There's even a sign when you first come in.

He beat himself up for a while after some guy got handsy with Emory when she worked here. He came out with his bat a little too late for her boyfriend Elliot's liking—except, at the time he wasn't her boyfriend, she actually hated him.

But that's a *whole* different story.

"You'd never have another customer if I answered that." I say.

"How's Vera?" Sam is the only person who knows just how scared I was when Grams had her stroke six months ago. It was right around the time we lost my grandpa, so it was hard to even function.

"She's fine. The nurse makes sure she eats healthy and takes her daily walks."

"How are you holding up? You've been going non-stop since losing your grandpa, and I'm worried." I'm more of a smile so no one suspects anything kind of girl. It's just second nature not to involve people in my problems.

"What is this, a therapy session? Hour is up, old man. I got tables to wait on." I put the box down and quickly walk out, ignoring his attempts to call me back.

"Kat, can you make seven lemon drops? I have to go put in a food order and I'm swamped." Nicole's high-pitched voice snaps me out of my daze. "Sure, no problem."

I go into waitress mode and assemble all of the ingredients.

Vodka, lemon juice, and simple syrup. There's a reason I'm not a bartender, but lemon drops are one of the easiest drinks to make.

"Hey Kat." All my muscles tense up when the deep voice rolls through me. I know that voice.

I eventually look up, into a set of brown eyes, not hiding my agitation at who's sitting on the other side of the counter.

Shit.

CHAPTER 5

Andrew

I had every intention of leaving Kat alone, but I was pulled to her as soon as I walked in. Now, I'm a deer caught in headlights, except the headlights are her emerald-green eyes. I remember when I first saw them last summer. It was as if she cast me under a spell.

She has beauty that's impossible to ignore—her long brown hair complimenting her delicate, almost flowerlike features, and her pearly cheeks and sun-kissed skin naturally radiate.

"Be careful what you say next, Andrew."

The acid in her voice is disturbing, since she usually always radiates kindness and compassion. Her justified coldness towards me makes me feel even emptier than I did before. I didn't even know that was possible.

I scramble for the words. "I just wanted to see how you've been."

"Busy. Sound familiar?" A strange twinge of guilt settles in my stomach. I deserve that. It's the excuse I gave her every time she tried reaching out to me last summer.

"Can we talk about it?" I should quit while I'm ahead, but I want to put this behind us.

She snickers and goes back to pouring drinks. "I'm working."

"After." She pauses, giving me hope.

"No. Now can you leave me alone so I can work please?" I take the polite rejection with a grain of salt and turn to walk towards Chance and Hiro. She's justified to be pissed, but I wish she wasn't so maybe we could at least be friends.

I see the booth Elliot and I always sat in when we'd come here, and it haunts me, like so many other things now. There's a lot of good memories here, but they're all blurred by sadness.

"Drew!" Hiro's obnoxious, slurry voice echoes through the bar. Their table is covered with beer bottles; I should have known they'd already be hammered.

"I leave you alone for ten minutes, and you guys are already shit-faced?" I ask, sliding into the seat across from them.

"More like an hour. What took you so long?" Chance slurs.

Trying to come up with an excuse not to come.

"I had to shower, and from the look of it, you could use one too." I gesture to his shirt that's still wet from the gym. He must be spiraling worse than I thought, because he wouldn't be caught dead in sweaty clothes.

"I got my heart ripped out of my fucking chest, leave me alone." He miserably takes a swig of his beer. It's unsettling seeing him this way since he's always so put together.

"I take it you decided not to take Izzy back?" A sloppy smile curves at his lips while raising his bottle.

"Thanks to the advice from the cute waitress, I'm just gonna say fuck it and move on. There's a lot to celebrate, like you finally coming out with us."

"What waitress?" I ask curiously.

"Katherine, the wise brunette." Hiro sings with a wide grin. I know all the girls here, and there's no Katherine, so he was probably too drunk to remember her real name.

"I know something this occasion calls for." Hiro announces as he stumbles out of the booth.

Chance turns to me as soon as he's gone, seeming more sober now. "How are you, D? No bullshit."

"I'm good." If the pill didn't kick in before I got here, I'd feel the tightness in my chest from his unconvinced stare.

"You think you can bullshit me after how long we've been friends?" I want to let him inside my head, but he can't help me, so why bring him into it?

"I didn't come here for a therapy session. You're the one that needs it." I instinctively scan the room for brunette hair I've became so familiar with, but bring my attention back to Chance's glossy eyes when I don't see her.

He's locked in on me, determined to get information out, I'm sure. Before either of us can say anything else, a familiar tune catches everyone's attention.

Hiro struts back to our table, mouthing the words to *Before He Cheats* by Carrie Underwood.

"I'm going to kill you, Aquino." Chance snarls at him.

"Get a sense of humor. It's a right of passage after getting cheated on," a wide grin plasters across his face, as if he's having the time of his life. Truthfully, you could put him in a room by himself and he'd find a way to have a good time.

"This is about a guy cheating," I point out. Everyone seems unfazed by both the song and Hiro's off-key singing. "Same shit, a cheater is a cheater." He shrugs his shoulders and quite literally falls back into the booth. Despite his resistance, Chance suddenly smiles brightly from ear to ear.

"C'mon, Drew, sing along." He playfully hits my shoulder.

"I'd rather swallow a jean jacket." I've done a lot of embarra-ssing shit—like sneaking on the football field in high school and peeing on the goal post—but shouting Carrie Underwood lyrics in public will not be one of them.

"Suit yourself." They shout the lyrics, grabbing the attention of everyone around us. Some of them even start to mouth the words too. Who knew this song was a universal language?

"I wish Izzy had a car so I could slash her tires." Chance is barely comprehendible.

"I'd help." Hiro chimes in. Their pleading eyes turn towards me.

I let out a deep sigh. "I'd keep watch so you two dumbasses don't get arrested." They seem pleased by my answer and go back to singing. I try to fight it, but I let a small smirk grow on my face.

I look down at my phone to see a text from Mom checking in on me. She never used to do that, it's like she's afraid I'm going to go off the deep end while I'm out with friends.

I find Kat with my eyes right away, as if I sensed her presence close by. I can't help but feel agitation eat at me seeing a man leaning over, trying to get her attention. I notice the way she tenses up the closer he inches to her, which makes me spring into action.

"I'll be right back." I stalk over to the bar and intentionally bump the older man who's too close to her for my liking.

"Excuse you, I'm talking to her," he says curtly, turning to face me, but I'm only looking at Kat.

On the outside, she looks annoyed that I came to her rescue, but I catch a glimpse of relief flash through her almond shaped eyes.

"Now I'm talking to her. You can go." I turn to pierce him with threatening eyes.

She's probably accustomed to guys hitting on her by now, and I know she's capable of taking care of herself, but I have a gut feeling that she actually wanted my help.

The stranger combs his hands through his beard and finally storms away from us. "I didn't need your help." *I knew she'd say that.*

"I helped anyway because that's what friends are for." I try to ease us into the conversation I've been avoiding.

"We're not friends," she replies dryly, trying to balance plates as she walks away.

"We could be." I follow behind while she tries to escape. I take advantage that this might be the only time I have to corner her into talking to me.

"You don't have to pretend you want to be friends so you can have a clear conscience, Andrew. We hung out a few times, I thought you liked me, turns out you didn't. I'm over it." There's an edge to her tone implying that maybe she's *not* over it.

I try to resist basking in the sweet scent of her perfume that smells like citrusy fruit.

"I told you about Elliot." It burns my throat to say his name.

"I get that you were having a rough time, Andrew, I really do, but we both know that isn't the reason you started avoided me. You haven't even said you're sorry. I can't be friends with someone like that." She walks away, leaving me to ponder over her words.

I could take this rejection and never cross paths with her again, but the thought of that suddenly twists a pain in my gut I've never experienced before.

CHAPTER 6
Kat

IT'S THE END OF THE SCHOOL DAY—FREE AT LAST. I LOVE BEING around my students, but I also love the peace and quiet I get when it hits three o'clock. It's my first-year teaching, but the kids like me so I take it I'm not doing too bad.

I'd usually be scrambling to change into my uniform for my four o'clock shift at the bar by now, but Sam gave me the day off. Most people would be ecstatic, but all I can think of is the money I'm missing out on. I've become so accustomed to my everyday chaos, I don't know what to do when I have time for myself. A nap sounds amazing, but it'd be nice to hang out with Grams for more than two minutes on my way down the hall.

I crawl into my slightly rusted Volkswagen Beetle. It's older than me, and I have to say a silent prayer before starting it up, but I don't have the heart to get rid of it. The day Gramps brought it home, freshly painted my favorite color, is forever ingrained in my mind. It used to be rustic yellow, but he had it customized to Sage green.

It struggles to start, as usual, but eventually does after countless pleads. The noises sound expensive, so I drown it out with loud music.

The drive home consists of listening to Gramps' old CD of every *good* 80s song you can think of. I've listened to it a hundred times, but I'll never grow tired of the way it jogs the memories of my grandparents. If it wasn't for them, I wouldn't love music as much as I do.

I get distracted by a notification on my phone as I'm stopped at a red light. I expected it to be Sam asking me to come in after all, but my heart sinks down to my stomach when Andrew's name pops up on my screen.

> ANDREW
> You're right. There was another reason. Can we talk?

I stare at the message, wide-eyed and shocked. I thought for sure I would never hear from him again after our run in at the bar. I could ignore it, and tell him to leave me alone, but curiosity eats at me to know the truth.

I thought Andrew was different, but he ended up being just like every other guy. I went through several stages after his silence: sadness, anger, then acceptance—I meant it when I said I was over it.

I don't like to hold grudges, so if he's willing to be honest, I'll hear him out. Whether we're friends afterwards depends on him and his explanation.

I SMILE AT THE SCENT OF GRAM'S PERSIMMON COOKIES AS I STEP inside my house. I'm taken back to when I would watch her make them as a kid and getting my hand swatted away when I tried to read her secret recipe.

"I'm home." I shout, hanging my bag up in the closet near

the door. Her nurse Kayla's jet-black hair is the first thing I see as she peaks around the corner.

"You picking something up before heading to the bar?" she asks with a delicate voice as she wipes her hands on a kitchen towel.

"Actually, Sam gave me the day off." The obvious surprise in her honey-colored eyes makes me chuckle.

Maybe I do work too much.

She nudges her head towards the kitchen, "She insisted on making cookies for you today."

Warmth overcomes my chest when I walk in to see Grams sliding a new batch of cookies into the oven.

"What are you doing home, lovey?" she brings me into a tight hug, engulfing me with her comforting smell.

"I have the rest of the day off, I'm all yours." I say with a smile. I try to ignore the message from Andrew waiting for my reply in my back pocket. Kayla gathers her purse and snags a cookie before heading out, "I'll see you tomorrow, Vera."

Today's mail sits on the countertop, begging to be opened. I shuffle through the letters, taking in all the companies shouting at me to pay them. I'm getting swallowed whole by past due notices.

"I could go back to work, you know. I could help with those." Grams says, gesturing to the stack.

"No. You took care of me, let me do it for you now."

"Oh, Kat, you put too much on your shoulders." She drags her finger across my cheek with a worried look on her face.

"What do you want to do today?" I change the subject.

"Let's just eat cookies and be couch potatoes." *Sounds like a great plan.*

I groan when my phone rings in my pocket. *Andrew.*

How ironic that I once waited for his name to pop up on my screen, and now it has twice in one day. I rush down the hall and into my room so Grams won't overhear the call.

"You couldn't wait for a text back?" I greet curtly.

"I had to make sure you didn't block my number."

"I should have." A few moments of silence hang between us before he speaks again. "I thought about what you said at the bar. I want us to at least be friends, so I'm ready to talk if you're ready to hear me out."

I think it over silently for several seconds, just to torture him.

"Fine. I'll hear you out." I don't miss the sigh of relief coming from the other end of the line. "Meet me at Sam's in an hour?"

"I can't today. I have the day off so I'm hanging out with my grandma."

"No problem. We'll just plan for another time." The line goes dead after we say our goodbyes, and I feel the weight of Sage on my lap. He purrs deeply when I scratch behind his ears.

"Who was that?" Grams startles me when I see her small figure leaning in the doorway of my room.

"A friend. They wanted to hang out today, but I'd rather be here with you," I say, changing out of my work clothes.

"You need to be out with people your own age, lovey, not an old woman like me. Sage and I will be just fine here." The thought of being anywhere else when I already don't see her as much as I'd like to fills me with guilt.

"I like hanging out with you. How else am I going to hear stories of when you were a groupie in the 70s?"

She was very *adventurous* before meeting my grandpa. She traveled everywhere with her friends in a van, and they attended rock concerts as if it was their job. My obsession with that era comes from her.

"You've heard those stories a million times. Go out and have some fun." She waves her hand dismissively and walks back out. I guess I have no choice.

> ME
>
> Sam's in an hour. If you flake on me, I'll drive to your house and pull you out myself.

I can't help but smirk as I hit send.

> ANDREW
>
> I would expect nothing less. See you then

Immediate dread plunges into me when I read his message. Here goes nothing.

I ARRIVE AT THE BAR BEFORE ANDREW, BUT I'LL GIVE HIM THE benefit of the doubt since I'm a little early.

"Didn't I give you the day off?" Sam narrows his eyes in suspicion as I approach the bar where he's drying cups.

"This place would be a shit show without me, I figured I'd pop in." I help myself behind the bar to a Shirley Temple since I don't drink. Growing up around addicts repelled me at an early age.

"Giving you the day off was more to get a break from you." He tries to keep his composure, but the corners of his mouth tips up.

"Please—we both know I'm the only source of entertainment you have here." I drop a cherry in my cup and sit on the other side of the counter, trying to hide my disappointment that Andrew hasn't walked through the entrance yet.

"What are you really doing here, kid?" It's a bad idea to tell him who I'm here to see, but I don't really keep secrets from Sam.

"If you must know, Mr. Nosy, I'm here to meet Andrew." I regret the words as soon as I look into his judgmental eyes.

"Andrew Cortes?" His face is puzzled as I nod my head and wait for the lecture I know is coming.

"Andrew's a good kid, he's been through a lot. Just be careful. He used to tell me about his dates with a different girl every week." I had an inkling that he was the player type, but hearing it out loud puts a lump in my throat that I can't swallow down. I can't believe I fell for him in the first place. I'm usually smart when it comes to guys.

"Relax, okay? Nothing is going on."

I grow irritated as I subtly take another glance at the door and there's no sight of him.

"I'm leaving anyway. I'll see you tomorrow, old man." I gulp down my drink and turn to leave. I'm not waiting around for Andrew like some lost puppy. I can't believe I fell for his shit *again*.

As I swing the door open, I collide with a brick wall that's someone's chest.

"Sorry I'm late. I lost track of time." I hate that I like the sound of his deep, husky voice. He towers over me in height, forcing me to look up to him.

"Well, I waited long enough, see ya." I purposely bump him as I walk outside into the fresh air. I don't get too far until his firm grip tries to pull me back by my arm.

"I got caught up with something, Kat."

"I've heard that one before." I boldly meet his gaze. He has these rich brown eyes that have a way of sucking you into his orbit.

"Can we put the guns down for five minutes and talk, please? I'm sorry. I was doing something on my truck and lost track of time, I swear."

The only reason I don't turn to leave is the pain hidden in his eyes. When I first met him, he was full of light, and now, he seems empty. Grams has always said that I'm a magnet for people in need. Maybe she was right.

"Five minutes," I say sharply, making my way back inside the bar. He follows quietly behind, and I take a seat at a nearby table that overlooks the busy street.

My eyes glance down at the way he's fidgeting already. "You want something to eat or drink? It's on me," he offers.

"No, thank you." I keep my voice as calm as possible despite my impatience.

"So...how have you been?" He asks. I almost say something snarky, but seeing his hands subtly trembling stop me.

"Good, I got a job teaching the second grade when I'm not here," he smiles an infectious grin. I hate that his smile is cute.

"That's great." Silence hangs between us again. I'm the one to break it, "You didn't invite me here to talk about my job, Andrew."

"I'm just nervous, alright? I've never had this conversation before." He says in between shaky breaths. "Promise you won't call me an asshole or whatever names I know you have ready?"

"Promise," I say. I did have a snide comment or two for him, though.

He takes another deep breath, before giving me his undivided attention. "You didn't deserve what I did. I'm really sorry. It's just...I have this rule—I don't hang out with a girl more than once to avoid a relationship. You were the first person I broke that rule with, and it scared the shit out of me, so I avoided you. You don't have to believe me, but I *do* regret it. I really want us to be friends." I search his face for any indication that he's lying, but it's not there.

"You should have told me you didn't want anything serious." I say, leaning in closer to him. The few times we did hang out, there were moments where I'd catch him smiling at me when he thought I wasn't looking, or his hand would creep towards mine but stop when I'd notice. I thought he might have liked me, but I guess it was in all in my head.

"I know. I usually have that conversation beforehand..." He looks right into my eyes as he speaks softly, almost in a whisper.

"I just like being around you." I can't help the way my lips tug at the corners, threatening to form a smile. His eyebrows arch like he's surprised those words slipped from him. I can sense bullshit on anyone, but my gut is saying he's telling the truth.

"Thanks for finally being honest." I relent.

"So...truce?" His tight smile seems forced.

"I guess it wouldn't be the worst thing in the world, now that I don't have feelings for you." Whatever feelings I did have for him fizzled out.

He smiles, and this time, it seems genuine. It's hard to look away from him.

"Oh, c'mon, I know you still find me attractive." He oozes cockiness, but I know he's being sarcastic.

"Now that you mention it, I'm not even sure how I did in the first place." I joke. He throws his head back with undiluted laughter, and it's so contagious, I can't help but join him.

Maybe being friends with him won't be so bad after all.

CHAPTER 7

Andrew

THE HOUSE IS EERILY SILENT AS I EAT MY BREAKFAST AT THE table. My eyes keep darting to where Elliot used to sit. Mom keeps his placemat as if she's still expecting him to join us. Every corner in this house holds a memory with him, a moment in time I can't get back. The only way I can explain how I feel is being in a constant vortex of darkness. The scariest part is that I don't know what can pull me out.

Ruckus near the front door makes me jump up, but when I see Dad scrambling through the doorway, annoyance settles into me. *I would rather encounter a burglar.*

"I left my lunch," he says, rushing to the kitchen. I think about running upstairs, but I'm still hungry. "You have plans for today?" he asks, digging in the fridge for the container with last night's lasagna.

"Don't know," I say coldly.

"Maybe forgetting my lunch was a sign that we should go out to eat." It irks me how much hope he holds in his voice.

"I'm good." I take bigger bites of food so I can leave before he pesters me with more questions.

"How about we go to Sam's and watch the game on

Sunday?" My jaw tightens. "That was Elliot's thing, not mine, Dad." Calling him Dad feels like acid burning my throat. Me and him haven't been close in years. I can't recall my last good memory, since he spent most of my childhood too drunk to even remember my name. I tried making sure Elliot only saw the good side of him for as long as I could, but the worse his addiction got, the more impossible it was to hide.

"I know we haven't been close, Drew, but we have to be there for each other now that Elliot is gone." It repulses me how easily he admits it, while I can't even say his name without choking up.

My hands start to shake, and my chest starts to constrict from being near him for this long. I already took a pill this morning, but I'm going to need another after this encounter.

"Yeah, well, we needed *you* to be there for us years ago!" I didn't mean to shout, but it made him stumble back, and I don't regret it. I slam my bowl into the sink, unconcerned if it shatters. He's eerily still when I forcibly bump into him as I walk out of the kitchen.

I'm in an inescapable hell, both mentally and physically.

A sigh of relief escapes when the hard slam of the door lets me know that I'm alone again. The bottle of pills screams at me from my drawer.

I don't need them. I don't need them. I close my eyes and try to recall good memories. Usually, I can pull up at least one, but the bad is outweighing everything else. I see my mom and dad screaming at each other when I was a kid, my brother in a hospital bed, holes in the wall.

I bury my head in my trembling hands, tears threatening my eyes as I try to conjure up anything good. I gasp for air like all my oxygen was just snatched away.

Fuck it.

As if it was timed perfectly, my phone rings just as I grab the knob to the drawer. I linger over the decline button as our graduation picture and Chance's last name come across my screen.

"What, Barrett?" I ask, making my irritation obvious.

"Well fuck, good morning to you too, sunshine." I rub my sweaty hands together to soothe the uneasiness. I shouldn't take it out on him.

"I'm sorry." He moves past it, just as we do with all our tiffs.

"You can make it up by doing me a favor." I knew whatever he called me for wasn't going to be good.

"What is it?"

"We all got invited to a party on Friday, but Izzy and that fucking tool she cheated with are going to be there..." I let him control his heavy breathing on the other end of the line. "I need to find a date for the party so it looks like I've moved on."

"But you haven't moved on. You've been bitching and moaning since it happened." I wish he'd moved on. It would mean I'd stop hearing him curse her name one second, then cry over her the next.

"I need to make it seem like I have, though." I don't think I've ever heard him sound this desperate. I don't know whether to laugh or pity him, but I guess I can multi-task.

I'm afraid to ask, but I let the words slip. "Where exactly do I come in?"

"I need you to find me a date, preferably one who's cool with pretending to be my girlfriend." I'm stunned into silence. *I should have declined the call.*

"Chance, this is the dumbest shit you've ever came up with."

"You pulled Camila Valdez, and you're telling me you can't find me a date for one night?" He's never going to let me forget that.

Camila was a freshman in college our senior year of high school, and there wasn't a guy that didn't want her. We went on one date, but Chance holds it over me like some kind of accomplishment.

43

I run my hands through my hair, tugging at it out of frustration. "No girl will go for it, Barrett." It's not something you can just ask. Even if I wanted to do it, it's fucking impossible.

"C'mon, D, please? I know it's crazy, but it's all I've got right now." Fuck, now I'm the asshole if I say no.

I sigh, full of regret already. "I'll try, but I'm not making any promises."

"Yes! I owe you big time." And I *will* hold him to it.

"Meet me at Sam's around five," I say before hanging up. The only way anyone would agree to this dumbass plan is if they had a little alcohol in their system.

AFTER ABOUT THE FIFTH DRINK IS THROWN IN MY FACE, I DECIDE to take a break from seeking out a pretend girlfriend for Chance. Who knew that girls don't feel comfortable being used by a stranger? As shitty as the circumstances are, all of this has gotten my mind off the exchange with my dad this morning, so I'll take it as a win.

"I'm fucked," Chance complains from the other side of the booth.

"I just want to put on record that if you had stayed single in high school, we wouldn't be in this position," I say, drying myself off with a towel I grabbed from Sam. He witnessed all five drinks thrown at me and chuckled after every single one.

"Why can't you just call one of your old conquests and ask if they can be Chance's fake girlfriend?" Hiro chimes in now.

"Because that'd be breaking my rule of not talking to them again."

Speaking of breaking rules, Kat's ethereal features suddenly catch my eye. She's behind the bar, talking to Sam while pouring out beers faster than my brain can comprehend.

Her hair is different today, in a messy bun instead of flowing down her back in loose waves. Her skin, glistening from the sweat, looks like a natural glow. The way she smiles when she interacts with people is so charming. No wonder all the guys swoon over her.

Why the fuck am I watching her? I snap my attention back to the guys.

"What the hell are we gonna do, D?"

"You're going to that party with Hiro, and you're gonna have a good time while not paying any mind to your shitty ex-girlfriend."

"You have to come too," he says firmly.

"Absolutely not." A few months ago, I would have been the one dragging *them* along, but I can't be at a party when the wound of Elliot is still open.

"We always go to parties together, Drew." Hiro says.

I know they both want me to go back to our normal routine of parties every weekend, the girls, the booze, but I can't.

"You guys will be fine."

I can tell Hiro wants to protest more, but before either of us say anything else, someone in the corner grabs my attention.

"I'll be back." They look confused as I slide out without another glance in their direction. Kat concentrates as she wipes down tables, while I concentrate on how the black apron that ties around her waist accentuates her subtle curves.

Damn it, stop looking.

"You missed a spot." I sit in one of the chairs to face her. She was tan last summer, but now her naturally rosy cheeks shine through her ivory complexion. Her light colored freckles are more obvious to the eye now too.

A sudden jolt surges in my gut when she makes eye contact and throws me a dimpled smile. "What are you doing here?"

"My helpless friends needed me to execute a plan," I say with embarrassment.

"What's the plan?" She stops to give me her full attention. If you look close enough, her green eyes have a ring of blue around them, and they're intoxicating.

"My friend wants to bring a girl to a party so he can make his cheating ex-girlfriend jealous."

"So what's the problem?"

"I forgot the best part: he wants her to pretend to be his girlfriend." Her entire face twists. "Sorry to break it to you, but women don't want to be an accessory, especially for a stranger."

"I tried convincing him to forget about it, but..." A thought forms in my mind. "Maybe if he hears it from you, he'll change his mind." I can tell I peaked her interest by the way her eyebrows raise.

"I get to tell a man off? I'm in." She throws the towel down and prances behind me as we walk over to Chance and Hiro. Their faces brighten at the sight of her, like they're seeing an old friend.

"Katherine!" Hiro sings with his arms reached out to her.

"I should have known you guys were friends." She shakes her head while a small chuckle escapes her. "Someone catch me up. How do you guys know each other and why does Hiro call you Katherine? I thought your name was Katlyn?" I look to all of them, baffled by their familiarity.

"She's the girl who gave me the advice on Izzy." I don't like the way Chance tilts a smirk at her.

"My name *is* Katlyn." Her eyes point at Hiro, then to Chance.

"Andrew told me you're trying to rent a girl for the night." A breath of amusement escapes my lips at her directness.

"When you put it like that, it sounds really bad, but all I want to do is make my ex jealous because she's going to the party with the guy she cheated on me with."

"Why don't you go to the party like a normal person and not

pay any attention to what she's doing?" I don't know how she can be harsh, but nurturing at the same time.

"I like her." Hiro's smile widens in approval. In the little time I've known Kat, I've noticed she just fits in. She came to sit down with us, and it's like she's always been a part of our group. She never seems out of her element.

"I know you guys think it's stupid, but I want her to know that her cheating on me didn't flip my world upside down after all."

I'm surprised at his vulnerability around someone he barely knows. Then again, Kat has a nurturing energy that gets you to admit things you thought you'd never say out loud. *I would know.*

Kat's face drops like she's about to do something she'll regret.

"*Hypothetically,* if I helped you, we'd need some rules." It takes several seconds to process her words, and my friends look just as confused as me.

"You want to help me?" Chance asks, full of hope.

"No, I hate the idea of being used…" Her shoulders slump. "But who am I to stand in the way of your payback?"

"We'll do it on your terms, whatever you want." he spews out.

"You can hold my hand, but if you *think* of touching anything else, you'll be on your way to the ER." Her intimidating smile makes her threat even scarier. "And no kissing."

Chance hisses through his teeth. "How is she going to believe we're dating if I can't kiss you?"

"Trust me, there are plenty of ways to convince her." The more I listen, the more this sounds bat shit crazy. Izzy will see right through their charade, and it'll backfire on Chance.

"Alright, let's do this," he says, satisfaction spread all over his face as they shake hands from across the table.

"Too bad you won't be there to witness it, D." It dawns on

47

me that I have no choice but to go to the party now. Kat is more than capable of taking care of herself, but I'll feel better if I'm keeping an eye out for her.

That's what friends do, right?

"Actually, I'll go." I don't appreciate the mischievous look Chance throws at me.

"I gotta get back to work now that I've sold my soul. See you boys later."

I didn't realize I was watching her confidently strut away until Hiro clears his throat and brings me back.

"I wonder what made Drew change his mind about going to the party, Hiro." They both exchange sly grins.

"Like you said, we always go to parties together." Clearly, they don't buy the reasoning behind my sudden change of heart.

Besides, not only do I have to keep an eye out for Kat, I have to be there when all of this blows up in our faces.

This ought to be good.

CHAPTER 8

Andrew

I'VE CAME UP WITH EVERY SCENARIO THAT COULD GET ME OUT OF going tonight, but ultimately, I decided against it for Kat's sake. I trust Chance, but not when he's trying to make Izzy jealous. Plus, I don't trust my friends to stay sober so that makes me the designated driver.

I look around my room to assure I have everything before I leave, eyeing the bottle of pills on my bed. I took a couple earlier, but I could slip some in my pocket. Just in case.

No. You don't need them.

Guilt claws at me when I look in the mirror.

My brother is probably somewhere cursing at me that I have the audacity to go out and have fun while he's gone. *Fuck.*

I shake out four pills into my hand, slide them in the front pocket of my jeans, and rush out of my room.

"I'll be back later Ma, don't wait up," I shout over to her in the living room.

"Wait—can I talk to you for a second?" Her voice is warm but with a hint of concern.

I name off all the things she could need to talk about. *Did she find my pills? Is it about what happened between me and Dad the other day?* I sit next to her on the leather couch that takes up way too much room. "What's up?" My leg starts to bounce.

"Adónde vas?" She never used to ask where I was going until recently.

"A party with Chance and Hiro." I leave Kat's name out on purpose because she would never stop prying.

"I'm glad you're going out more now."

"Not by choice." My voice hardens.

"You used to stay out until odd hours every weekend and now, you want to stay home?" She taps me on the head.

"Things have changed, Ma." I shouldn't have said that. The energy turns cold as soon as the words leave my mouth.

"It's okay to admit you're having a hard time, mijo." It almost slips out that I'm having a *really* hard time, that everyday I wander around like I'm lost and I don't know how to get back. How I have to take pills in order to cope with Elliot being gone.

Instead, I just say, "I'm fine. Don't worry about me."

"I just wish you had someone to help you…heal." I don't see myself *ever* healing, but that isn't what she wants to hear.

"Let me guess, when you say someone, you mean a girl?" I ask, shaking my head.

She's never accepted that I don't want to settle down, not knowing her and Dad are the reason for it. Years ago, they'd bicker so much, I would wish for them to just divorce so I wouldn't have to

hear them anymore. I swore off relationships so I would never put myself in a position to be like them.

"All I'm saying is look how Elliot perked up once he had Emory."

Elliot was in love with Emory before he even hit puberty, of course he was ecstatic when she finally returned the feelings. Even when he was in the end stages, if she was there, he was happy.

Sometimes, I envied how he was still capable of love, even

after getting a front row seat to the shit show of our parents' marriage.

"I gotta go before I'm late." I peck her quickly on the head and run out the door before she can lecture me about anything else. I know there's a lot of unsaid words hanging in the air with us lately, and the only thing worse than going to this party would be finding out what they are.

"Dammit, I wanted to get there before Izzy." Chance is fixated on his social media while I drive. I suggested he remove Izzy, but of course he didn't listen.

"It's perfect. Now you can make an entrance with a girl on your arm." Hiro inserts himself in the conversation from the backseat. The thought of him using Kat as arm candy makes my fingers tighten on the steering wheel until my knuckles turn white.

"I know Kat agreed to your plan, but don't treat her like a piece of ass tonight, alright?" I grit out. They both twist to look at me, puzzled with confusion.

"This is coming from the guy who treats every girl like a piece of ass. Did something happen with you and Kat? We can blow the whole thing, D."

I avoid eye contact with him as I focus on the stretched out road ahead. "We're just friends, but she's a good person and she's doing your ass a favor, so treat her with respect." I look over in time to see his eyebrows flicker with interest.

I could tell them what happened between me and Kat, but that's between us.

"Damn, give me some credit. I'm not an asshole." He hits my arm hard enough for me to flinch just as we pull up to Kat's house.

There's a full garden of daisies and white roses planted in front of her porch, and a built-in swing hangs from a tree. She made it clear to text when we arrive, so I send her the message and wait.

"Be a gentleman to your fake girlfriend and get in the back seat, Barrett."

All three of our heads snap to Kat as she walks up to us. It's hard not to give her all of your attention, she demands it without even trying. It's as if my mind is slowing her strides down, making me get sucked into her presence the longer I look.

"Since no one else will say it, I will: your fake girlfriend is way hotter than your real ex-girlfriend, Chance." Hiro's practically drooling over her as he stares. I know he'd never go for her, but he doesn't shy away from looking, that's for sure.

"Why are you guys staring? Should I change?" she asks, adjusting the green maxi skirt that flows down her legs. Her style is what most girls are afraid of trying. She perfectly blends colors and patterns, and makes it edgy.

Chance stumbles over his words. "No, you look good—a little too good. People might think you're out of my league."

"They would be correct." I chuckle to myself at her remark. I forgot how refreshingly funny and witty she is.

"You sure you're up for this?" I whisper to her as she climbs into the passenger seat.

"I didn't wear a shirt that makes my boobs look good for nothing." The white crop top under her leather jacket looks like she might have crocheted it herself. My eyes trickle down to her breasts, and she catches me smiling to myself before I look away.

"Are you sure you're the driver tonight? Most people say that but end up passed out by the end of the night."

"Drew never has more than one drink. It's a sacred rule. He's been our DD since high school," Hiro says, hovering between us to adjust the radio.

I can feel Kat's piercing gaze waiting for clarification, but I don't pay her any mind—as hard as it is. I'll save her the boring, sad details of having a drunk as a dad being the reasoning behind it.

Having one drink is metaphorical—my way of control. I can stop at one while my dad never could.

There's hardly anywhere to park in front of the mansion at the end of the cul-de-sac. Luxury cars fill the entire street. Parties thrown by rich kids usually mean booze galore.

To my surprise, Chance opens the door for Kat as we trickle out of the truck. "Thank you, fake boyfriend."

"Anytime."

Hiro looks over at me and silently gags. *Same here.*

"Okay, Chance and Katherine will go off and gloat in front of Izzy, me and Drew will hang back and watch it all turn to shit. Sound like a plan?" he says it sarcastically, but it's probably exactly what's going to happen.

"Relax. Izzy will see me with Kat and realize I've moved on, then we'll leave and go get some burgers on me."

This is the stupidest shit we've ever done, and that's saying a lot.

"Let's just get this over with." I brush past everyone to go inside, my skin already crawling when I enter the circus of people. I reach into my pocket to assure my pills are still there—it seems like I'm going to need them.

Chance and Kat follow behind me holding hands, trying to pass for a happy couple, while Hiro is already busy greeting people.

It's going to be a long ass night.

CHAPTER 9
Kat

Feel So Close - Calvin Harris

Until today, I never went out of my way to show up to parties. Even in high school, I was always too busy working my after-school job to attend them. Who would have known the first one I attend would be on the arm of a guy I hardly know, posing as his girlfriend?

I feel like crawling into a hole when all eyes snap to me and Chance walking in, hand in hand. I don't know if my mind is playing tricks on me, but I swear, every girl scowls with disgust as I pass by.

Even when I tried warning a girl that her skirt was riding up, she seemed repulsed that I even tried to speak to her. I don't feel insecure from others' opinions of me anymore, but even if I did, it's all about faking it 'til you make it.

"Since D won't tell me, how'd you two meet?" Chance starts the conversation as we approach the wide spread of booze. I decide to stick with a water bottle I found by some miracle. I wish I did drink, though, just to have some liquid courage to get me through the night.

"I'm friends with someone he knows, she introduced us at the bar last summer."

"And nothing ever happened with you guys?" The devilish smirk on his face implies that he already suspects something.

I ponder whether to tell him, but if Andrew hasn't mentioned anything, then it's probably for a reason. Besides, it saves me the embarrassment of admitting that he ghosted me.

"How'd you guys meet?" I ask, directing the subject off me. He chuckles, like he knows exactly what I just did.

"He was the new kid our junior year of high school, me and Hiro took him under our wing. He's been unable to get rid of us ever since."

I notice the way his eyes search the room. "Tell me more about this girl we're here for," I say.

"Izzy was always around in high school, so naturally, our friendship became more. I thought she would be the girl I'd marry, but shit changes, I guess." He shrugs his shoulders and takes a big gulp out of his red solo cup.

"Now that you've given me the rundown of what you tell everyone else, how do you *really* feel?" His wide-eyed look tells me that no one has ever called him out like that before.

"Alright...I loved Izzy more than anything, but I also felt like I had to be someone I wasn't to keep her. Nothing I ever did was good enough." He stops mid-sentence, embarrassment is all over his face.

"I can keep a secret. You can tell me." I'm satisfied to see the glimmer of relief flash in his eyes. "I'm only here to show her that she didn't completely break me. I know it probably sounds pathetic."

"I wouldn't be here if I thought it was pathetic. I know we just met, but I can confidently say that this girl didn't deserve you. If a little revenge is what you want, then that's what we'll get."

He's glowing as he stares back at me, but it's not a look you give someone you like. It's more someone who understood you for the first time. "I can see why Andrew likes you around."

I'm not sure how to respond, so I smile and take a sip of my water.

"Also, if you tell anyone what I just said, I'll have no choice but to flee the country." I make a zipping motion over my lips, which gets him to laugh.

"Okay…" I take the solo cup out of his hand and place it on the counter. "Let's go find that ex-girlfriend of yours and make her regret cheating on you." I grip his rough hand with mine, and my eyes find Andrew and Hiro through the mix of people. Hiro looks like he's having a blast, while Andrew sticks out like a sore thumb as he leans against the wall, not engaging with anyone. I watch as his eyes move straight to where my hand is entwined with Chance's, and I almost pull back.

"Chance!" An unfamiliar face shouts from the couch. I'm tugged away to the group of people passing a joint around to each other.

"Long time no see, Steven." The girls who occupy his friend's lap scrutinize me, as if they know this isn't my typical scene.

"Who's this little number?" I instinctively roll my eyes at the obvious misogynist. "This is my girlfriend, Kat." Chance pulls me in closer and wraps his broad arm around my shoulders.

"You upgraded from the last one. Speaking of, she passed by not too long ago." Steven leans all the way back on the couch as he takes a puff of a joint, his eyes never peeling away from me.

"I'm gonna go find the bathroom," I whisper in Chance's ear. I don't need to use the bathroom, but I'm in desperate need of fresh air.

"Do you need me to go with you?" he asks. I know it's the bare minimum, but I find it sweet that he'd leave his friends to walk me to the bathroom.

"I'm okay. Stay here with your friends. I'll be back." I jolt for the door before I inhale more smoke. The tension in my body starts to dissipate once my feet touch the grass and I get the first taste of fresh air. I had to get out of there—being around drugs my entire childhood made me never want to be around it in my adulthood.

"Where's your boyfriend?" I startle at the low voice behind me.

"Don't sneak up on me, asshole." Andrew comes to stand beside me with a proud look on his face.

"I didn't take you for the type to get scared easily." He scoots closer to me so our hands are almost touching, and it suddenly feels like we're in our own little bubble. I've always noticed that there's a comforting energy whenever I'm near him, like I'm weirdly supposed to be there.

"I don't, but there's pervy guys in there, and I don't feel like using my taser tonight." I pat my purse to display where I keep my protection. "I thought you were DD?" I ask, gesturing to the cup that looks so small engulfed in his big hand.

"It's water." He tips it enough for me to see the clear liquid.

"If you don't mind me asking, what's with your one drink rule?" It took Hiro mentioning it for me to realize he's never ordered more than one beer at the bar.

He stares off into the distance, not saying a word, and I accept that he isn't going to answer. "Let's just say I have a bad experience with alcohol." I don't ask for clarification. His tense shoulders and irregular breathing tell me it probably took a lot for him to admit that.

"Now it's my turn to ask a question," he says, admiring the stars.

"What do you wanna know?"

"Why'd you come outside? Seemed like you and Chance were close in there." If I'm not mistaken, there's hostility in his tone.

Now it's my turn to hesitate. "Let's just say I have a bad

experience being around people doing drugs." I've been around things *a lot* worse than weed, but I still wouldn't choose to be around it.

We don't say anything else. Instead, we stare in comfortable silence at the moon that shines brightly over us.

"Before Elliot died, he told me that after he's gone, to look for the brightest star in the sky and that's where he'll be." He goes still. I don't think he meant to admit that to me.

Before I can muster up something to say back, he takes a sip of his water and clears his throat. "How's Chance at being a fake boyfriend?" The quickness of the subject change gives me whiplash, but I recover quickly.

"No complaints. He might even give you some competition. You opened the car door for me on our first date, but Chance poured me a drink." I laugh deeply as I pretend to swoon. I recall the memory of the first time we hung out on a beach trip with Elliot and Emory. I remember having the most fun I'd had in a long time.

"Oh, c'mon, my little brother and your best friend were there. It shouldn't even be counted as a date, I can do better than that." His infectious laugh cuts through the humid air.

There's a brief moment where we're both motionless, soaking each other in. I don't know if it's the leather jacket I'm wearing, but it suddenly feels a few degrees warmer the longer I stand here.

Our odd moment is cut short when Hiro interrupts it with a stoic expression. "Houston, we have a problem."

We follow him back inside to see Chance leaning against the wall with a girl who's not me. She looks comfortable being so close to him as her manicured fingernails drape over his shoulder. I take it this is the famous Izzy. I can see why Chance was under her spell: she's absolutely breathtaking. Her long black hair falls flawlessly down her back in curls, and her pink dress fits her slim figure perfectly. She's like a Barbie doll.

"Katherine, go get your man...or your fake man. Do not let Izzy dig her claws in him again." Hiro barks the order at me, and I look to Andrew, who nods his head in encouragement.

Showtime.

I walk up to the two of them, who seem very cozy with each other, and make my appearance known by swatting away her hand and replacing it with my own. He seems relieved to see me, while Izzy looks at me like a bug that needs to be squashed.

"Babe, let's go dance." I say in a low, seductive voice as I try to pull him away.

"Who are you?" She doesn't even try to hide her distaste.

"His girlfriend." If looks could kill, I'd drop dead right here from hers. "I see you picked the first girl you could find to replace me." I'm a firm believer in following girl code, but I think I can throw the rule book out the window to defend my honor.

"Is it technically replacing if I'm an upgrade?" Her mouth gapes open with shock, and by everyone's collective gasp, I take it no one has ever confronted her before. I finally pull Chance away and walk to where our friends greet us with delighted grins. I'm surprised they didn't make popcorn while I was gone for the show.

"You're a fucking legend." Hiro takes a swig from his beer while Andrew admires me fondly.

"What the hell was that? You drag me here to make Izzy jealous but snuggle up with her the first chance you had?" I snap at Chance. I'm not jealous—it's just the principle.

"I'm sorry! She just came up and started telling me she misses me, and we should get back together. I tried finding you but then I saw you outside with Drew."

"That was strike one. Get to strike two, and I'm leaving." I point my finger at him with piercing eyes. He looks intimidated, even though he's at least five inches taller than me.

"It won't happen again, I promise."

59

The plan was to leave when we confronted Izzy, but the music blaring over us is catchy despite it being way different than the music I usually listen to. I smile at how everyone looks like they're having a blast with their friends, dancing freely under the colored lights. With all the drama, I didn't stop to enjoy my first house party experience. It feels like a milestone I missed in high school.

"C'mon, let's dance." I manage to drag them all closer to the makeshift dance floor, but they don't move a muscle. I used to love dancing in the living room with my grandparents. Music has this way of making me feel at peace. Hiro starts to move to the fast tempo, and I wait around for the other two stooges to join in on the fun. They're still as statues, looking bored as ever.

"Have you losers never danced at a party?" I pull Chance in first, giving our bodies enough space not to touch. "You're my fake boyfriend, so by definition, you have to dance with me." He looks around warily at everyone, but they're not paying any attention to us.

"Get out of your head for once and just enjoy the moment."

He lets go of my fingers, looking more confident. Before I know it, the three of us are screaming the lyrics to the song at each other and laughing like idiots. Andrew is the only one keeping his distance. Usually, he owns any room he's in, but right now he just looks *lost*.

I can't imagine what'd it'd be like coming to a party so soon after losing someone important to you, but he *is* here, and that counts for something. I make it my mission to make it memorable for him. I reach over to grab one of his hands while the other stays stuck in his pocket. Without hesitation, he grips onto me as if he's drowning and I'm a life preserver. Our eye contact doesn't break even as the chaos ensues around us. Even in a crowded room, his presence draws me in. Just as I'm about to remove my hand from his, he grips onto it tighter, not wanting to let go. Chance and Hiro are oblivious to what's going on as they continue knocking back beers.

I take advantage of the iron tight grip on Andrew by moving us to the music, but he resists the more I try to persuade him.
"It's okay to have fun, you know." His entire body freezes. I almost take it back before I notice the shine in his eyes that wasn't there a second ago. His face is doing all the talking his lips aren't.

He catches me by surprise when he grabs my arms to wrap them around his neck. He has to bend down for us to be at eye-level, but he doesn't seem to mind. I try to keep the same gap of distance as I did with Chance, but he closes it so we're touching. While the music is fast, we sway together as if it was a slow song. Heat starts to build on my neck and travel up to my face, and for a split second, I swear time stops. There's no music, no crowd of people, just us alone on the dance floor, consumed in one another. He tucks a loose strand of hair behind my ear with shaky fingers. He's careful, like I'm fragile and can break at any moment.

"Katherine, you're up." Hiro demands my attention when he calls my "name", making me break away from Andrew.

Before I can ask why I was summoned, I lock eyes with Izzy who's staring us all down in the corner with her friends.

"I thought you said she'd be here with someone. I don't see a guy with her." I thought she'd be more distracted, but instead, she's practically eye fucking Chance from across the room.

"He left earlier, which is why she was flirting with me. She was just bored." His somber face is like a puppy getting kicked.

Fuck.

"Kiss me." I cringe as I rush out the words. They all snap their necks to me hard enough to get whiplash.

"You said not to kiss you," Chance says with caution.

"Just do it so she can see you're not paying attention to her anymore." I brace myself as he cradles my face in his hand. The kiss is short, but he definitely doesn't hold back. He manages to slide his tongue in before I push him away. I'll admit he's a good kisser, but I didn't feel fireworks or butterflies. I'm starting to think that type of kiss is just made up. Andrew is turned away from us when I finally look at him again.

"We've got company," he warns as Izzy storms towards us, her friends following closely behind.

"Chance, what the hell? You bring a girl here to flaunt in front of me to what? Make me jealous?"

Actually, that's exactly what we're doing. She's addressing him but looking at me like she wants to set me on fire.

"I don't care what you think anymore, Izzy. I'm actually glad you cheated, because you don't deserve me. So, thank you." Her face washes of color, her once pink cheeks now red with embarrassment.

I hide the proud smile forming on my face. I'd like to think I gave him the ammo for that response.

"So that's it then? You throw us away for this slut?"

I don't know what comes over me when I get directly in her face. "I could be wrong, but aren't you the one who cheated? I think that term would be better used for you, but hey what do I know?" I know my words cut deep from the way she turns red with rage.

Before I can react, she shoves me hard enough that I slam into Chance's solid chest. I shove her back even harder, hoping she'll stop, but her movements are quick as she grabs a handful of my hair and drags me down to the floor.

Andrew is the first to react and rip her off me, then Chance and Hiro jump in. Once I'm free from her grasp, anger takes control of me, and without thinking, I throw us both to the ground again. I've never been in a fight before, but I do manage to get a few scratches on her. I'm lifted effortlessly and thrown over Andrew's shoulder as he rushes us out the front door, me still squirming to get loose from his firm grip.

"Is it weird that I found that kind of hot?" Hiro asks as soon as we're clear of the house.

"That wasn't exactly how I planned to end the night," Chance says, fighting a grin.

Andrew plants me in the passenger seat, buckling my seatbelt like you would a toddler. As we drive away, I start to untangle all the knots in my hair, and I can't help but burst into hearty laughter.

They all look at me, ridden with confusion. "My first house party lived up to the expectations." The energy in the truck is now ten times lighter than it was seconds ago.

"You're officially one of us." Chance chirps from the back.

"Thank you," Andrew whispers. I catch him admiring me from the driver's side.

"For getting my ass handled to me in your friend's honor?" I tease.

His lips curl into a crooked smile. "No, that was cool too, but thanks for getting me to have fun. I haven't done that since…" He winces, as though the next words will physically hurt to say out loud.

"Anytime." I turn away to look at the trees quickly passing by before I can get sucked back into him. I won't let what happened last summer happen again. Just being his friend has its perks anyway—like being a part of this odd little friend group.

CHAPTER 10

Andrew

Hits Different - Taylor Swift

THIS IS THE THIRD TIME I'VE TRIED AND FAILED AT MAKING myself breakfast without burning it. I keep spacing out on memories from last night. I was fully prepared to occupy the wall all night, then drive Hiro and Chance's drunk asses home, but Kat made all the difference—not just for me. I've never seen Chance and Hiro smile so much, and it was all thanks to her. She just waltzed into our group as if she's known us her entire life, and somehow, it feels that way too. Being friends with her is easier than I thought it would be—then again, being around her in general is easy.

The moment my uneasiness completely vanished when she acknowledged me plays on a constant loop in my head. I was seconds away from excusing myself to sneak a pill, but when she grabbed onto me, I suddenly couldn't fathom walking away from her. I needed her close, or it felt like I was going to run out of air.

My perfectly toasted bagel finally comes out at the same time my phone starts to ring in my back pocket. "What, Barrett?" I greet Chance with a snap.

"And here I thought you'd be in a good mood after last night." Even though I dreaded it, I knew that was coming.

"What are you talking about?" I decide to play oblivious.

"C'mon, D. Kat was my date but spent most of the night with you." I can't deny it, even though it was completely unintentional.

"Whatever, man. What'd you call me for?" I successfully change the subject.

"I called to get Kat's number so I can thank her. Izzy's been blowing up my phone. I just blocked her, and I wouldn't have been able to do that before last night."

"It's about fucking time," I say with my mouth full.

"We should hang out with her more—we like her." I'm not surprised at all that she won them over with her charm.

"I don't know if she'd want to after last night." I don't think she'll be too eager to hang out with three guys all the time, especially with friends like mine.

"There's one way to find out. Is she working at the bar?"

"How should I know? I'm not a stalker." I actually do know that she's working today; she's always there on Saturday.

"Then we go find out. Meet us there in an hour." The line goes dead before I can protest. How naive of me to think I'd be able to stay home today. My fingers are already on the button to call him back, to tell him to count me out, but Mom comes waltzing into the kitchen in her purple silk robe.

"Hey. You got in late last night. How was it?" She goes to her coffee maker to start a fresh pot, just as she does every morning.

"It was fun, I guess." I try to be subtle because I'm definitely not letting her in on the details.

"Well, at least you're starting to get out there again."

Silence only hangs for a few seconds before she says in a sly voice, "Speaking of getting out there again..." *Shit.* "We're having dinner with one of my work friends tonight, and she has a daughter around your age." I almost miss the last part because she says it so quickly, but panic settles into my gut when I sense what she's up to.

"Absolutely not." My voice is stern, screaming that I'm not budging. There is no fucking way.

"Cálmate. She saw your picture on my desk when she came by and said you were cute." The subtle joy she has from admitting that terrifies me.

"I'm not being set up by my mom." I should have seen this coming. She always holds out hope that I'm going to change my mind one day and fall in love like Elliot did.

"It's not a set up when no one is making you date her, but I also wouldn't disapprove if you guys hit it off."

I can feel a headache coming on as I rack my brain for any idea of how to get out of this. Plan A would be to move across the country, but then something else clicks.

"I can't, Ma. I wanted to keep it a secret, but I'm seeing some- one." It wasn't my best idea, but I have nothing else. Her eyes almost bulge out of her head once the lie is out in the open.

"Why would you keep that from me?"

I pause. "Because it's not serious enough to mention, and I know how you get."

Her face glows with delight. "I want to meet her."

Nausea plunges into my stomach. "This is exactly why I didn't want to tell you. No you can't meet her." Mainly because there is no *her,* but even if there was, I wouldn't bring her in my mom's vicinity.

"It wasn't a question. Bring her by sometime so I can meet the girl responsible for my son finally settling down. You know I'll keep asking if you try and put it off."

Well, I'm fucked. She ruffles her hands through my hair before nearly skipping out of the kitchen with happiness, while I'm left with the consequences of my own doing.

I obviously didn't think this through, otherwise I would have seen exactly how this was going to backfire on me. I let empty ideas float in my head as my face is buried in my hands.

Think Andrew. Think.

Suddenly, brown hair and a dazzling smile flash through my mind, and a light bulb goes off above my head. *Kat.*

My mom already knows of her, so it'd be perfect. She did it for Chance, of course she'd be willing to do it for me.

"HELL NO," KAT SPITS OUT AS SOON AS THE WORDS LEAVE MY mouth. I don't blame her, but she's my only hope.

"Why not? It worked out for Chance, and we're friends aren't we?" I plead while helping her wrap silverware.

"It's different. That was just to make some girl jealous for one night. You're asking me to pretend to be your girlfriend to fool your family for who knows how long."

I feel like scum for asking this of her when I placed so much judgement on Chance, but I'm already in too deep. I can't go back to my mom and say 'actually, just kidding. I don't have a girlfriend.'

"Kat, please…I need you." I don't think I've ever said those words to anyone, but I mean it. Without her, I'm fucked.

"No."

"I'll do whatever you want," I plead again.

"I'm not a pawn you and your friends can pass around." Her words are jagged, and I feel even worse seeing the twisted expression on her usually bright face.

I relent. "You're right. I'm sorry. We all really want to be your friend, and that was shitty of me to ask." I'll just figure out some bullshit excuse to tell Mom. It wouldn't be the first time.

"Thank you." I'm relieved to see a sincere smile touch her freckled face again.

"Drew!" Hiro's high-pitched screech makes the entire bar turn when he enters, but he loves the attention. "Katherine!" he shouts again when he spots Kat sitting next to me.

"I spent enough time with you losers last night, so excuse me while I go wait on tables and flaunt around for tips." She gets up and walks away gracefully, greeting people as she walks by. She owns any room she's in, but her inability to be cocky about it despite being fully aware of the effect she has on people is striking. I'm in awe of her.

"What were you guys talking about?" Chance asks insistently.

"About what happened last night." They would never let me live it down if they found out what I asked of Kat, so I add this to list of things I'm keeping from them.

He narrows his eyes at me in disbelief but moves to the next subject. "You should invite her bowling with us next weekend."

I wince, but not at the mention of bringing Kat—we used to go bowling every weekend but stopped when Elliot got sick. Between the party and now this, I don't want to get in over my head.

"Bowling is the guy's thing," Hiro chimes in. We made up the rule that it would always be just us guys, no girlfriends or dates.

"Well, change is good, right, D?" Chance tries to convince me. I almost decline the invite, but something tells me that whether I go or not, they'll invite Kat, and there's no way in hell I'll let her go alone with them. Who knows what embarrassing memories they'd dig up in my absence?

"Sure, I guess." I say, shrugging my shoulders. If she's part of our friend group now, she should be included in our traditions. We've never really considered adding a fourth person to our group, but in a weird way, Kat is like the missing puzzle piece we didn't know we needed.

I SHOULD BE HOME, BUT I JUST HAD TO FORGET MY GODDAMN phone at the bar. Since it's past closing time, I had to go on a scavenger hunt in my house to find the spare key Sam gave me.

I pull into the parking lot expecting it to be empty, but I see a familiar figure pacing back and forth in a panic. She's hovering over her green car in defeat, but nearly collapses with relief when she sees me get out of my truck.

"What are you still doing here?" The dark parking lot is right next to an alley, adding to the eerie feeling. No one, especially her, should be stranded out here alone at this hour.

"My car won't start. I called roadside assistance an hour ago, but as you can see they're not here. I don't know what to do or how I'm going to get home, I have to work tomorrow too and…"

"Hey, relax. Take a deep breath." I grasp her shoulders and coach her through slow, deep breaths until she calms under my hold. I've become very familiar with breathing techniques.

Her cheeks aren't rosy like they always are, and her eyes are wet from tears. I have the urge to touch her and wipe them away.

"Thank you. What are you doing here, by the way?" I miss her warmth when she moves away. "I forgot my phone."

She reaches into her purse and pulls it out. "Oh yeah—I found it in the booth you were sitting in. I was gonna bring it by for you."

"You were gonna drop it off at my house?" It's a small gesture, but that might be the nicest thing anyone had ever done for me.

"It's sort of what friends do, Andrew." That's what's so refreshing about her—she does nice things for people like it's second nature, being a reminder that not everyone in the world is shitty.

"Let me return the favor by giving you a ride home." It's not exactly a request, since leaving her here isn't an option.

"It's okay. Roadside assistance will be here soon." She doesn't sound convinced, and neither am I.

"We both know they won't be here 'til morning. Let me take you home and we'll have them tow it to my house tomorrow." I place a gentle hand on the small of her back and guide her to my truck before she can object again. She's so stubborn, she'd stay out here all night just to prove that she doesn't need help.

"Why your house?" she asks, stepping onto the side rail to climb inside.

"So I can fix it."

"You don't have to do that. I was just gonna let it sit in my driveway and catch Ubers in the meantime." It's like looking in a mirror. Her first instinct is to not accept help from anyone. I guess we're more alike than I thought.

"You'll be wasting money on Uber rides."

"I don't have any other choice," her defeated look makes my stomach churn.

"You have me," I rush out. "Just take the help, Kat. This is what friends do." You'd think I was pulling teeth with how hard it is to convince her to accept my help.

"What do you want in return?" She can make anything that comes from her lips sound good, but not distrust and loathing. I can't help the rude scoff that escapes me.

"Has no one ever done anything nice for you? I don't want anything. I like working on cars, and I have a lot of extra time." I bite it out harsher than I intended. I might not call girls back after taking them out, but I'd never take advantage of one, and I don't want her to think I'm that kind of guy. For some peculiar reason, I actually care about what this girl thinks of me.

"I'm sorry I asked. I guess I don't know how to accept help, and I remembered what you asked me earlier, and I just thought…"

"I wouldn't give you an ultimatum. I meant it when I said I want to be your friend, so can you just let me help you?" I know she believes me when a gentle smile takes up her face.

"Who knew you were such a gentleman?" *There's the Kat I know.*

"There's a lot of things you don't know about me," I fight the urge to look over at her as we're stopped at a red light.

"Oh yeah? Tell me something no one else knows. I promise I can keep a secret." There's an unfamiliar voice in my head telling me I can trust her, and that doesn't happen often.

"I went to the party feeling guilty I was even there in the first place after losing Elliot, but you made it *sort of* bearable." I meant to say something lighter, but that was sitting on my tongue, waiting to be admitted out loud.

"Having fun doesn't mean that you're forgetting him. You're trying to move on with the new reality without him."

She captures all of my attention, the road no longer interesting me. Her tone doesn't carry sympathy I've grown used to hearing these past few months, but more understanding than anything else.

"My grandpa died less than a year ago. Well, he was more like my dad. For awhile, I felt guilty any time I would laugh or have fun. I thought it meant I was forgetting him, but then I thought that he'd probably be pissed if he saw me moping around."

Elliot would probably be pissed too if he saw me now, maybe even disappointed.

We pull into her driveway, but before she climbs out, she reaches over the middle console to peck me on the cheek. It was quick but I still feel the warmth in every crevice of my body.

"Thanks for the ride. I'll see you tomorrow." she says from outside the car window.

"Night, freckles." It's the first time the nickname slips out, but it feels right. I like the freckles on her face, they're like a roadmap to her captivating green eyes.

I wait for her front door to close before driving off back to my house. With my free hand, I touch where she kissed me to feel the stickiness of her lip gloss left there. *Fuck, why do I not hate this?*

My truck still smells like her sweet scented perfume, but I breathe it in like oxygen. Even though our friendship is still rather new, I've noticed this feeling I only have around Kat—like the whole in my chest is temporarily filled.

I'm not sure what that means, but I could get used to it.

CHAPTER 11
Kat

Thirteen - Big Star

As if I didn't have enough on my plate, my car finally decides to crap out. Everything keeps piling on, and I'm getting closer to buckling under the pressure. I had a shift at the bar today, but Sam gave me the day off after I had a slight panic attack on the phone with him.

I thought for sure Andrew would have forgotten about helping me and I'd have to figure this out on my own—which I'm used to—but he texted me before the sun even came up that he'd be waiting for my car to get dropped off at his house.

Not only was it a turn of events that he ended up helping me, but also that I've come to actually enjoy our friendship. The weird tension is gone now, replaced with a comfort you usually only have with people you've known for years.

I walk into Grams' room to find her watching an old western in black and white—she said they remind her of a simpler time.

"Morning, Grams." I snuggle under the blankets with her, just like I used to when we'd have sleepovers as a kid. This house always felt like my safe space, but when I got older, I realized it wasn't the house—it was her and gramps.

"I didn't see your car in the driveway. I thought you left with-out saying bye." Her face lights up when she sees me.

"I would never forget. My car is sitting in the parking lot at work." It's probably getting towed to Andrew's house as we speak.

"Wouldn't start again?" I nod in disappointment. The car belonged to her in the 90s, so she knows all too well the trouble it can be. "I say you sell that old thing and get a new one."

Obviously, she doesn't have the same attachment to it as I do.

"Absolutely not. It was yours, it's an heirloom," I say with a trace of laughter, which gets her to smile. She has the kind of smile you look for on a bad day.

"You think too highly of your grandma, kid." She squeezes my hand, and it's comforting to see she's starting to gain her strength back after her stroke.

"Want me to do your hair?" I ask, hoping she'll say yes. She used to do my hair as a kid, and now, it's the other way around.

A warm smile curves her mouth. "That'd be perfect."

She lets me walk her to the bathroom a few steps away, and I sit her on the stool before starting to stroke each gray strand tenderly. She once had the most luscious blonde hair, the kind you'd see in salon magazines. Time and age got to her, though, and eventually, it faded into the brittle strands it is now. She still tries her best to keep it healthy.

"Remember when I wanted pigtails for picture day, so Gramps spent all night looking up videos so he could surprise me?" I smile fondly at the memory.

Even though I lived with my highly unfit parents until I was a teenager, most days I was here with my grandparents. If it were up to me, I would have been here everyday: I finally moved in permanently at sixteen.

"It was the funniest thing to watch him fiddle with the

apps. He was so confused." She chuckles so hard, she nearly looses her breath. The smile on my face faints, holding a hint of sadness now. It's nice to reminisce, but then comes the pain of remembering. I go back to brushing her hair to distract myself.

"She wrote again." I never thought she could say anything that would make me instantly nauseous, but those three words did it.

"It'll join the others in the trash," I say with no remorse. It's been eight years since my mom peeled away in a strange car, leaving me in the dust as if I never existed. If it wasn't for my grandparents getting full custody when I was sixteen, who knows where I would be now.

When I say I don't hold grudges, that doesn't apply to her. I really thought she would have came back for me, but instead, she was my first heartbreak. Therefore, I have no interest in any of the letters she's sent me recently. I'll give her the same silence she gave me.

"I support whatever decision you make, lovey, but I'm not going to be here forever. If she wants to be a part of your life, I think you should let her." Grams has a soft spot for her, but I can't blame her—no matter what she's done to us, that's her daughter.

"You've been my mom in every way that counts. I don't need her." She turns to face me now, tears welling in her blue eyes, but our moment is suddenly interrupted by the doorbell ringing.

"It's probably Kayla checking on you." I leave her where she is and run to answer the door. To my surprise, Andrew is confidently standing in my doorway. "What are you doing here?" I ask warily.

"Your car got dropped off at my house, but I didn't have the key."

"Shit, sorry. I'll be back." I don't invite him in, because if Grams sees a guy in here, she'll never let me live it down.

"How did they know where to take it if I haven't called yet?" I shout as I scrounge around my purse.

"Sam was there when they finally showed up, I told him to give them my address." I pause to let a satisfied grin touch my lips at the gesture. After what seems like forever, I find my keys and hand them off to him.

He scans my face fiercely, finally stopping at my eyes.

"What? Do I have something on my face?" I ask.

He shakes his head and speaks through a shy smile. "No, I've just never seen you without makeup."

That's when it dawns on me. "I just woke up. I know I look crazy."

The way he eyes me up and down while leaning against my doorway makes me swallow down a lump in my throat.

"Not even close, Harrison." I'm not used to being called by my last name, but with him, I don't mind.

Before I can say anything else, I silently curse at the sound of Grams slippers hitting the tile behind me. "Who is it, lovey?" *Shit.* I can't exactly hide Andrew—he's hard to miss, touching the top of our door with his head.

"Who is this?"

"I'm Andrew. Nice to meet you, ma'am." He averts his eyes quickly to me. So, he actually has manners.

"Ma'am was for my mother; you call me Vera." She reaches out to grab his hand, and it's ginormous compared to hers. He's gentle with her, which I appreciate. "Nice to meet you, Vera. I'm sorry for just stopping by, but Kat's car is at my house and I didn't have a key."

I can't believe what I'm seeing when she turns to me and winks subtly.

"No need to apologize. You're welcome any time, especially since you're helping fix that piece of..."

"No trash talking my baby," I interrupt before she can insult my car—even though it is a piece of shit sometimes.

"You can come by and check on it anytime, Kat." Andrew says before walking to his black Chevy truck parked in my driveway.

"She'll go now!" *I what?* I snap my head to Grams, trying to figure out why she's volunteering me.

"Andrew doesn't want me in his way." I say.

"It's no problem. My parents are at work, I could drop you off later." I look over at Grams again.

"Can I have a minute?" I ask, slowly shutting the door behind me.

"What was that?" I rush out. She grabs a hold of my shoulders and speaks softly. "Kat, I love you, so I'm going to tell you that a handsome guy like him doesn't come knocking on the door every day. Don't waste it."

"We're just friends," I say defensively. She doesn't look convinced, which irks me greatly.

"Whatever you are, being with him is better than sticking around here with me, so go." Her tone is firm, so there goes any chance I had of getting out of this.

❈☙❦☙❈

I HAVEN'T BEEN BACK AT ANDREW'S HOUSE SINCE THE DAY OF his brother's funeral. I forgot how mesmerizing it is. Once you drive through their iron gate, you go up the long, narrow driveway that leads to their two-story house with black trimming. They have this small statue on the grass, gracefully spewing out water. Clearly, they have money, but thankfully they're not the stereotypical rich, snobby people.

As we pull in, my eyes find my green car that sticks out like a sore thumb next to a blacked out Jeep and a BMW. I move to open my door, but Andrew beats me to it. I didn't think guys still opened doors for girls these days. He's kind of a gentleman when he's not a pig.

"You want something to eat or drink?" he asks, closing the front door behind us.

"No, I'm okay, thanks." I move to look at the photographs lined up over the fireplace. They're all of him and Elliot, seemingly chronological in order of their ages.

"I'm gonna change. I'll be right back."

I'm too interested in the pictures to acknowledge him. The first is the two of them in matching plaid shirts. I'm sure their mom made them take that one, which would explain their bored faces. The last picture catches my attention more than the others, though. It's the only one not professionally taken, but it's the most natural, a candid of Andrew's bright smile as he looks over at Elliot. I didn't even know someone could smile that big.

"Alright, let's go see what's up with that piece of..." I snap my head to him, "artwork." The sarcasm is obvious, but I ignore it as we walk outside. I'd be lying if I said it wasn't a *little* attractive to see his muscles contract as he lifts the heavy garage door over his head with ease.

Right away, I notice the walls full of tools—he must know what he's doing then. The first thing he grabs is an unknown machine before walking out to my car.

"What is that?" You'd think I'd know a little about cars from my grandpa, but he'd mostly tell me which tools to hand him and how to hold the flashlight.

"It's to diagnose your car and figure out where to start." He swiftly connects the cord, like he's done this a thousand times.

"When did you get into cars?" I ask, hoping he won't shut down my attempt to know him a little better. To my surprise, he doesn't even hesitate.

"I think I was eight. I learned about cars first, but Elliot still knew more than me so he taught me a lot. He lived and breathed them. He rebuilt that truck himself before he…" The words get stuck, so I save him from trying to finish the sentence.

"My grandpa owned a bunch of classic cars, but he sold them so he could buy my grandma her dream house." The picture of them from the day they bought their house hangs in our living room.

"Can I ask you something personal?" This would be the first time he's asked something about me, of course I have to answer it.

"Depends on what you ask," I tease. Typically, I'm an open book, but some subjects, I'd prefer not to dig up.

"Why are you always at your grandma's house? Do you live with her?" He ducks his head under the hood of the car as I silently debate whether to answer.

"I moved in with my grandparents when I was sixteen," I admit.

"Where are your parents?" I wince at the words I feared were coming. I've never told *anyone* about my parents.

It's a definite conversation killer to admit they're addicts, and my mom ditched me to go live a new life, while my dad is who knows where, doing who knows what.

"They died," I say, dodging eye contact. It's not technically a lie—to me, they've been dead for a long time. They feel like ghosts that only exist in my nightmares and bad flashbacks.

"I'm sorry." His sorrow filled voice gets me to look at him. *There's that feeling again*—like I'm being pulled towards him by this invisible string. I know his sympathy is genuine which makes me feel shitty for lying, but it sounded like the better choice at the time.

"Can I ask *you* a question?"

"Depends on what you ask." A smirk tugs at my mouth when he repeats my words.

"Are you guys rich?" It was meant to lighten the mood, but I really am curious after seeing their house again. He chuckles, like this isn't the first time someone has asked that.

"It might seem like it, but it's only because my grandma left us money when she died. My parents bought this house, the cars, and the rest was used for Elliot's medical bills. I've had access to a trust fund since I was eighteen." I didn't peg him for a trust fund kid, that's for sure.

"What music do you want to listen to?" I ask, changing the subject as I walk up to the radio sitting on his worktable.

"Surprise me," he says, distracted by the machine in his hand.

"I don't think you're gonna like what I listen to." Most people don't appreciate my music taste.

"Try me." I accept the challenge and play a song from my phone—one my grandpa used to play on the acoustic guitar. I wait for the same distasteful reaction I get from everyone else as *Thirteen* by Big Star plays, but I'm pleased when he doesn't react and keeps working instead.

His irresistible grin makes me slightly nervous. "I like this."

"Are you just saying that to get on my good side?" I ask, narrowing my eyes at him.

"I think fixing your car got me on your good side, so I'd tell you if your music taste was shit." I pick up a nearby towel and throw it at him, but he catches it with a swift reflex.

"Alright, smart ass, play one of your favorites so I can judge *your* music taste." I can't ignore the way my skin burns when our fingers accidentally touch as we exchange my phone. It wasn't a bad feeling, more the kind you miss when it's gone.

He laughs to himself before *Sunday Morning* by Maroon 5 starts to fill the silence. I was never into the boy band thing, but everyone knows this song.

Before I can register what I'm doing, I sing along.

Andrew's halt is what gets me to stop, his mouth slightly gaped open.

"I didn't know you could sing." He's seemingly astonished at the sudden realization.

"You can thank my grandpa." We used to sit at the guitar for hours and play covers of his favorite songs, but when he died, so did my love for playing.

The sound of my car struggling for dear life to start interrupts the moment, but Andrew doesn't seem fazed. It's refreshing to see him this way, in his element.

"To clarify, that wasn't my favorite song. I just wanted to see if you'd judge me." He has the kind of dazzling smile that over shines the rest of his features on the rare occasions he shows it.

"I judged a little, but you knew what you signed up for when you begged to be my friend again."

"First of all, I did *not* beg." I hunch over in hearty laughter from his apparent frustration.

"Please. You were practically stalking me." Okay, he didn't stalk me, but I enjoy seeing the way his nose scrunches up when he's irritated.

"Oh really?" He starts to slowly stalk toward me, his brown eyes scanning me like I'm prey. He lifts his big, grease-stained hands and threatens to touch me with them as I slither away and run around the car to avoid him.

"Andrew, I'll kick your ass if you touch me with those." I try to sound threatening, but I'm actually terrified of him coming any where near me.

He races around the car, but I hurry to the grass to dodge him. His rich laughter from behind me is pleasant to my ears. I don't think I've smiled this much since Gramps died. It wasn't on my bingo card that Andrew would be the cause of said smile. He surprises me when he lifts me up off the ground, grabbing onto my waist as if I weigh nothing.

"What were you saying? You were going to kick my ass?" he whispers in my ear, making goosebumps rise on my arms. He holds me still in his muscular arms like a trophy, but after some pleading, he plants me back on the ground.

The distance between us doesn't last long, though, before he closes it to tuck a strand of hair behind my ear. He did it at the party too. How does such a small gesture give me butterflies? Thankfully, he's mindful of our height difference as he bends to be eye-level. His strong jawline, clenched as he concentrates on my face, but the sound of a woman's throat clearing snaps him out of whatever trance he was in.

Emily, his mom, is watching us with a confused look on her face as she holds a bag of groceries. She's absolutely stunning, with thick, dark hair cut to her shoulders and perfectly tanned skin. Her small stature forces her to look up at Andrew as she approaches us.

"What are you doing home so early, Ma?" He suddenly goes stiff. "I got off work early, but never mind that." Her attention turns to me now instead of her son.

"Hi, Mrs. Cortes we've met before, but I'm Kat." I reach to shake her hand, but she disregards it and hugs me instead.

"I remember you. Nice to see you again, Kat." She lets me go and widens her eyes at Andrew, who is obviously uncomfortable.

"I knew you were the girl he was seeing." She seems happy at the idea of us together, and I don't want to take that feeling away. By the washed out look on Andrew's face, he's nervous about her finding out the truth. *Goddamnit.*

"Actually, Ma, we're..."

I cut him off before he can finish. "We're taking it slow. Sorry for keeping it from you, Mrs. Cortes," *Too late to turn back now.* He almost breaks his neck to look at me, but I stay focused on his mom's wide smile of approval.

"I'm glad he found someone so beautiful." Her compliment makes me smile like a little kid. The only compliments I get are from the drunk guys at the bar, but I don't count those.

She disappears to go inside, leaving Andrew stunned.

"What…uhh…" I help him as he scrambles for the words.

"Relax, Casanova. Call it returning a favor since you're doing me one." I didn't plan on pretending to be someone's girlfriend for a second time, but hey, life is full of surprises.

"I'm not fixing your car so you would do that, I swear." It's funny to see him frazzled.

"I know, but friends help each other out, remember?" He doesn't have to tell me he's relived; his face says it all.

Pretending to be the girlfriend of a guy I used to like who is now my friend—can't be that bad, right?

CHAPTER 12

Andrew

"I KNEW I'D FIND YOU OUT HERE." OF COURSE HE'D BE OUT here with his head buried under the hood of his truck. It's where he always was. I hang back just to watch him in action. I'm the older brother, but it was me who ended up looking up to him.

"You gonna help or just watch like a weirdo?" he asks with the same bright smile you could always expect on his face.

I'm overcome with this feeling of sadness mixed with relief when I reach him. When I see Elliot in my dreams, I imagine him the way he was before he got sick again—healthy, happy, and strong.

"What?" he asks, confused at how I can't stop staring at him.

"Nothing. I just miss you, little brother," I say, fighting a sob. The words feel like they're buried under cement in my throat.

I can feel myself starting to wake up, but before I can pull him in for the embrace I've been longing for, I'm pulled back to reality by the loud alarm going off on my phone.

Heaviness overcomes me when I remember the only way I can see, hug, or talk to Elliot is in my subconscious. I know when I'm dreaming about him, but it feels so real, I let myself believe that it is for a brief second.

For that moment, everything is right.

I grab my phone off the dresser to turn off the blaring alarm and see a text from Kat.

> KAT
>
> Good morning! Thanks in advance for the ride to work. I'll bring out a coffee for you. See you soon!

She sent that at six in the morning. I can't even function before nine. I didn't know being a good friend meant waking up at the crack of dawn, but here we are.

Kat is a teacher, so she has to be at school by seven thirty, and it's six forty-five now. At least this will give me more incentive to finish fixing her car.

I spring out of bed to open the drawer where my pills are and have the same mental battle with myself I do every morning. After my dream, I could use something to help me deal with my reality, but I also could try to face the day without them for a change.

One won't hurt. One barely does anything. No one will notice.

The goddamn voice in my head wins as I shake out a pill and swallow it down along with the remorse. The house is quiet, which means I can sneak out while my parents are still asleep. The last thing I need is for them to question where I'm going so early

I quickly jolt down the stairs and scurry around for my keys that I'm somehow always losing.

"Hey, where you headed?" *Damn it. I thought I was in the clear.* My dad's deep voice rolls in from behind me. *I was so close.*

"Out." I try to turn the door handle, but he stops me again.

"Drew, where are you going this early?" I finally turn towards him with clenched teeth. "I'm picking up a friend for work. Any more questions, *Dad?*" The last word burns as it comes out.

I take his silence and walk out into the brisk air I desperately needed, squinting as my eyes adjust to a sunrise I haven't seen in a while. I quicken my pace when I remember I'll be seeing brown hair flowing in my passenger seat soon.

KAT WALKS OUT IN A WHITE T-SHIRT AND JEANS, WHICH IS ODD because she usually incorporates color. The closer she gets, the more I notice the colored flowers hand painted on her jeans. The bottoms of them are cuffed, making her white socks and sneakers more visible.

The way she dresses is oddly satisfying.

She's struggling to balance two cups of coffee in her hand and also adjusting the straps on her tote bag, so I help her out by grabbing them.

She looks at me full of surprise as I lean by the passenger door, waiting for her to get in. Honestly, I surprised myself—I've never opened a door for a girl. It wasn't to be a jerk, but it never crossed my mind until her.

I try not to be phased by her captivating smile as she climbs into the car, only taking back one of the coffees in my hand. I'm not a coffee drinker, but I don't have the heart to tell her that after she went out of her way to make it.

"I don't know how you drink your coffee, but you peg me for a cream and sugar guy." She's beaming as she waits for me to drink it.

Keep a straight face, even if it's gross. After it stops burning the shit out of my tastebuds, the flavor doesn't agree with me, but I keep a brave face to avoid hurting her feelings. It's not horrible, but it definitely didn't change my mind about coffee.

I'll drink as many as she makes me, though, if it means I get to see that smile.

"It's good. Thank you." I try to mask my inner turmoil as I drive, the conversation with my dad this morning still imprinted in my mind.

"You okay?" Her delicate voice pulls my attention to where she's fixing her makeup in the mirror. It's easy to be mesmerized by her doing the simplest of tasks. I have to admit that she buries any girl I've ever encountered, and not just with her looks.

"Yeah, I'm fine." I take another sip of the hot coffee just to avoid the scrutinizing gaze of her green eyes.

"I know you have this thing where you don't like to share, but I'm here to listen if you need it." She speaks with such a genuine soft-ness that it's on the tip of my tongue, but I prefer not to open the Dad box. I don't even talk to Chance and Hiro about him.

"Thank you, but really, I'm fine." She purses her glossy lips like she knows something is up, but to my relief, she doesn't push any further.

"Shit! I forgot my lunch on the counter," she shouts, emptying her bag frantically. "I'll just have to get shitty cafeteria food today." I get this weird feeling in my stomach seeing her disappointed. I would do anything not to see her like that.

We pull up to the school minutes later, and she directs me to where we can avoid the long drop off line filled with parents.

"Thanks for the ride," she says while pulling her hair back with the green scrunchy she always wears on her wrist.

"I'll be back later to pick you up." As I watch her walk away, the unsettling feeling grows in my gut when I think about how she has to eat cafeteria food for lunch. It's been years since I graduated, but I remember vividly that school food isn't great. I can't have her eating that shit.

Why do I even care? What the fuck is happening to me?

I'M SHAKING AS I WALK WITH MY HEAD DOWN TO CLASSROOM seven, a bag of food in my hand. I don't get why I'm so nervous as I get closer, this is just a friend bringing another friend food.

The echo of children's laughter is what gets my head to pop up to the playground full of kids. I remember pushing Elliot on a swing set we had as kids. I swear, I can still recall what his laughter sounded like even back then, but I shake it out of my mind before opening the door to Kat's classroom.

She looks so peaceful as she writes in a notebook. So this is her when she's not getting drinks for people at the bar. The room is very *her*—vibrant colors everywhere, kind messages, and references to the 80s are all over the walls. She's unaware of my presence since the unfamiliar music playing in the background drowned out my entrance. I think about just watching her be, but that's fucking weird.

She startles when I drop the bag in front of her, but once the shock fades away, I notice the glow of delight.

"What are you doing here?" she asks.

I gesture to the food. "It's not much, but there's this deli near my house that has the *best* turkey pesto sandwiches you'll ever have."

She looks suspiciously at it, then at me. "Why did you bring me lunch?" People really must not do nice things for her if she's wary of a turkey sandwich.

"No friend of mine will eat shitty cafeteria food," I say firmly. Her face pouts like she's about to tear up, but she recovers quickly.

"You're already doing too much for me but thank you." She signs contentedly when she smells the inside of the bag. It oddly fills me with pleasure that I put that look on her face.

"Oh, you thought this was out of the kindness of my heart? The sandwich was thirteen fifty, then the gas, so let's just call it an even forty bucks." I try to keep a tight-lipped face as I reach my hand out, but break character when she throws a piece of bread at me.

I glance down at the notepad she was writing in while she's busy eating.

In big bold letters at the top, it reads, *THE AGREEMENT.*

"What's this?" She puts her food down and grabs a pink pen that's sitting on her desk. "If I'm pretending to be your girlfriend, we need some rules set in stone, a pact if you will, so we're on the same page literally and figuratively." The weight of her words settle in, and I can't believe we're actually doing this.

I never thought there'd be a day I had a fake girlfriend, but I guess if I had to have one, I'm glad it's her.

"Ok, what do you have for me, Harrison?"

The Agreement

1. No one can find out
2. Call it off when someone wants out
3. No kissing ~~(unless Kat changes her mind)~~
4. Dinner at Andrew's house to please his mom
5. Break up after 3 months + fake devastation
6. No hurting each other or our friendship
7. No falling for each other

x <u>Kat . Harrison</u>
x <u>Drew Cortes</u>

October

CHAPTER 13
Kat

EVERY YEAR, I DREAD THE CROWDS THAT COME WITH SUNDAY football games. I learned to stay away from any man whose team is losing, they tend to get a little dramatic.

"I need you at the bar to cover Jen's lunch," Sam shouts at me over the game. "Don't even think about making a face, Katlyn." he says sternly before I can even muster up an eye roll. I dread working the bar.

I walk over to the crowd of people hovering over each other, trying to order. I used to get overwhelmed by the big crowds, but I've been here so long, it doesn't even bother me anymore.

"Can I get two scotches on the rocks?" The man in a suit and tie thankfully orders an easy drink to make.

I can usually guess what kind of drink someone will order before they even open their mouth. Older men typically get booze neat or on the rocks, while younger girls get mixed drinks or a shot with some provocative name, and then you have the macho looking guys who just order beer.

I pour out his drinks and charge his card before moving onto the next.

"I'll take four Coors Lights and your phone number," a man

in a football jersey says with a proud grin, as if he just made the smoothest move.

There's always that one guy.

"I've never heard that one before." My sarcasm rings through as I pop the tops off the glass bottles. "Twenty-eight even." I don't even entertain the advances anymore. Most of the men either have no idea how to talk to a woman, or worse: they're married.

"Do you have a boyfriend?" This guy looks old enough to be my dad, making it even more disturbing.

"Twenty-eight even." My voice hardens.

"Oh c'mon, don't you ever smile?" *The infamous line.*

"She does, but only for me." The assertive voice comes from Andrew, who slid into the seat next to the man without my notice. I feel relieved when I look over to see him, not only because he saved my ass, but because he's just here.

"And you are?" His jaw tightens at the man's rude tone before a devilish smile takes over his face.

"Her boyfriend. She said twenty-eight bucks, and add an extra ten for a tip." I've never heard his voice so cold. It sends chills down my back, and I'm not even on the other end of it. Call me crazy, but he's wildly attractive when he's protective.

The guy relents, putting two twenty-dollar bills on the counter before he walks away with a huff.

"My hero." I pretend to swoon over him, and he eases into a smile at the ego boost.

"It's fun pulling the boyfriend card. It's like a threat," he boasts with a puffed-out chest.

"I get customers like that twenty times a day, and you can't pull it on everyone," I unfortunately admit.

"Damn. This is what I get for having an attractive fake girlfriend."

I roll my eyes at him but turn my back so he won't sense the warm glow travel through my chest from his compliment.

Someone else comes up to the bar to order a drink, but my concentration is on Andrew as he watches me work attentively. I pretend not to notice, but lately, I've caught him looking at me like he doesn't care about what else is going on around him —the place could be burning, and he wouldn't budge unless I did. While it's flattering, I can't help but think of how many girls he's looked at that way.

Anyway, we're friends, so I shouldn't look too much into it.

"What are you doing here? You just dropped me off not too long ago." He's been picking me up in the morning to take me to my first job, bringing me here at four, then giving me a ride home in early hours of the morning. He's not even taking the money I offer for gas. I'm persistent on taking Ubers, but he doesn't entertain the idea, not even for a second.

"It's about your car..." His distant tone doesn't settle well with me.

"Bad news first." I hold my breath as I wait.

"It's the clutch." *Of course it is. It couldn't be something easy, like oil.*

"How much?" I grimace.

"The part is eight hundred." My chest aches at the blow. I was expecting a high number, but not that high. With most of my money going to the bills and Grams' nurse, it'll take me months to save up that much kind of cash.

"Is there good news?" Knowing my luck, there isn't, but I ask anyway.

"The good news is that you have a friend that likes to work on cars and give you rides in the meantime." I don't think he's ever heard of modesty.

"I don't have that kind of money right now." There's no speck of judgement on his face, even as I cower with embarrassment.

"Don't worry about it. I got it." There's *no* way he's this nice without wanting something in return.

"I can't ask you to do that when you're already doing way too much."

"Well, it's not free. I do want one thing." A mischievous grin grows on his smooth face. I knew it; he was too good to be true.

"Come bowling with me, Chance, and Hiro on Friday. They cheat, so I could use the extra help. Plus, it's a friend thing and you're one of us now." I let out a sigh of relief, but I also feel guilty for assuming the worst. "I guess I can spare some time."

I never expected to get along with the three of them so well, but overall they're good guys. They're all so different but somehow they work.

"Alright, it's settled. I'll see you later. Tell the next guy who looks at you that your boyfriend knows how to fight." He leaves a twenty on the counter despite not ordering anything, and walks out before I can give it back.

I didn't realize I was watching him leave until Sam blocks my view with a disappointed look on his wrinkled face.

"What?" I ask defensively.

"I don't like that look on your face." There's no trace of humor or amusement in his voice.

"I could say the same about the judgy look on yours," I throw back with resentment.

"I thought you said there wasn't anything going on between you guys?" He's scolding me like a dad who just caught their kid doing something they're not supposed to.

"Relax. We're just friends." He doesn't look sold on the truth.

"Right, because friends call themselves your boyfriend. Is that a new thing with you kids?"

I can't tell him about our arrangement. One of our rules is to keep us a secret, but I also can't have him thinking that Andrew is my actual boyfriend.

"Can you keep a secret?" I'm already regretting this, but one person knowing won't hurt, right?

He puts everything down and listens attentively, like a school-girl hearing drama. "Of course."

"We're not actually dating. It's fake."

His thick eyebrows arch. "Bullshit," he spits with a ripple of amusement.

"It's true. Andrew needed me to pretend to be his girlfriend in front of his family." Saying it out loud to another person makes me realize how stupid it sounds.

"Let me get this straight: to everyone else, you're friends, but the second you go around his parents, you're a *pretend* couple?" He's obviously trying to piece everything together.

"Exactly, and what he said earlier was just making fun of the situation. I swear, we're *just friends*." I try to emphasize the last part so he can grasp that I'm not lying.

"That can't end well, right?" His question is valid, but it still irks me.

"Since we don't have feelings for each other, there's no risk."

"Just be careful, Kat. I care about both of you, and I don't want this blowing up in anyone's face." We might talk shit and get under each other's skin, but we care for each other like family, which is why he pries, and why I actually listen to his input.

"I'm always careful, Sam." I pat him on the shoulder and walk to the back for a break. Andrew comes to mind when I sit down.

I didn't agree to this arrangement because of the pressure of his mom, but because since I've met him, I've felt pulled to him.

I thought it was romantically, but I guess it's platonic. We carry ourselves in a similar way, in the sense that we both put on brave faces instead of letting people in. He doesn't think I notice, but I can see glimpses of sadness through the cracks of his mask. I just have this feeling that he needs my help, and not just to be his fake girlfriend.

I have the urge to wake up Grams to say goodnight, but it's late, and I don't want to disturb her peaceful slumber. I miss her during the day, but Kayla texts me updates to make me feel included in her routine.

Sam had to threaten some guys when they refused to leave so I left the bar later than usual. It's nearly three in the morning, and I have to be up in three hours for school. My body is overcome with exhaustion, but a hot shower is calling my name.

I greet Sage before putting fresh food and water out for him, then check on the plants I have scattered around my room.

Gramps loved plants, he'd get me a new one every time he went to the farmer's market. Before I knew it, they were engulfing every corner of my room. I'm a shitty plant mom, but I feel the need to keep them alive since they were from him.

Sage comes to join me on the mattress as soon as my body sinks into it. My eyes get so heavy with sleep, I can't hold them open anymore until my phone's ringer blares in my ears. Andrew's name flashes across my screen, but he just dropped me off minutes ago.

"Miss me already?" I ask in a sleepy voice. His laugher on the other end comforts me.

"I forgot to say goodnight when I dropped you off."

I'd be lying if I said my heart isn't racing now. "Don't get sappy on me, Cortes." I poke at him. I've never called him by his last name, but he always calls people by theirs, I guess it's growing on me.

"You wish, freckles," he mumbles. I thought I misheard when he called me that the first time, but it's clear now. "Freckles?"

"It's your nickname. It's also a compliment since I like your freckles." It's a good thing he can't see me smiling like an idiot right now.

"Can I tell you a secret?" He asks in a whisper.

"Of course," I say, fighting my sleep.

"I like how easy it is with you. I forgot how nice it is to smile or laugh, and I don't do it this much with anyone else."

His admission makes my eyes well up with tears. It's the nicest thing anyone has ever said to me. I never imagined such sweet words could come from him. "What are friends for?" I say, smiling up at my ceiling.

"Goodnight, freckles."

"Goodnight, Andrew." As soon as the line goes dead, I find myself wishing I could still hear his deep voice. I drift off to sleep with the peace that comes with knowing I get to see him tomorrow.

CHAPTER 14

Andrew

My sleeping schedule has been shit lately—from taking Kat to work early in the morning, then taking her home late from her second job. I honestly don't know how she juggles it all and still manages to stay upright. I'm convinced she's superhuman.

"Andrew Cortes," The nurse shouts into the empty waiting room of my doctor's office. With everything else going on, I almost forgot about the check-up I had scheduled today. Without this visit, I can't get refills on my medication, so needless to say I jumped out of bed when I remembered.

"He'll be in shortly." The nurse closes the door behind her, leaving me in the cold, brightly lit room.

Doctors' offices have made me uncomfortable since I can remember. I tagged along to every appointment of Elliot's, even when we were kids. I remember when he cried after getting his first flu shot. I asked them to give me one too, and I pretended to cry so he wouldn't feel alone.

My chest feels heavy as the memory gets more and more vivid. My fingers graze the pills in my front pocket, begging to be acknowledged.

I shouldn't.

One won't hurt. It would make it all go away.

I'm shaking as I put two pills on my tongue, swallowing them dry. I lay my head back, counting down from ten, but I'm interrupted when my doctor enters with a smile.

"Andrew, how's my nephew?" he asks, sitting down on the stool in front of the computer.

"I'm good." He doesn't react to my short tone—he's used to it by now. Unlike our family gatherings, our visits are brief and to the point, which I like. He's my Mom's only brother, so I see him often, but thankfully he's kept these visits between us.

"Any new issues I need to know about?" I hide my shaking hands in my pockets, away from his view. I can feel the loose pills wiggling around.

I almost bring up how old memories are starting to come back to me in random flashbacks and nightmares, but I shake my head instead. I know he'll just try to recommend me to a shrink, just like everyone else in my family.

"Your trembling hands you're trying to hide tell me otherwise. That's new."

Here comes the prying. "It's just anxiety, that's why I need my medication refill."

"What triggered it this time?" He types away on his computer.

"Being here." I answer bluntly.

"What exactly about being here makes you anxious? I've known you your entire life. Tell me what's going on. That's what I'm here for."

My hands stop shaking and are now balled into fists at my sides. "I remembered something about Elliot being at the doctor." I say. I only answered so I can get out of here faster. He rolls his chair over to me, but keeps a safe distance.

"Andrew, you've been through something traumatic, and very recently at that. I know I diagnosed you with anxiety and depression, but you have all the symptoms for Adjustment

Disorder as well. It would explain why you're having a hard time coping. You need to learn how to deal with your feelings in a healthy way instead of medicating yourself. You went through your monthly supply quicker than usual. I let it slide because I'm your uncle, anyone else would cut you off, but I didn't prescribe the pills for you to use as a crutch."

And here I thought this would be a quick visit.

"When you say deal with them in a healthy way, you mean talking to a shrink?" I ask tightly. Sitting in a room with a stranger for an hour talking about feelings sounds worse than the nightmares I'm already having.

"I think it would help you, you might even be able to grieve Elliot and move on."

Move on? Losing Elliot isn't something I can move on from. My brother was the only person who understood me. How do I grieve someone like that? *I don't. I can't.* I just learn to live with the pain that comes with not having him around anymore. If taking pills is the only way for me to do that, then so fucking be it.

"Can I just get my refill please?" I say through gritted teeth, trying to suppress my rage. He breaks eye contact with me and goes back to his computer.

"It'll go to the same pharmacy. I know you're having a tough time, Andrew, and I just want to see you get some help. I'll come by the house and check on you guys soon," he says before leaving me alone in the cold room again.

"I know you're having a tough time." Tough time doesn't even scratch the surface. I feel like there's a pit of darkness following me around, waiting for me to fall in so it can consume me.

As I stay in the chair gathering my thoughts, my phone vibrates with a text from the group chat.

HIRO

> Hope you and Kat are ready to get your asses handed to you in bowling later. 10 o'clock.
> Don't be late!

I'm not in the mood to go anymore, but they would never let me live it down if I flaked. Not to mention, Kat asked to get off an hour early just so she could go, it'd be a dick move if I backed out.

Guess I'll tough it out as usual. Anything to keep the illusion going, right?

❦

K<small>AT</small> <small>BROUGHT</small> <small>EXTRA</small> <small>CLOTHES</small> <small>SO</small> <small>SHE</small> <small>COULD</small> <small>CHANGE</small> <small>AFTER</small> work, saving me the trip back to her house. The light blue jeans that hug her hips are very flattering to the lower part of her body, while her floral crop top compliments her chest.

I'm certain she could wear a trash bag and still make it look good.

"Stop looking at my boobs, you perv." She smacks me on the arm while laughing from the passenger side. From her point of view, it may have looked like that's what I was doing, but really, I was trying to read the letters engraved on the crystal necklace dangling from her delicate neck.

"Get over yourself. I was looking at your necklace. But now that you mention it, they are pretty nice." My eyes find them now, and my lips tug at the corners in an unconscious smirk. The rosy tint of her cheeks tells me she accepts the compliment, but she bites her lip to hold back a smile. Just seeing a sliver of it makes my bad mood from earlier dissipate. It's comical how completely unaware she is that she can do that.

I already see Chance's black Lexus parked in front of the

bowling alley. Kat reaches for the door, but I reach over to stop her.

"I got it. Chivalry isn't dead, you know." She follows me with her eyes as I walk over to her side of the truck.

We're side by side walking into the building, our hands mere inches away from grazing. The inkling to grab her hand alarms me. I try to avoid it with other girls. Kissing is one thing, but holding hands seems more intimate than I was ever willing to be.

"Damn, Katherine, you look good," Hiro compliments her as we make our entrance. Six months ago, I used to flirt with anything that walked too, but he has the crown now.

The bowling alley is packed, as expected on a Friday night. We always come this late—after ten o'clock on weekends, they replace the regular lights with LED ones, and the pins glow in the dark.

"You're lucky you're on D's team Kat. He likes to cheat if you're playing against him," Chance warns as we walk to get our bowling shoes.

"I don't cheat! They just can't accept that they suck," I boast as I pass my card to the worker to pay for everyone. We all switch off on paying, but since Kat is here, I'll take the hit.

"Hey, Andrew," a high-pitched, familiar voice chimes from behind the counter, and I almost pretend I don't see her.

"Hey, Nat." *Fuck, I forgot she worked here.* We went out one time, and then she got pissed when I didn't call her after, even though I told her that I don't date.

"Long time no see," she says blandly. Kat is on my side, but she's laughing about something with Hiro and Chance instead.

"I haven't had the time to come by." I'm shaking with eagerness to leave this conversation, but the worker is slow to grab our shoes.

"Or time to call." Her blonde hair is pulled back into a bun, showing off her piercing hazel eyes. Sometimes, I feel bad for not calling girls back, but none of them can say they were surprised. I always set my boundaries early. If that makes me an asshole, I won't apologize for it.

"Ready?" Kat comes to my side and grasps onto my arm as if she sensed my distress, and my teeth clench with anger when I see Nat sneer at her.

"Absolutely." The worker finally comes back and we leave the counter, but her arm doesn't unwrap from mine as we walk close together.

"I could tell you needed a little help with that," I get a whiff of her sweet scent when she leans in close to whisper. I appreciate that we have this unspoken language, that we just know when the other one needs help.

Chance is first up to bowl. He grabs a ball and gives me a sly grin. I'm not threatened by him at all—I wasn't joking when I said they suck. I get a kick out of seeing them get pissed off though, which is why I enjoy coming. He throws the heavy ball down the lane, and it goes straight into the gutter.

"Who needs to cheat when you're shit at this?" He flips me the middle finger at my insult and sits down next to Hiro.

"Fuck you. It was a warm up."

When Kat is up, she picks a heavier set ball.

"Don't hurt yourself." I shake my head with pity at Chance because I already know what's coming.

I haven't known her that long, but I know she loves to prove people wrong—especially a man. She smirks at him before turning to throw a strike. I clap so obnoxiously it gets people from other lanes to turn their heads.

"And here I thought you'd actually be competition." She snarks.

I notice a group of guys in the lane next to us ogling at her as she strides back to us. My jaw clenches so tight, I can feel my teeth grinding. They shouldn't even be able to breathe the same air as her. I don't think anybody should, even me.

To no surprise, Kat and I won both games, and of course Chance and Hiro were sore losers. After about five minutes of bickering, we called a truce and decided to hash it out over some arcade games.

Me and Chance always go up against each other in basketball, so we head there first. We're beside each other, waiting for the buzzard, then he moves away and lets Kat take his place at the last second.

"I'll take it easy on you, Harrison." I say, throwing the first ball into the net.

"Don't. That way when I beat you, I can say it was fair."

Competitive looks really good on her.

We hurry to get as many baskets in a minute. Kat was keeping up on her own, but her score doubles when Chance and Hiro start to help her out.

"You fucking cheaters." I shout, picking up the pace.

I lose by a few baskets, and usually I'd be upset, but if I was going to lose to anyone, I'm okay with it being her.

It isn't until their hockey score is 3-0 that I notice Kat isn't standing near us anymore, and my eyes quickly scan the entire room for brown hair. I almost think she went to the bathroom until I see the back of her floral shirt facing an unfamiliar tall figure.

His hands are glued to his pockets as he sways side to side nervously while he talks to her. How she can make any guy fold is beyond me.

"C'mon, you're not even trying." Chance's annoyed tone pulls me back to the game, but my eyes don't leave Kat.

Why is his face so close to hers? My fingers clench onto the air hockey handle so hard, I'm afraid I'm going to break it.

It bothers me that she doesn't seem to mind that he's in her space. *Why does this bother me?* We're only fake dating, so techni-cally, she can talk to whoever she wants, but the idea tugs a string inside of me I didn't even know existed.

Something comes over me when she throws her had back, laughing at something he said. I leave the game, ignoring the angry pleads from my friends as I head straight for her before I can stop myself. I know I shouldn't, but my legs won't stop their pursuit.

"Are you doing anything next week?" I overhear him say before I approach.

"Yeah, me. I'm her boyfriend, so you can go." I wrap my arm around her waist and eye him in a challenge.

"Sorry, man, I didn't know. Have a good night." I'm content when he backs away from us with his hands up.

Kat shakes off my arm as soon as he's gone. "Andrew, what the hell?" she blurts out coldly.

"Hold on—are you two dating?" Hiro butts in on the convers-ation, and I'm suddenly aware that they overheard everything.

"No," we say sharply in unison.

Hiro doesn't buy it. "See, you say no, but just a few seconds ago, you called her your girlfriend. I need some clarification."

Chance nods as they look from me to Kat, waiting to see which one of us is going to answer.

"Can you guys just give us a minute?" One look at my face, and they leave us alone in awkward silence.

"What gives you the right to get involved in my business?" she asks, her arms folded across her chest. I have to look down at her because of our height difference, but somehow, she still scares the shit out of me.

"I thought this was one of those times I had to pretend to be your boyfriend," I lie. I know she didn't want me to get involved, but I wanted to. I can't tell her that, though, so I go with the latter.

"Well, it wasn't. I think it was obvious I wanted to have a conversation with him." It *was* obvious—I just didn't like it.

"I'm sorry." I'm not sorry for interrupting her little moment with that douchebag, but I am for erasing the smile on her face. I can tell the second she decides to relent. Her eyes soften and her lips purse.

"I forgive you, but don't do it again, not unless I look in distress." I can't promise her that, so I wink instead.

"We're waiting." We look over at my friends: I guess we have no choice but to let them in on the secret.

It's our very first rule in our arrangement, yet here we are, breaking it.

Some rules are meant to be broken, though.

CHAPTER 15
Kat

TODAY IS THE DAY MY BIG MOUTH PAYS THE CONSEQUENCES. Rule number five of our arrangement—I have to have dinner with Andrew's family to convince them we're this happy couple. Even though we're fake, I still feel the pressure of needing to leave a good impression. I can usually charm anyone, but this is a whole different ball game. I can feel the nerves starting to bunch together in my stomach. I'm wearing one of my favorite maxi dresses, hoping it'll bring me luck. It's a neutral color, but with small pink flowers on it so it still feels like me.

Since my car is still being held hostage in his garage, Andrew had to pick me up. I've been over once a week to help him work on my car, and by help, I mean picking the music and passing him tools.

I've enjoyed seeing firsthand how our friendship has developed over the past several weeks. Even when we're just hanging out in his garage, it's more fun than I'd have with anyone else.

When we pull up to his driveway, my body stays planted in the seat while I try to gather myself.

"You'll be fine, I promise." Maybe it'd be easier if we were actually dating, but not only do I have to leave a good impression, I have to pretend to be head over heels for their son.

No pressure.

I rub my hands on the silky fabric of my dress, trying to calm my nerves. I've never met a guy's parents before, but I imagined it'd be under different circumstances.

"How are you so calm?" I look over to see him cool and colle-cted in the driver's seat.

"Trust me, if I was with anyone else, I'd be throwing up on the sidewalk right now."

The more I study him, the more mesmerizing he looks. He must have gotten a haircut, because his thick, wavy hair is now a little above his ears, resembling a young James Dean. I take in the rarity of seeing him in something other than a t-shirt. He looks great in them, but he should wear black collared shirts more often.

"How do I look?" I ask, trying to hide the tremor in my voice.

He scans my entire body like he's trying to undress me with just his eyes. "You look beautiful, but what's new Kat?"

His crooked smirk is what makes the nerves disappear compl-etely. I know he's genuine, because when he's telling the truth, his brown eyes dilate and the muscles in his face relax. When he's angry or irritated, the muscle right next to his ear clenches.

He opens my door before I can even try to do it myself, as usual. I'm gonna miss the gesture when I have to open my own door again. I gain a new level of bravery when his warm hand grabs mine as we walk up the steep driveway together.

There's a split second when he squeezes my hand where it almost feels real—like this moment is for us and not for his parents.

It passes as quickly as it came.

We walk straight to the kitchen, still holding hands, to find

THE DARKNESS THAT FOLLOWS US

his mom standing over the stove while his dad sets the table. Now that I get a good look at them both, Andrew is the perfect mix. His dad's light-colored eyes compliment his dark hair and full mustache. While Andrew looks a lot like him, I still see Emily in his eyes and on the rare occasions when I see his bright smile.

They don't notice we're here until Andrew clears his throat to get their attention. I freeze when their eyes find me, and I suddenly miss when they were distracted. I face drunk people every day at the bar, but I have never been this intimidated before.

"Kat, I've heard so much about you. I'm Miguel."

I note the way Andrew's hand suffocates mine the closer his dad gets to me. It's not until Emily rushes to hug me that our hands separate. I miss his warmth as soon as it's gone, and I notice the way his hand flexes in the absence of mine.

"I hope you're hungry. I pulled out my best recipes for you." She taps her long fingernail on my chin in an endearing way.

"I saved my appetite—I'm starving." Just then, my stomach grumbles with hunger. "Do you need help with anything?" I can't cook for shit, but it's polite to ask anyway.

"Absolutely not. You're our guest. All you need to do is sit down and eat."

I wouldn't be too much help anyway. Before I can sit down, I feel Andrew's strong hand on my back as he pulls the chair out for me. His mom seems stunned at the gesture, but I'm not. I look over to notice an extra placemat set up. I didn't know there was someone else joining us, but I ignore it to focus on Andrew's dads voice.

"So Kat, tell us about yourself," his dad says from the other end of the table. I've always hated this question.

"I teach second grade, which I love, but I also work at Sam's, which I don't so much." I wish I had more interesting things to

112

say, but when you work two jobs, there's hardly any time for hobbies.

Thankfully, Emily puts the final dish on the table in front of us and takes a seat next to her husband. Andrew's practically drooling over the food, and I don't blame him.

"My mom only makes her enchiladas for special occasions, so dig in." He catches me off guard when he serves my food first, but I should have expected he'd do that.

"Who knew my son was just a gentleman?" Emily boasts, holding a hand over her chest as she admires me and Andrew.

I shift nervously under her gaze but decide to just go with it.

"He's been great. You raised a good person, really." Andrew's eyebrows shoot up in surprise, and I hope he knows that wasn't a lie for his parents. Deep down, I think he knows. I can feel his gaze soften on me.

"You're very sweet, thank you." Emily's eyes almost shine with tears at my compliment.

"I've seen you working on her car. How's that going, Drew?" his dad speaks up, but it's met with Andrew's obvious hostility. His fingers start to tap, and his leg starts to shake vigorously under the table. There's a sudden frost hanging in the air now that I feel helpless to fix.

I take the risk of doing the only thing I can think of, and place my hand on his leg to hopefully give him comfort. I immediately regret it and try to pull back, but he grabs onto it like it's his lifeline.

"It's going good. It's her clutch, so it'll take awhile, but it's getting there," he finally answers, still holding onto me for dear life.

Just then, his mom announces dessert. "Oh! I made chocoflan."

"Chocoflan?" My eyes must be bulging out of my head with excitement. Andrew nods.

"It's this dessert my grandma would make when she'd visit

from Mexico. It's chocolate cake under a custard with caramel on top."

"Can I have some of that now, please?" They all seem delighted by my excitement, and I suddenly think of Grams and her apple pie.

Guilt plunges into me that I'm here instead of with her. I hardly have free time, but whenever I do, it's spent with Andrew now. I can't help that I like spending time with him. He makes me forget about all the problems waiting for me.

Andrew picks at his food, seeming disconnected from his parents' conversation.

"I forgot to tell you that you look really nice today," I whisper closely to his ear. I don't know why I said it; all I know is that I don't like the somber look on his face. His eyes shine again, as if my voice

brought him back to the moment.

"Not as good as you," He whispers back, followed by a wink.

"Duh." I flip my hair back, getting him to laugh. His parents don't seem to mind that his laughter interrupted them. In fact, they look relieved that it did.

I hope the rest of the night goes as smoothly.

I'M HELPING EMILY DRY THE DISHES WHILE ANDREW WAITS IN the living room. He offered to help but was shewed away by his mom to spend time with his dad, though he didn't seem too happy about it.

"You should know that I knew it was you he was talking about when he said he was seeing someone. I'm glad I was right."

I'm full of questions, but I start with the obvious. "How'd

you know it was me?" I keep at my task of drying dishes as I wait for her answer.

"The first time I saw you at the hospital with him, I knew there was something, whether or not you two knew it yet. When he's with you, he lets his guard down, and I don't even think he realizes it. He's gentle, he smiles, and you brought back his laughter when I thought I'd never hear it again."

I have to admit, I'm shocked. How could she have seen some-thing then when we didn't talk for weeks prior?

"He's a really good guy." I'd feel shitty for telling her another lie, so I say something I know is true.

"What are you two gossiping about?" Andrew's voice makes me jump.

The sleeves on his shirt are cuffed now, exposing his toned arms. He must have been ruffling his hands through his hair, as it's messy the way I've come to like it. I suddenly can't pry my eyes away from him.

"Kat?" When I snap my attention back to Emily, she smiles knowingly, and my cheeks turn hot from the embarrassment.

"Andrew said we could do this again, so you should pick our next dinner." I'm stunned by this new information, but I decide to go with it anyway. "Uhh, that'd be great. Thank you."

"I'm calling it a night. Kat, it was great to see you. You're welcome anytime." She embraces me with a warm hug that I sink into before she walks up to Andrew and kisses him gently on the forehead.

"Goodnight, mijo. Don't forget to lock up."

"Kat, it was nice to meet you." His dad enters the kitchen and waves to me from a distance. If I wasn't looking, I would have missed the way Andrew's back tenses when he feels his dad behind him and eases as soon as he's gone.

We're alone for the first time tonight when they go upstairs.

"They like you." He pulls himself up to sit on the countertop with no struggle at all.

"What can I say? I know how to win people over." I shrug my shoulders.

I meant it as a joke, but I faintly hear him whisper, "I know." I pretend I didn't hear it in case he didn't want me to.

"Can I ask you a question?" I ask hesitantly. A hint of fear covers his face, but he nods anyway.

"What's up with you and your dad? You seem tense when he's around." He shifts uncomfortably and starts to pick at his nails. I feel terrible for asking when he finally looks up, and I'm able to see the sadness in his eyes. "You don't have to answer. I'm sorry I asked."

"No, you have every right to ask. I just don't know where to start." His chest starts to move faster as his breathing gets heavier, and his hands start to subtly shake. Before I know it, I'm in front of him, holding tightly onto his hand, trying to take all the light I have in me and give it to him.

"We don't have to talk about it, really." I take his hand and move it to linger over his heart.

"Feel that? When you feel overwhelmed, just focus on your heartbeat. How fast it's going, the intensity, the feeling under your palm."

When I try to drop my hand, he pulls it back on top of his like it belongs there. There's a force that seems to be pulling us closer together the more we try to resist it, and my pulse starts to race when he glides his index finger across my face. I'm conflicted by my response to his touch; I've never reacted that way around him before, but then again, he's never touched me like *that*.

"I've never seen someone with green eyes like yours. There's this little strand of blue that you can only see in certain lighting," he

whispers in a husky voice. We're so close, all it would take is one of us to flinch, and our lips would touch. This moment isn't a façade—his parents aren't around. The pull I'm feeling towards him isn't fake. The comfort I tried to give him wasn't for show. *But we're not real.* We're friends.

I'm grateful for the alert that goes off on my phone, because it allows me to pull away when I was physically incapable of doing so. He may have pulled me in for a second, but I have to look at the bigger picture. What we have is good, and I don't want to ruin that by becoming just another girl on his long list.

If I didn't know better, I'd say he's disappointed that I backed away. Being close to him rose my body temperature a few degrees, so I clear my throat and try to cool myself down.

"Let me take you home." He jumps off the counter and checks his pockets for his keys.

"Actually, I beat you to it and ordered an Uber. The alert on my phone was my ride saying it'll be here soon," I gloat, showing him the order confirmation.

"You're not taking an Uber," he spits out with a tight expression.

"Watch me." Now I have to take the ride to show him that he can't tell me what to do. He shakes his head but smiles at my defiance like he finds it fun.

"Fine but stay on the phone with me until you step foot inside your house," he demands.

"Whatever you say." I mock his voice as best as I can but it's hard since it's so deep. The app says that my ride will be here in a few so I start to gather my things to avoid keeping them waiting.

"I have to grab something, but don't leave without me so I can walk you out." He runs upstairs before I can protest.

I don't know if it's because we're friends and there's no longer any pressure, but Andrew wasn't like this last summer. Sure, we had fun, but it never felt like this. He never made it feel like I was the only girl in the room. I never felt this pull to him whenever we were close. I just can't put my finger on why this time feels so different.

117

My phone goes off, telling me my ride is parked outside, but Andrew is still absent, and I don't want to keep them waiting. I almost leave, but since he asked me to wait, I go upstairs to find him. I've only been up here once, so I try to be as quiet as possible as I snoop around.

Thankfully, there's a door cracked open that I assume is his, but he's nowhere in sight when I enter. I've never been in his room, but it's very *him*. Posters of old trucks and cars line the white walls, books are scattered on his desk, and shirts are thrown on his bed.

Right before I'm about to walk out, my eyes catch sight of an open pill bottle next to his bedside table. I shouldn't go through his private things, but curiosity eats at me. My eyes go wide when I see *Xanax* printed on the label above his name, and they go wider when I see this was given to him two weeks ago and it's nearly half empty. The drawer that's cracked open also contains empty bottles with the same label.

I don't stay around to confront him, instead I quietly leave down the stairs and run outside to where the car is waiting for me.

As the car drives toward my house, I conjure the worst possible scenarios of what I just saw.

There are so many questions—what are they for? How long has he been taking them? If he's supposed to be taking them, why be so secretive about it? You don't keep bottles of pills in your night-stand unless you don't want anyone to find them. Is it because he has an addiction?

I could have let him explain himself, but when I saw those pills, I was transported to the old trailer home where I used to watch my parents get high. Mom and Dad started off just taking pills, but then it escalated, and my entire life was fucked. Andrew would never do that, I know, but I can't help but think the worst.

I promised myself I would never willingly be around

someone who did drugs or took pills. I almost thought about breaking that promise tonight, but as much as I like our friendship, promises with yourself have to be sacred.

I decline his call as it comes in. I know I have to talk to him about this, but I can't right now, not when my brain is scrambling. A text comes through the moment I decline the second call.

> I thought you were going to wait? But anyway, call me so I can make sure you don't get kidnapped

There's no evidence that he knows something is wrong, so he must have not heard me storm out. I've tried burying my past so deep that the only place it exists is in my occasional nightmares, but it finds me in my everyday life.

Since I was fourteen, I've felt like there was this darkness latched onto me that I can't escape.

I've mastered the art of pretending it's not there, but it always comes back to remind me it's lingering. The shitty thing about your past is that it finds a way to follow you.

CHAPTER 16

Andrew

I'll Look After You - The Fray

It's been a week since Kat and I have spoken, and the only indication I have that she's okay is the text saying I didn't have to pick her up because she'd be taking Ubers. I even went by the bar a few times just to see her, but each time, Sam lied and said she wasn't there.

I wish she'd just talk to me. I want to know if I did something and how to fix it. I didn't realize how engraved she'd become in my everyday life until my days felt empty without her. I miss tasting the coffee she brings me, seeing her hurry to finish getting ready in the passenger seat before school. I miss her smile. I've gone over every scenario she could possibly be upset about, and the only one I came up with was maybe she got weirded out by our moment in the kitchen when she came over for dinner.

I say that because it weirded me out too. For one second, it felt real. It scared the shit out of me, but once I realized it was with Kat, it faded away.

"D." Chance's voice echoes in my ears as he snaps his fingers to get my attention.

"Yeah?" I try to play it off like I wasn't just a million miles away.

"I asked if you wanted to get in the ring today or just hit the bag."

"Let's run some drills in the ring," I suggest as I set my bag down on the floor. I've been using my free time to join Chance and Hiro in the gym, but even though I'm here physically, I've been checked out the past week, replaying every detail of the last time I saw Kat and where it went wrong.

"You've been extra mopey lately; what's up?"Chance asks as we circle around each other in the ring, Hiro hanging on the ropes. "I haven't been mopey." I hit the mats on his hands with a little extra force than I intended as the words bite out.

"Cut the shit. We know something is up." He taps me on the head, making my neck crank with frustration.

"Nothing is wrong, Barrett." I switch stances and hit with more urgency and purpose now.

"If I had to guess, it'd be that you and Kat haven't talked."

I stop and eye Hiro warily. "How do you know that?"

He smiles mischievously. "I couldn't get a hold of you on Tuesday, so I texted Kat, and lo and behold, she said she hasn't talked to you lately."

"How'd you even get her number?" I don't know why *that's* the first thing I acknowledge. I remember giving her number to Chance when he asked for it, so I'm sure he passed it along.

"Relax, Drew; I'm not trying to steal your fake girlfriend. I have it because we're all friends now, remember?"

I roll my eyes at his smart remark.

"Anyway, that's not the reason." I lie. I only hit the mat a few more times before I go back to the bench. I'm tired of pretending I don't want to be anywhere Kat is right now.

A girl has never had this much of an effect on me, and I don't know what the fuck to do about it. When Chance and Hiro are mad, I just let them cool off and reach out when they're ready, but with Kat, I'm constantly checking my phone, waiting for crumbs.

They both come to join me on the bench, but we don't say anything for several minutes.

"You're our friend, but if we have to endure another day with your broody ass, Drew, I might have to fight you, so fess up." Chance says.

My leg shakes vigorously before I force the words out. "Kat hasn't talked to me in a week, and I can't fix it because I don't know what the hell I did. It's only been a week, but I miss her, like actually miss her. Isn't that fucking weird?"

Their eyes shoot to each other so quickly, I almost miss it.

"Why do you think you like being around her?" Hiro typically gets uncomfortable in conversations where he can't crack a joke, so I'm amused to see him serious for once.

It shocks me when I don't have to think long for an answer. "I don't know. I guess that, with her, my mind can shut off. To her, I'm not the guy who just lost his brother—I'm just Andrew. It's different with you guys. I can tell you walk on eggshells around me." My throat tries to lock up, but I push through. "Then, when she just drops off the face of the Earth, all those feelings come back with a fucking vengeance."

Pressure releases off my chest from the word vomit, and I almost think that's the end of the conversation with how long we're all silent. It finally occurs to me that we're sitting in the middle of the gym having a therapy session which is definitely a first.

"I'm sorry if we ever made you feel that way, D. We know how important Elliot was to you, and I guess we just try not to trigger anything."

"I know," I say sincerely. Chance and I have given each other lectures when the other does something stupid, but we've never sat down and talked like this. He's probably the only person who would understand exactly how I feel— he lost his older brother in a car acci-dent years back, and I know it kills him every single day.

"If Kat makes you feel like, that then you need to talk to her and fix your friendship. That pain you have after losing someone doesn't just go away, Drew. You found someone who helps make it easier to bear, so keep her around." Chance nods, agreeing with Hiro. I suddenly miss when he'd crack jokes.

"She doesn't want to talk to me."

"Then you're going to have to try ten times harder for her to listen." I never thought I'd see the day I'd be taking advice from him, but there's a first time for everything. I pat them on their shoulders and gather my things to leave.

"Let's not do that again. It creeped me out seeing you guys so serious."

"Hey, D." Chance's booming voice makes me turn around to face them just as I'm walking out.

"Just so you know…with us, you'll always be Drew and not the guy who just lost his brother."

I don't know what I did to have friends like them, but I pity anyone who doesn't.

SINCE I CALLED THE BAR AND WHOEVER PICKED UP SAID KAT wasn't in, the next best place to check is her house. I've avoided going by because I didn't want to intrude on her grandma, but now I'm desperate.

It takes longer than expected to gather up courage to knock on her door. I'm on the verge of throwing up into her bushes, but I hold it back. I assume no one is home when my knock goes unanswered until I hear rustling, and the door swings open to reveal her grandma's welcoming face.

"Andrew? What are you doing here?" she asks with a lively smile. They both have the same smile that could brighten anyone's day.

"I'm sorry to bother you, Vera, but I was looking for Kat." I speculate that she's not here either; otherwise she'd be the one on the other side of the door right now.

"No need to apologize. You're welcome any time. Kat had a car pick her up to get some groceries, but she'll be back soon if you wanted to wait inside."

"Oh, that's okay I don't want to intrude I'll just come bac—" She interrupts me before I can finish speaking. "Nonsense. Come in and wait for her."

I do as she says and duck through the doorway to a retro-decorated living room. Vera directs me to take a seat on the couch while she rocks in her recliner.

Every inch of the yellow wall is covered in pictures, and my eyes find one of Kat when she was a kid right away. If she forgives me, I'll have to tease her about the glasses she wore back then. I didn't realize I was smiling at the photo until Vera points it out.

"That was the day she started third grade. She loved those glasses. Her grandpa had them, so she felt like part of the club."

She reaches over to retrieve a photo album and hands it to me with trembling fingers. I'm hesitant to look inside, but the curiosity of seeing more pictures of Kat as a kid consumes me. The first picture to catch my eye is of her when she's no older than six, rocking an awkward cut bob and a missing tooth. I'll have to tease her for that too. In all the earlier photos of her, she has blonde hair. I always assumed she was a natural brunette.

The more I flip through pages, the more jealous I grow of how content her childhood seems. My fingers linger on a more recent photo of her. She couldn't have been older than fifteen, hyper focused on playing the acoustic guitar in her lap, totally oblivious to the camera. Her hair is pulled out of her face into a messy bun and she's still in her pajamas, but even a grainy photo catches the natural glow she had even back then.

"That was Christmas morning seven years ago. She was always jealous of her grandpa's guitar, so we decided to get her one too. She was absolutely awful at first, but eventually, it turned into my favorite sound." She smiles fondly, making me do the same as I picture a younger Kat jamming out to the guitar with a smile on her face.

"I didn't even know she played." I don't break concentration from the photo as I speak. I was mesmerized when I found out she could sing, but playing an instrument is new to me. There's so many layers to her, and I want to learn every single one.

"She hasn't since my husband died. It seems like when he left, he took the music with him, but I miss it." Her eyes turn sad.

"Thank you for showing me these." I pass the album back to her waiting hands.

"I don't know what's going on between you and Kat, but whatever it is, I'm glad you're around. She's always been the one who figures it out for us, always puts the family first, but she's never lived. With you around, she does more than just work herself to death, so thank you." The sound of the door closing makes my heart race before I can muster up a reply.

"Grams, whose car is parked in the drive—" She stops in her tracks when our eyes meet for the first time in a week. I drove my mom's Jeep here, so of course she didn't recognize the car.

"What are you doing here?" She tries to mask her anger, but I still catch it.

"I came here to see you." The way I say it with such ease startles me. She doesn't say anything as she walks into the kitchen and starts to unload the groceries she brought home.

"I'll be in my room." Vera gets up to walk away, but not before winking at me, nudging to where Kat is making a ruckus in the kitchen. The more I'm around her, the more Kat's personality makes perfect sense.

"Can we talk?" I finally break the eerie silence as I join her in the kitchen. Her obvious detachment gives me a feeling of unfamiliar misery. I want to know what I did for her to look at me like I broke her.

I'm both shocked and relieved when she pulls me down the hall and into a room I assume is hers. It's exactly how I pictured it would be—colorful, earthy, vintage rock band posters hanging on the walls, vinyls scattered across the floor. In the corner sits a beanbag chair next to a stack of books.

"I was trying to avoid this conversation for as long as I could, but you're here I guess it has to be now. We can't be friends anymore, Andrew. I can't fake date you, and we can't hang out. I'm sorry." I was expecting her to be pissed, but she's more disappointed and crushed than anything, which is ten times worse. I stiffen with shock as my face flushes from her sharp words.

"I'll accept that you don't want to be friends anymore if you tell me what the hell I did." If she truly doesn't want to be friends after this, then I'll respect her decision, but I'll never forgive myself if I don't ask for an explanation first.

Her face pales, like she's looking at a ghost, before she lets out in a gasp. "I found your pill bottles...I can't be around someone like that, Andrew I just..."

I feel a new level of pain at hearing the way her voice cracks. I'm at a loss for words. I'm embarrassed. I slowly walk over to her on the bed, wincing when she moves to the other side, avoiding me. I never wanted to say this out loud, but if this is how I keep her around, then so be it.

"The pills...I've had them since before Elliot died. No one knows. I feel like there's this darkness that's constantly following me around, and I have to fight everyday for it not to swallow me. The pills help." My voice breaks as tears prick my eyes and slide down my cheek. Before I can wipe them away, she rushes to my side and does it for me. I'd be repulsed at crying in front of anyone else, but not with her.

"I'm sorry you saw that. My dad gets me a little on edge, the pills help make everything more bearable." I'm not trying to make excuses, but she needs to know the truth.

"You don't have to pretend to be okay around me." My breath hitches in my throat as I stare at her perfect face, unable to get any words out. She's the first person to see right through me, past the mask.

"Everything is easy with you. It's easier to breathe, to think, to pretend I'm the old Andrew, even if it's just for five seconds." I don't know why I admit it out loud, but it feels right. She grabs my hand, similar to what she did that day at dinner when I was anxious talking to my dad. I like holding her hand. It's always painted with sage green polish that compliments her creamy skin.

"I'm sorry. I just assumed the worst, and it's probably not my place to say anything, but the pills aren't going to help you grieve Elliot. Your problems will still be there when they wear off."

I don't know what comes over me when I let out a gut-wrenching sob that's been lodged inside of me for months. "It should have been me." Her face drops as I repeat it over and over like I'm possessed.

"It should have been me, not Elliot. It should've been me." I collapse into her lap, and she cradles me as I cry. Her sniffle makes me aware that she's crying with me. I feel shitty for pouring all of this out, but she's a safe haven for vulnerability.

"It's not easy being the one left behind, but you can be grateful you're still here. I am."

The words *I am* pull on a particular string of my heart that's never been tugged before. Her fingers start to ruffle through my hair, soothing me to the point where my eyes feel heavy enough to sleep.

There have been other girls, but none like Kat Harrison. She's her own genre of a person. Fun and grounded. Empathetic and graceful. Beautiful but not cocky. She's witty but generous.

Now, she has a piece of me no one else does. On one hand, it's a relief, but at the same time, it's utterly fucking terrifying.

CHAPTER 17

Kat

Landslide - Fleetwood Mac

Monday is usually the toughest day to get through. The kids are still tired and grumpy from the weekend, but I feel the same way today. I'm supposed to be grading the spelling test I gave last week, but instead, I'm using some time to call someone I've been meaning to for weeks.

"Look who finally remembered I exist." She was never one to hide her sarcasm. Emory can be a hard pill to swallow at first, but she means well. Once you get to know her, she'll do anything for you. She used to be a lot grouchier before she softened up with Elliot.

They were the epitome of love, the classic love story, except Emory didn't get the happily ever after with Elliot, at least not in a literal sense. Witnessing their love story unfold made me believe that love still exists. She was beside him every waking minute until he died. She's only twenty, but she's stronger than most.

"Sorry I've been so busy with the two jobs. Then my car had some problems, so Andrew's been helping out and—"

"Pause. You've been hanging out with Andrew?" Her shock makes me regret opening my mouth.

"He's helping fix my car." I can't give her the whole truth—she'd tell me I'm crazy for being his fake girlfriend. A month ago, I'd say she was right, but it works for us.

"And that's it?" I can smell her insinuation even from three hundred miles away.

"Yes, nosey. It's been nice hanging out with someone since you're off at your fancy school, and besides, he likes the company now that…" I bite my lip to stop myself from speaking Elliot's name. Last time I let it slip, I could hear her silent sobs on the other end.

"I'm glad he has you around. Elliot was really important to him. I imagine he needs someone to get him through this." She speaks softly and shakily. While I'm glad I'm here for Andrew, I can't help but wonder who's there for her while she grieves. I can only do so much living in another state.

"How's school?" I ask, attempting to change the subject.

"Hell. I underestimated how hard these classes were gonna be, but thankfully, I've met some smart people to copy notes from." I want to believe she's joking, but I know she isn't.

"Good thing you only have four years to go." I just know she's flipping me off right now.

"I hate you," she bites out in between lighthearted laughter.

"Are you coming back for winter break?" I know it's a stupid thing to ask when her laughter dies off and I hear her breath hitch.

"I think I'm gonna stay here. I can't be there—not yet." It shatters my heart to hear her stumble for the words. Of course she wouldn't want to come here. It's only been two months since the love of her life died; why would she want to return to the place where he's everywhere? *Nice going, Kat.*

"I get it. I'm sorry I….asked" My sudden pause is caused by

Andrew almost giving me a heart attack leaning in the doorway of my classroom, silently watching me.

"It's okay, but I gotta get to class. I'll call you soon."

"Call me if you need anything." She doesn't say much else before the line goes dead. If I had the chance to go to San Diego to be with her, I would take it in a heartbeat, but I can't afford to miss work, and Grams needs me. I wouldn't know what to do if I left Phoenix anyway.

"What's wrong?" Andrew asks while taking a seat in a chair meant for an eight-year-old.

"Nothing. I was just talking to my grandma." I try to hide my face so he can't tell I'm lying. Emory would kill me if I told him she was having a rough time.

"Is that what I think it is?" My gaze falls to the familiar bag in
his hand.

"Turkey Pesto, especially for you. I asked for the bread that just came from the oven, so it's fresh."

I bite into it as if I haven't eaten in days and sigh with contentment when it hits my tongue.

"I have lunch, you know." I say between bites to avoid talking with my mouth full. I wouldn't necessarily call a tuna sandwich from the cafeteria lunch, but I didn't have much to pick from.

"I'm sure that sad-ass sandwich is great, but I figured you'd want this instead." I wonder if he's aware how captivating his smile is; it has become one of my favorite sights.

"I don't want you looking at me eat like a creep, so here." I say, sliding the other half of my sandwich to him as I suppress a giggle.

"How's my car?" It feels so familiar hanging out with him this way, just having casual conversation like we've been doing it for years. "Good news and bad news." Last time he said that, I almost fainted from the hit.

"Good news first." I always prefer bad news last. That way, I can sulk directly after if needed.

"It's almost done." His voice is bland, and his expression reads nothing but disappointment. "And the bad news?"

"We won't get to hang out in my garage anymore." I try to ignore how my pulse is pounding against my skin. He has a way of making all my senses spin out of control without warning.

"We'll just find something else to do then." He keeps a tight-lipped expression, but his eyes tell me something else by the way they light up. No one looks at me the way Andrew does; I can't imagine how'd he'd look if he were in love with someone. Just the idea of that is laughable, though, he's never shy of showing his resistance to relationships.

He starts to fiddle with the ring on my index finger, making me ignite from his gentle caress. Being close to him this way is like being under a blanket of comfort.

"Shit. The kids are coming back in two minutes." I throw myself around like a rag doll as I frantically assemble chairs for reading time. I blame Andrew and his stupidly cute smile for distracting me.

"You go round up the kids. I'll set up the circle thingy." Chills run up my spine as I feel the pressure of his hand come to rest on my back. I know it shouldn't, but my body feels powerless to even his gentlest touch. Clearly, I'm embarrassingly touch deprived.

While I appreciate his offer, I furrow my brows at him with uncertainty—he knows I like things done a certain way.

"Can you just trust me and not be so weird about it?" He pushes me towards the door just in time for the bell that indicates it's time for the kids to come back inside.

It makes me smile to see my class already lined up in single file—they might actually respect my rules. The first kid in line is Ella, who's the sweetest but very shy. She looks up at me through her thick glasses.

"You're pretty, Miss H." She says timidly. I bend down to be eye level with her and squeeze her little hand.

"You're prettier." You would think I just told her she's going to Disneyland from the smile that covers her face now.

"Alright little ones, use your inside voices and sit in the reading circle." I shouldn't have doubted Andrew, because all of the chairs are evenly lined up in a perfect circle. I couldn't have done it better myself. The kids all look shocked at the stranger, but they also look intrigued by him, like he's an artifact.

"Guys, this is my friend Andrew. What do we say?"

"Hi, Andrew." I'll never get tired of hearing them shout things in unison. Andrew tightly waves at them, and the confidence that naturally radiates off him falters. Being the subject of twenty kids will do that to anyone.

"Are you reading to us today?" one of the kids asks, looking up at him like he's a skyscraper.

"No, I'm just setting up chairs." He mutters uneasily. It's sort of funny seeing him get so nervous around kids.

"Miss H, can your friend read to us?" another student asks, making everyone turn their full attention to me.

"Sorry kiddos, Andrew has things to do so he can't stay." They whine with disappointment, and Andrew's eyes shoot to me as he playfully winks.

"Actually, I can stay, but only if you guys promise to always listen to Miss H." Why do I feel like he's going to start using my teacher name against me? I can't exactly protest him sticking around when the kids seem so excited. They'd hate me for the rest of the year.

I grab the book I was going to read and hand it to him with a slight grudge. I actually enjoy reading to the kids, but they forgot that I existed the second they saw him.

I sit at my desk while he starts to read out loud with a shaky breath. I subtly snap a picture of him in the chair that's *way* too small for him and send it to Chance and Hiro.

To my surprise, he turns animated, interacting with the kids as if he's gaining courage the more he reads. Witnessing it strikes a chord inside of me that's been untouched until this very moment.

※※※

I'M STILL HEAVY WITH EXHAUSTION AS MY PHONE WAKES ME from my deep slumber. I just closed my eyes not too long ago, after getting home from the bar.

"Hello?" I greet groggily with my eyes still shut.

"Hey." Andrew's broken voice has me wide awake.

"What's wrong?" I shoot up, startling Sage. His silence is frightening, making me bite my nails as I wait.

"I had a nightmare. Usually, I take my pills when it happens, but when I went for the bottle, I thought of you." His voice is low but equally alarming; I know the sound of defeat when I hear it.

"I'm glad you called. What can I do to help?" I ask, rubbing my eyes to eliminate any lingering sleepiness.

He speaks in a shattered whisper. "Can you play a song for me on the guitar?"

Now's my turn to go still. I gaze over at my once-favorite acoustic guitar collecting dust in the corner. I haven't touched it since we lost Gramps. I meant to put it in the music room after the funeral, but I didn't have the guts to go inside. Now, it just haunts this space. A ghost that occasionally calls out my name.

"How did you know I played the guitar?" I manage to get the words out somehow. No one except my grandparents know I played. It's not something I advertise to people.

"Vera showed me pictures of you playing." *Of course.*

There's a dull ache in my chest from the idea of declining

him, but my hands are trembling as I recall running my fingers across the same strings my gramps' fingers did not too long ago.

"You still there?" he asks after several minutes of my panic.

"I haven't played in a long time," I whisper.

"I won't judge if you sound a little rusty...well, I won't judge *that* much." His husky laughter unravels my knot of anxiety.

"Don't ever say I'm a bad friend after this." I put my phone down on the bed so I can walk over to the haunted corner.

I run my fingers across the golden strings and almost tear up at the sound. I'm transported to the day I unwrapped this guitar on Christmas, my grandparents watching with excitement. I never played as well as Gramps did, but no one could in my eyes. We learned a new song every week, and once I perfected the playing, he taught me to sing too.

"Miss you, Gramps." A tear falls down my face quicker than I can catch it, but I gain the courage to walk back to the bed and lay it in my lap. It's ice cold as it touches the skin of my thigh, but it also feels right.

"Any requests?" I put the phone on speaker while pulling the old guitar strap over my shoulder. My chest vibrates when my fingers strum the dainty strings.

"Your favorite song to play."

I smile faintly at his ability to make *me* feel important even when this gesture is for him. There's a song embedded in my memory that I'd ask Gramps to play for me until I finally learned to play it myself. I almost think to play another song, but I trust Andrew with this part of my past now.

I start to play *Landslide* by Fleetwood Mac, the strings singing to me as though they missed me. I'll never sound as amazing as Stevie Nicks, but I'd like to think I have a voice that's pleasing to the ear.

I let my eyes tear up when I think of what my grandpa would think—I'd like to think he's somewhere watching me. I never wanted to give up on music, but I never had the strength to go back to it until now.

Until Andrew.

I manage to get through the song without choking up, and I grow insecure at how silent Andrew is. I can't even hear him breath-ing.

"Sorry, I've never been speechless before. I'm trying to process," he finally says.

I thought playing again would be scary, but playing for him made me feel at peace. He doesn't even know he mended a piece of me that was pleading to be fixed.

"I'm already fake dating you, Cortes. You don't have to lie to get on my good side," I joke, but I'm relieved he didn't say I sucked.

"I'm not lying. Seriously Kat, that was amazing. I didn't know you were that good."

If it weren't dark in my room, I would see my flushed cheeks in the mirror. "Thanks, you're the only one I've played for other than my grandparents." I was never comfortable playing around anyone else, but he came in and changed all of that.

"Well, you're doing the world a disservice by not playing for them." His words are laced with silk. Anything he says sounds like poetry.

"Did that help at all?" I ask.

"Yes, but now I'm wide awake and want to hear more."

I chuckle; I've never laughed as much as I have since we re-kindled our friendship. "I aim to please. What do you want to hear?"

An hour and three songs later, I finally hear his calm breath-ing on the other end of the line. He thinks I helped him tonight, but he helped me. I always feared I'd never find a reason to pick up a guitar ever again, but I did.

Him.

CHAPTER 18

Andrew

I'VE NEVER BEEN ONE TO TALK ON THE PHONE. IT FEELS TOO personal, but every night for the past week, Kat's voice is the last one I hear before I shut my eyes. Sometimes, we just talk; other times, she plays the guitar, her voice a calming lullaby. Not only have I not been reaching for my pills as often, but I don't wake up every morning dreading the day, since I know I get to see her face.

I'm at the stove making eggs when my mom walks into the kitchen, clearly very apprehensive about seeing me cook.

"Who are you, and what have you done with my son?" She narrows her eyes.

"What? I can't make myself eggs?" I ask playfully.

"I didn't even know you knew how to turn the stove on." Sarcasm pours out from her lips.

"Does your good mood have anything to do with a certain brunette I've been hearing you on the phone with every night?" She tries to hide her raised eyebrows under the mug as she takes a sip from it.

"Have a good day at work, Ma."

She pouts when I don't give in to her prying, and I duck

down so she can kiss me on top of my head. Once the door closes behind her, I'm completely alone with my thoughts. Usually, that would scare me, but nowadays, my mind is more occupied with something—someone—else. I never knew being friends with a girl could be so fun. I decide to eat upstairs today so I can watch TV in bed, but I regret it when I notice the door to Elliot's room is cracked open. I pass by it every day, and it's never open. It's one of the house rules we all established after he died.

I want to close it, but I can't promise myself that I won't try to go inside. I can't go inside, though. Time is frozen inside of that room, everything exactly how he left it. Mom hasn't even washed his clothes, so they'll have his scent forever.

I'm saved by the doorbell ringing downstairs, and I jolt to answer it just to get away from that suffocating hallway.

"What are we doing for Halloween?" Chance greets me as he nudges past, letting himself inside.

"Same thing we always do: nothing." I haven't made a deal out of Halloween since I was like eight. I prefer Christmas.

"C'mon, this is my first Halloween single. I owe it to my teenage self to go out," he pleads as he grabs my remote and starts to flip through channels. He's lucky he's practically family; otherwise, I would have thrown him out by now.

"Whose dumbass idea was it to get into a long-term relationship in high school?" I spit back.

"Touché. But seriously, D, I need you as a wing man. Just one party." I brush my fingers through my hair out of frustration. Deep down, I know I don't have any other choice.

"I'm not dressing up." My voice comes out in a mumble.

"Me and Hiro already decided that we're going as the three musketeers though." I'm seconds away from cursing him out, but he bursts into uncontrollable laughter before I can.

"Fuck you," I groan. He almost fooled me, and I try to repress my own laughter.

"You kiss your girlfriend with that mouth?"

"*Fake* girlfriend." Calling Kat by that title leaves a sour taste in my mouth, even though it's true. Now that our friendship has evolved, it sounds more like an insult. Hiro and Chance are my best friends, but Kat's friendship is different. She knows me on a deeper level than anyone else.

"Right...fake girlfriend." The way he elongates the words doesn't sit right with me. I threaten him with my narrowed eyes.

"Why'd you say it like that?" He puts his hands up in surrender at my defensive, curt tone. "I'm just saying, I don't buy that it's *all* fake when you're fixing her car and spending all your free time with her." My jaw ticks at his insinuation.

"Last time I checked, friends help each other out, Barrett." He laughs at my unintentional coldness. "If you say so, D." He excuses himself to the kitchen, leaving me with the echo of his words in my head.

Anyone with two brain cells would know he was hinting I like Kat, but how could he think that? I don't act any differently with her that would insinuate that I do.

Granted, she's the only one who knows my true feelings about Elliot, the only one I confided in about the pills, and I do smile more when I'm around her, but it doesn't mean I like her that way. It just means I enjoy our friendship. People can enjoy being platonic.

It's not in the cards for me to fall in love and live happily ever after. It happens for people like Chance, Kat, even Hiro, but not me. I've made peace with my fate.

I HAVE TO FORCIBLY PRY MY EYES AWAY FROM KAT AS SHE reapplies her cherry red lip gloss in the passenger seat. She curses under her breath as she scrambles for her favorite lipliner, but then she smiles like a little kid when she finds it at the bottom of her purse.

"So there's this costume party at work I have to attend on Halloween, and I wanted to see if you could go with me?" My deafening silence fills every inch of the car as she waits with hopeful eyes for my reply.

"Costume parties aren't really my thing," I say. I'm gonna kill Chance when I see him. He's put it in my head that I'm doing all these gestures for Kat because I like her—which I don't —but what if she thinks the same and I'm giving her the wrong idea? I don't want to make her feel like I did last summer. Our friendship is one of the only good things I have, and I can't mess that up.

The only indication she's disappointed is the frown that takes up her face briefly before she turns it back into a smile. She must be well rehearsed on doing that, because it would have gone unnoticed if I wasn't admiring her.

"No worries. I asked because everyone is bringing someone, but we're not actually dating, so it was dumb to ask anyway."

I wish she'd get mad instead of being understanding; maybe it would make me feel less like shit. "I'm sorry." Am I supposed to feel this crappy for saying no to her?

"Andrew, it's okay. It's not the end of the world if I go to a party alone." She gives me her beautiful smile, but I can sense the torment behind it. A new level of anguish settles into my heart knowing I could have prevented that look on her perfect face. In the same second, the torment is gone as walks into work with her head held high.

She looks confused when I walk her into the bar instead of leaving as I usually do. "What are you doing?"

"The guys wanted to meet here."

"Don't sit in my section." A glint of her humor returns, to my great relief. We've sat in her section on purpose ever since she voiced how much it annoys her, but we know she finds us entertaining; well, mostly Hiro.

Sam's gray mustache flickers when he sees me approach the bar counter to greet him. "I'd say I'm surprised to see you, but I've seen your face more in the last few months than I have in the entire five years you've lived in Phoenix." He pops the top off a beer bottle and hands it off to an unfamiliar face. "Table three, Angie." I brush off the way she runs her eyes over my face before leaving Sam's side.

"I've been giving Kat rides." I admit innocently.

"As long as that's all that's happening." His tone is playful, but body language says otherwise.

"Relax. We're just friends." He's not the first person to not look convinced. If one more person implies something about me and Kat, I'm gonna go fucking crazy.

Speaking of her, she manifests in front of me with a wide grin across her face that makes me wary.

"Don't make it obvious, but my new coworker over there is totally eye fucking you."

I can't concentrate on whatever she's saying, because her sweet, citrusy perfume distracts me. Not to mention that under the direct lighting of the bar, she glows even more than usual. My eyes keep going to her red glossy lips that look like they taste like cherries.

Why the fuck am I worried about what they would taste like?

I pretend to stretch so I can turn to see the girl who smirked at me earlier. "She's cute." I shrug my shoulders dismissively.

"I'll introduce you." She smiles devilishly, looking behind me and over at the girl.

"No you're not." I boldly meet her shiny gaze so she knows I'm serious.

"Oh c'mon, you must be having withdrawals without a date for this long." Usually, it'd be unsettling that I haven't been on a date in months, but lately, it hasn't even been on my mind.

"Actually, I don't. I already get my ear talked off with you, so there's no need for dates." She smacks me playfully on the side of my head with a towel.

"You know you love it." I save a mental image of the way her nose scrunches when she smiles. I thought I knew all her motions, but I'm still learning new details about her all the time.

I don't deny it. I really don't mind her talking my ear off. I'm more of a listener anyway, it's nice to let someone else do the talking. It does amaze me how she always has something to talk about, but at least I'm never bored.

"Angie, come over here for a sec," she shouts, motioning for the girl.

"I'm gonna kill you," I whisper through gritted teeth.

"Shut up, you'll be thanking me later." She gestures to me like I'm a prized trophy she's showing off.

"Angie, this is Andrew. Andrew, this is Angie. My job here is done. I'll be somewhere pretending to work." She skips away, but not before subtly winking in my direction.

The girl's amber eyes sear into mine like a siren as she waits for me to say something. She reeks of the kind of confidence you have to notice as she eyes me. Wispy bangs flow from her jet-black hair, complimenting her heart-shaped face. She's definitely my type. A few months ago, I would have already had her number, but now, I feel like a fish out of water.

"I meant to approach you the other day, but you talk to Kat a lot so I just assumed you were her boyfriend," she says in a high-pitched voice.

"We're just good friends." I give her a tight smile as my eyes wander. The smile she returns is dazzling against her tan skin, but I can't help but compare it to Kat's. When Kat smiles, she radiates warmth and undeniable beauty, and she has a dimple that only shows itself when she smiles big enough. I've only managed to make it appear once, but I'd be lying if I said I wasn't always trying.

"I'm usually not this forward, but maybe I can give you my number and we could hang out sometime?" Her light eyes bore into mine as she waits. She seems nice, and no one can deny that she's cute. Why wouldn't I say yes? *But,* I find myself searching her face hoping to find emerald-green eyes or freckles or plump, rosy cheeks.

It startles me when Kat's face appears in front of me before I see Angie's again.

"I'm sorry. I can't." By her stunned expression, she's probably never been told no. She walks away with obvious embarrassment, but I don't feel any regret as I watch her leave.

AFTER WATCHING CHANCE AND HIRO POUND BACK FIVE BEERS each, I decided to drive them both home and come back for Kat. She usually doesn't get out until two when she closes, so I had plenty of time.

Typically, I wait for her outside, but I fucking hate the cold, so I use my key to let myself in through the back door to wait inside.

The place is dark and eerie when it's not packed to the brim with people. Everyone from the kitchen is gone by now, but the dining area is still lit up. I start to hear a song I recognize right away playing loudly. I know Kat is the cause, she plays it frequently in my truck.

I follow to where *I Don't Want To Miss A Thing* by Aerosmith is coming from, and sure enough, I find her singing along as she wipes down tables. She hasn't noticed me yet, which is probably why she's gracefully swaying back and forth to the music. My feet are glued to the floor as I watch her in her raw form. I could watch her this way forever. She exists as if no one is watching, yet that's what makes everyone want to watch her.

She's a rare soul that you only get granted the luck to encounter once.

I make a noise when I trip over the leg a chair, making her turn around. Her face lights up when she spies me. No one ever lights up when they see me.

"You're back already? Couldn't wait to get back to me, huh?" She mouths the words to the next song as she wipes down tables.

"Don't flatter yourself, freckles." I grab a damp towel to help her clean.

"How'd it go with Angie?" Her soft smile wraps me in a cocoon of bliss.

"Uhh…it didn't work out." I silently hope she won't ask for any details, but who am I kidding—it's Kat.

"Why not? She's your type. She has a pulse and everything." Her laughter is more beautiful than the music playing on the jukebox.

I chuck the wet towel at her face, but she dodges it.

"Seriously, though, I'm sorry it didn't work out." Another thing I like about her is how sincere she is.

My mind reels, thinking about why her face came to mind earlier, and I come to the conclusion that Kat has just engraved herself in me, so now, I compare every girl I see to her.

Honestly, none of them even hold a light candle to her in my eyes.

CHAPTER 19

Andrew

I'M SPENDING MY LEAST FAVORITE HOLIDAY BEING DRAGGED TO A costume party and babysitting my friends. *Woo fucking hoo.*

Hiro decided to go as Tom Cruise from *Risky Business*, but honestly, I think it's so he didn't have to wear pants. Chance decided to go as a greaser from *Grease*, and it's really difficult not to poke fun at him when he has a whole tub of gel in his hair and his leather jacket keeps squeaking against my seats. They tried to get me in a costume, but I'd rather mop the ocean floor.

"I thought Katherine would be here." Hiro's discontent carries over the music playing on my radio.

"She's at a work party." My eyes stay glued to the road, but I can feel Chance's skeptical glare. My physical body is here in the car with them, but my mind is stuck on the fact that the only peep I've heard from Kat today was a picture of her costume, along with a quick rundown of *The Breakfast Club* when I didn't recognize she was dressed as Claire.

"Why aren't you there with her?" Chance asks, voice full of surprise.

I look over at him with a tight expression. "Weren't you the one who told me I spend all my free time with her?"

Before he opens his mouth to speak again, we start to hear loud music blaring down the entire block.

"Did this person invite the whole fucking city?" I ask as I circle around.

"It's a college party. What you did you expect, D?"

I haven't even been inside yet, and I'm antsy to leave, but after what feels like hours, we find a spot to park and head into the house lit up with red and orange lights. There's a tall skeleton holding up a sign that says *one jello shot for entry* when you walk through the door covered in fake spider webs, but I walk right past the liquid courage.

I always feel a little out of place at college parties, even though I'm the same age as most of the students. I thought it was crazy to expect an eighteen-year-old to decide his future right after high school, so I took some time off. It's now been almost four years, and I still haven't decided what I want to do, and I'm reminded of it every time we come to one of these parties full of people who know what their next step is.

Chance goes straight for the booze and pours himself a drink while I fail at finding water.

"Hey, Andrew." I turn towards the soft voice, and my face brightens at a familiar face.

"It's been awhile, Lacy." Since she's no taller than five foot, I have to practically hunch down to the floor to embrace her. Lacy was one of the only girls who was on the same page as me when it came to only having a one-night stand. We even stayed acquaintances for a little while afterwards.

"What are you supposed to be?" I ask, scanning her long blonde hair and ripped up clothes covered in fake blood.

"I'm Drew Barrymore after Ghost Face killed her in Scream."

I definitely see it now that she's pointed it out. Her costume is one of the few in here that looks like thought and effort went into it.

"What are you supposed to be? A man whore?" I know her

remark is in good humor since we left on good terms, so it gets a laugh out of me.

"Don't forget that you went out with me."

A teasing smile tugs on her dark red lips. "Touché. Call me if you're ever bored." She kisses the palm of her hand and pats my cheek before walking off to join her friends.

"I'd say that I'm surprised you hooked up with Lacy James, but who am I kidding? Of course you did." Chance shakes his head as he takes down a shot.

"Relax—it was two years ago," I say, rolling my eyes.

Before we can talk further, I watch as he gets pulled away by a brunette dressed as a cheerleader. It's nice to see him interacting with girls again. I thought for sure he'd be hung up on Izzy for who knows how long. I stay put, my back pressed against the cold counter, watching as people dance around without a care in the world. There's crowds of people either dancing, playing drinking games, or just laughing with their friends, and then there's me. When I pull out my phone, the room suddenly stops. Kat's name sits on my screen with a text from five minutes ago.

> I'm surrounded by millennials, yet no one has commented on my costume. I hope your party is better than mine. Be safe tonight!

I smile fondly at her message, but then a wave of remorse crashes over me that I'm not there to keep her company. Just the idea of her sitting alone makes me sick to my stomach.

"I love parties with rich kids because they have the high-quality booze." Hiro suddenly pops up with a full bottle of whiskey in his hand.

"If anyone could sniff it out, it's you." There was a time when I worried about Hiro's drinking, but I also know a drunk when I see one, and he's not it.

He pours some of the dark liquid into his cup and takes a

satisfied sip. He chugs the rest down and amps himself up to walk over to someone eyeing him across the room. I should have known they were going to ditch me. I'm occupying myself by agonizing over Kat's message. The more I imagine her there, the more I feel pulled towards her with an invisible string. Just as I'm about to type a reply, I feel someone searing their eyes into me.

"Hi." I look up to see a girl with model features peering up at me with interest. I can see her honey-colored hair through the red wig that's slipping. "Hi." My tone is short and edged.

"You don't remember me?" She inches closer to me, but her face still doesn't ring a bell.

"Am I supposed to?"

"Sophia Garcia, but you used to call me Soph? We had math senior year of high school." Now it clicks, but the only way I remember her is because she let me copy her homework.

"Oh, hey. It's good to see you again. Sorry for copying you all the time. I fucking hate math." She looks up at me through her long eyelashes, and since I can't exactly back up anymore, she has me cornered.

"I didn't mind—I had a crush on you back then." Her hand grazes my arm as she reaches behind me to pour vodka into a cup.

"Did you have a girlfriend back then? I never saw you with anyone, but I just assumed you did." I can tell by her swaying that the drink in her hand is definitely not her first of the night.

"No, I didn't." I look around frantically, trying to find Chance or Hiro to save me from this awkward exchange.

She smiles devilishly as she puts her red acrylic nails on my neck to whisper in my ear. "Do you have a girlfriend now?" The stench of vodka is strong on her breath.

"No." *Does a fake girlfriend count?*

"You want to go talk somewhere?" Of course, she doesn't mean talk, but I have no interest in going anywhere with her—or anyone for that matter. A glimmer of Kat's bright smile appears in my head, and I swear I hear her warm laughter too.

Great, now I'm fucking hallucinating her.

A sudden revelation hits me over the head like a brick. What the fuck am I doing here? Why am I wasting my time talking to these girls when the only girl I want to be around is Kat? Not just now, but all the time. Seeing her face while I'm talking to another girl once is a weird coincidence, but twice must be my subconscious trying to tell me something.

"Actually, I have to go." I leave her with a dumbfounded look on her face as I rush out of the crowded house. I stumble over the people passed out on the front lawn to get to my truck parked a bit away.

"Drew!" Someone shouting breaks the focus on my strides.

Chance and Hiro are sprinting towards me to catch up.

"What the hell happened?" Chance asks, trying to catch his breath.

"I know I'm supposed to hang out with you guys tonight, but I gotta go." They look to each other, like something clicked at the same exact moment.

"It's Kat, isn't it?" Hiro asks with a raised brow.

I hesitate to answer, but it just blurts out. "I was talking to that girl, and then suddenly, I see Kat's face. I just have this feeling that if I don't go be with her, I'm going to lose my goddamn mind. I don't know what's happening. I just..." My quivering breaths make it impossible to finish speaking.

"You feel something for her, D."

I scoff at Chance's remark. "No, I don't."

"You forget we've been around you guys for two months. The way you look at her...It's not fake, whether you're ready to admit it or not," Hiro jumps in without cracking a joke, making me realize the depth of his words, but there's no way I could like Kat. Theoretically speaking, even if I did, a girl like her and a guy like me could *never* work. She's the sun, and

I'm the storm that's going to swallow her whole if I get too close.

"What are you still doing here? Go."

I almost turn to sprint away, but I decide to stay and tell them one more thing. "I'm sorry for bailing. I get it if you guys are pissed."

"We're brothers, Drew. We can never be pissed."

Guilt washes away, replaced with a bundle of nerves at the thought of seeing Kat soon. I never believed people came into your life for a reason, but maybe the universe gave me Chance and Hiro because it knew I would need them when I lost Elliot. They might not be my brothers by blood, but they are in every way Elliot was.

"You know where you're going?" one of them shouts loud enough for me hear as I crawl into my truck. This area is unfamiliar, so technically, I don't know where I'm going, but there's one thing I have to do first.

"To a costume store!"

CHAPTER 20
Kat

Heaven - Niall Horan

IT'D BE AN OVERSTATEMENT TO CALL THIS A PARTY. SOMEHOW, time is moving slower here. I knew I should have just stayed home with Grams and handed out candy like we do every year. Everyone is occupied with their plus one while I occupy this basket of bread rolls. Andrew never replied to my earlier text, so there went my attempt at company. I'm sure he has his tongue down someone's throat right now.

"Hey, Kat." A masculine voice rings from behind me, and I see James, the PE teacher, coming to sit beside me.

Rumor has it, he's had a crush on me for a couple of months. His round glasses frame his well-groomed face nicely, and you can't help but look at his smile of pearly white teeth. His short, curly hair is hidden under the hat of his Indiana Jones costume.

"Hey, James." It's nice finally talking to someone after begging for human interaction all night.

"Why are you here by yourself?" he asks. His ocean eyes remind me a little bit of Chance's.

I take another bite of my bread before answering with disappointment, "I don't have a plus one." I pretend not to notice the pleasure that graces his face at my answer.

"Me either. I was supposed to come with my girlfriend, but she dumped me a week ago." I can tell he wants pity just by the pouty eyes he makes at me.

"I'm sorry," I say, looking around at everyone else having fun around us.

"Do you have a boyfriend?"

Shit. Do I lie? If I say no, he'll definitely come on to me, but if I say yes, he'll ask where my boyfriend is, and I'll have to come up with another lie. I fill my mouth with carbs to give me more time to answer, but I'm suddenly entranced when I look towards the entrance.

My jaw nearly drops seeing Andrew striding in confidently dressed in a costume. I can't take my eyes off him; I completely forget about James's existence as I leap out of my chair and pace towards him. The closer I get, the more at peace I feel. It could be the florescent lights, but his eyes shine as soon as they find me.

"Save the remarks. I told the girl at the costume store who you dressed up as, and she said I should wear this."

Who he's dressed as is obvious by the dark sunglasses and jean jacket hiding a red plaid shirt. I can't stop a smile from forming as I notice more details. I'll have to thank the girl at the costume store for this precious sight.

"You're John Bender, the bad boy who kisses Claire at the end of the movie." I can't take him seriously when he channels his inner 80s heartthrob by smoldering at me.

"So I get the girl at the end. Good to know." He pulls the character off really well, but I do miss his regular clothes that flatter his lean figure.

"What happened to your party?"

He avoids eye contact with me and instead looks at the ground as he answers. "I realized I wanted to be here instead."

His words start a gentle fire inside me and sends my pulse racing. Without another word, I drag him by his hand back to my table. Thankfully, James is gone, so it rescues me from the awkward encounter of telling him to move over for Andrew.

"Who was that guy you were talking to?" he asks with a hint of jealousy as he pulls my chair out for me to sit.

"It was just James. He teaches PE. You ruined his moment of trying to hit on me so he might hate you now." I smile politely at James, who's watching us like a hawk from a nearby table.

"Yeah, well, he can join the club." He finds James and waves at him, wrapping his hand around my shoulders. I guess we won't be greeting each other in the teachers' lounge any time soon.

"He looks like a tool anyway." Though it's rare, seeing his devastatingly handsome grin does something to my heart strings.

"I'm sure the girls you were making out with at your party weren't any better." I glow with enjoyment at teasing him.

"I didn't make out with any girls. I did see one I've made out with in the past, and a girl who would have stuck her tongue down my throat if I stayed, though."

I turn my body to face him. "You ditched a sure thing to come to a costume party with me even though you hate Halloween?" He searches my face, like he's trying to memorize every detail, before he stops at my eyes. I've never felt nervous around him, but his tender, yet seductive glare makes me shift in my seat.

Instead of answering my question, he nudges his head to where people are dancing. "You want to dance?" Most of them are middle aged, so they're pulling out dance moves that were cool years ago, but I'm jealous of how much fun they're having.

"You said you don't dance." He doesn't say anything as he gently grabs onto my fingers and pulls me out of my chair.

"Only with you, freckles." I'd be a liar if I said his nickname isn't growing on me. I've always loved my freckles.

Of course as soon as we step onto the dance floor, the song changes into a slower one. "We could sit and wait for a fast one."

I expect him to take me up on my offer, but instead, he drags me to where others are already swaying to the music. My breath hitches in my throat when he grips my waist and pulls me closer. He smells of the mahogany cologne I always see stashed in his truck.

It's endearing to see someone so masculine and commanding like him be so gentle and attentive, and I'm at a loss for words.

"Thanks for showing up," I say, soaking up every moment of our closeness. I don't know how he lifted me onto his toes without my noticing, but I appreciate the gesture. Now, I don't have to stretch to be eye level with him. I hope he knows the weight of my words. He didn't have to come, but he did, and as someone who always shows up for others, it's nice when someone does it for me. It tells me that our friendship actually means something to him, just as much as it does to me. I was scared of letting him back into my life, but he's shown me he's a lot more than what people peg him to be. There's so many layers to Andrew Cortes, and I find joy in learning every single one of them.

"I'll always show up for you." He says it with such certainty, I believe every word. Who knew six words could alter your brain chemistry so fundamentally?

People start to walk back to their tables, but we stay put. We're close enough that if we moved even an inch, our lips would graze. We've been in this position before, but this time, all my instincts are telling me to lean in closer. I'm not supposed to want to kiss him, but I do. His comforting warmth is radiating into me like a heater, and I can feel his shaky breaths in my chest.

Everyone races back to the dance floor when the song changes to a faster tempo, which ruptures the static air between us. I don't know if I should be thankful that the moment was ruined, or curse that it was.

Just when I think we're heading back to the table, he pulls me and starts to move them to the rhythm of the catchy song.

"Don't leave me hanging, Harrison." I didn't even realize I was frozen in place, watching him dance freely. Last time, I had to force him to do this with me. I snap out of my trance, and we dance around like idiots for what feels like forever in our own little bubble of peace. I can't remember the last time I laughed this much.

It's funny how him just showing up turned my entire night around, but that seems to be a normal occurrence now.

As soon as we're parked in my driveway, he rips away every piece of clothing that resembles John Bender's and throws them in the back-seat like trash he can't wait to be rid of.

"I thought you said you hated dressing up?" I ask over the soft music.

"I do…but I don't hate you, so I figured I could endure it." In his own way, that's one of the nicest things he's ever said to me.

"Thanks again for coming." I'm almost out of the truck when he grabs my wrist with pleading eyes. I notice the slight tremble of his hand as he holds onto me.

"Kat…" His voice is low and full of uncertainty, like he's fighting against the words. "I like being around you."

My heart flutters. "I like being around you too." This moment feels entirely different than the ones we've had over the past couple of months. The unspoken words float around us.

"I mean it. I've never met anyone like you. I don't know how you do it, but I can be the guy I've always wanted to be when

I'm around you." It's dark in the truck, but my garage lights shine on his flushed face.

"It's not me. You can be that guy all the time, but you don't let yourself." He gives me too much credit, but I also understand exactly what he means. When I'm with him, all of my problems at home are an afterthought when they're usually the only thing that occupies my brain. His tight lined expression eases into a smile. If he asked me to rob a bank with that irresistible smile on his face, I'd happily be an accessory to a crime.

Time stills when he moves in closer, the gap closing faster than I can process. Right before our lips touch, he jerks back, unsure. I didn't think he was the type to ever be nervous around a girl.

Should I let him kiss me? I don't want to ruin our friendship, but I'm also surprised by how much I *really* want to kiss him. His nearness alone makes my skin feel lit up with electricity. I can already taste his minty Chapstick on my tongue. I don't know who finally closes the distance, but everything clicks into place when his soft lips caress mine. I always pegged him to be rough, so it's surprising how gentle and careful he is.

No kiss has ever felt like this one. If we were standing, my foot would be popping like in the old movies. Our lips are eager, like they were waiting for each other, but it's also slow and patient. I swear, I see stars when he cups my face and wraps his fingers in my hair. Is it possible for something to feel so wrong but absolutely right at the same time? I'm the one to move away first; not because I want to, but because at least one of us has to have control over this moment.

"That was..." I suddenly can't form a coherent sentence anymore.

"Yeah." He brings his fingers to touch his lips, and his hearty laughter fills the car, easing the uncertainty in my gut.

"We just broke rule number three." It's impossible not to join in his laughter, but it dies off when he moves a loose strand of hair out of my eyes. "Goodnight, freckles," he whispers before kissing me softly on the forehead. I know we just made out, but that felt way more intimate.

"Goodnight, Cortes." I feel like this is a romance movie, and I'm the main character who falls against her door with the stupidest smile on her face. If I left it up to him, he wouldn't have stopped kissing me.

Whatever moment that was, I think we can both agree it wasn't fake. So, the question that remains: was that the best thing we could have done, or the worst?

CHAPTER 21
Andrew

I kissed Kat.
Holy shit. I just kissed Kat.

CHAPTER 22

Andrew

1 step forward, 3 steps back - Olivia Rodrigo

ON ONE HAND, I FEEL LIKE A FUCKING IDIOT FOR LETTING MY impulses win last night with Kat, but on the other hand, I've never woken up smiling like I did today. I don't know what came over me, but there was a void in my chest that could only be filled with the touch of her lips. I pull the memory from my brain of how her lips felt, and how her lip gloss tasted on my tongue. The vanilla scent of her hair sends me into a frenzy just thinking about it.

She always smells like the inside of a candle store during fall.

It's been less than twelve hours since I last saw her, yet I miss her. *What has she done to me?* Coincidentally, last night was the first time in a long time I didn't have any trouble sleeping—not one night-mare.

I pick up my phone to see no messages from her, which is weird because she always sends me good morning texts that I used to hate.

The sound of bacon sizzling in the kitchen raises my

eyebrows—we haven't had a family breakfast in months. I'm even more shocked when I see Dad at the stove, helping Mom cook while Spanish music plays in the background.

"Good morning, mijo." Mom greets me as she squeezes my cheeks together.

I hate it now just as much as I did when I was eight, but I let her do it because it makes her smile. My dad and I lock eyes, testing each other to see who's going to greet the other first, but I decide to bite the bullet. "Morning."

Mom looks pleased that I actually acknowledged him, while he's just stunned. I reach over to snag a piece of perfectly cooked bacon sitting on a tray before drinking straight from the orange juice carton sitting on the counter. Everyone hates when I do that, so they started getting me my own carton.

"What's got you all chipper this morning?" She eyes me with a knowing smirk.

"First of all, I'm not *chipper,* and second of all, who the fuck says that?" I can't hold back my laughter when Dad spits out his coffee at my remark.

"He's right, Em." he says, smiling over at me. I don't want to give him the idea that we're friends or something now, but I don't feel like being an asshole today, so I return a forced smile of my own.

"Watch your mouth, Andrew Mateo Cortes." The last time she called me by my full name was when I was caught stealing a shirt in seventh grade.

Mom sets the table with all the food while Dad makes her coffee just the way she likes—two pumps of pumpkin creamer, no sugar, and oat milk. He was never this attentive and caring for her until he quit drinking. Now, he makes her coffee, makes sure her car is warmed up in the mornings, and everything in between. While I'd like to one day give him the benefit of the doubt, I'm not as forgiving.

We sit and eat breakfast like we always used to, trying not to make it obvious that we all notice the missing piece. We haven't had breakfast together since we lost Elliot. He was always up before the sun, so on Saturdays, he'd wake up the house with pancakes, bacon, muffins, you name it. My eyes dart to where his spot at the table used to be, and I'm overcome with a gust of nausea.

The only thing that gets me through sitting here is the fact that any minute now, Kat's name will come across my screen and turn my day around, just like it always does.

I'M GOING STIR CRAZY. I'VE NEVER BEEN IN THE POSITION OF waiting for a text. It's fucking miserable—the overthinking, the constant checking of your phone. I used to be the one who'd kiss a girl and not talk to her again, and now, Kat is giving me my karma. *Fuck this.* I grab my keys as I rush out the door.

"Adónde vas?" Mom shouts from the couch.

"A friend's house," I say in a rushed tone. Her tired eyes shine with contentment, like she knows where I'm going. It's nice to see her resting for once instead of working herself crazy. She was starting to get dark bags under her eyes that matched mine.

I can't stop thinking about Kat as I speed towards her house. I just need to know what she's thinking. Does she regret what happened last night? Is our friendship ruined? The high I felt this morning is long gone, replaced with panic as I contemplate my entire life at this red light. It's so like me to fuck up something good. Our friendship has become one of the most important things in my life, and it's possibly ruined because I couldn't go without kissing her.

All of a sudden, a sense of calm washes over me when I catch sight of Kat's favorite lipliner on the floor of my truck. It's the same one she puts on in the passenger seat every morning, which happens to also be the one she paired with the cherry flavored lip gloss she had on last night. I still had some of it left on my lips after she left.

An obnoxious car honk from behind me is the only thing that snaps me out of my flashback, sending me flying towards Kat's block. Coincidentally, she's the one to help me when I'm feeling nervous. I can already feel a pull towards her as I park in her driveway.

I ring her doorbell and wait on the other side of the door, my hands in my pocket to avoid fidgeting. *Please be home.*

I've seen her every day for months, but I never get tired of being greeted by her wavy brown hair and green eyes.

"Hey. What are you doing here?" She folds her arms over the pink crewneck she's wearing.

"I was in the neighborhood." She knows I'm lying, since I live twenty minutes in the opposite direction. I haven't known her long, but I know her better than I do most people, which is why I know she only chews the inside of her cheek when she's anxious. I have this urge to fix whatever's making her uneasy just so I can see her smile again.

"I wanted to talk about last night..."

I get cut off mid-sentence by her sharp voice. "Can we just pretend last night didn't happen?"

I try to play it off like I didn't just get stabbed in the chest. I don't know what I was going to say, and I didn't even really have a grasp on what last night meant to me, but all the air got knocked out of my body as soon as the words left her lips. *Act cool.*

"Yeah, sure. I was coming over to say the same thing," I lie again, hoping she doesn't see through it.

"I just don't want to ruin our friendship and ultimately our arrangement just when your mom is pretty convinced we're dating." Her voice breaks as she forces the words out.

She's right. I know she is, but I can't help but wish I was hearing something different. I wish she said that last night wasn't a mistake, because I don't see it as one.

My brain tries to stop my mouth before I say it, but it's too late.

"I agree. It didn't mean anything anyway." *You fucking idiot.* The only thing I know how to do is pretend like everything is fine, which means I'll say anything to convince people it is. I deflect. If I could take back any words I've ever said in my twenty-three years, it would be the ones I just said to Kat. She shrivels, and the shimmer in her eyes dies, along with a piece of me. I didn't know there was anything left in me to kill, but I felt it when I took her smile away.

"You're right—it didn't." Her retort is laced with anger; her voice and strained face say one thing, but her eyes are clawing for me.

"I have to go help Grams, so I'll see you later, Andrew."

Hearing my name fall from her lips usually fills me with content, but this time, it makes me feel like shit. I deserve it. She could slam the door in my face and never talk to me again, and I wouldn't blame her, but that's not Kat.

She's too good to hurt those who hurt her. It makes me hate myself even more.

I thought I hit rock bottom when I lost Elliot, but I was wrong.

This is it.

CHAPTER 23

Kat

I wish I could say Andrew's five words haven't been on constant replay in my head since he said them a week ago.

It didn't mean anything anyway. The words cut through me with a jagged knife, because it confirmed I was just another girl he wanted to add to his long roster. I thought he was different this time. I thought *we* were different.

The shittiest part of it all is, I think I was falling for him. I was hoping for a different outcome when I told him we should pretend the kiss never happened. It was a test to see if he would catch me if I put myself out there, and he failed. I wanted him to fight for me, to say I was wrong, but instead, he said five words that he can't take back.

I guess it's for the best. I want something real, and with him, it'll always be pretend. I deserve to be someone's first thought when they wake up and the last before they go to sleep. Maybe that only happens in movies, but I've always held out hope for that kind of love.

We've talked about a handful of times since that day, and each time, I have to pretend my heart isn't crushed just hearing his voice. Our friendship means so much to me, but it's hanging on by a thread, and we both know it. What if we opened a wound that can't be sewn back together?

I have the house to myself for a couple of hours while Grams and Kayla are out running errands. I follow my morning routine—feed Sage, water the plants, journal, and sort through past due bills.

Among the bills sits another letter from my estranged mom. If only she put this much effort into being part of my life years ago; maybe I wouldn't toss the letters in the trash without reading them.

I almost ignore my phone vibrating with an incoming call, but since it's Chance's name across the screen and he never calls me, I decide to pick it up. "Hello?" I answer hesitantly.

"Hey, I hope you don't think this is weird, but me and Hiro wanted to invite you to hang out later." My face twists with confusion because Andrew's name wasn't mentioned, and the only times we've been in the same room together is if he's there too.

"Just us three?" My mind continues to reel as I try to get all the details.

"Yeah, it's not weird if we're all friends." His voice tells me he's got something planned. The two of them never do anything without Andrew; they're a package deal, so something is off.

Besides, even if it's weird with me and Andrew right now, it'd feel even weirder to hang out with *his* friends without him.

Wait a second. What if they invited him too, but he declined because I was going to be there?

"Why is Andrew not going?" I ask.

"Uh, he's busy." His hesitation is off-putting but telling. Any hope that our friendship can be salvaged goes out the window with his answer. I'm glad no one is here to see the pure devastation roll through me.

"I'll go. Why not?" I say distantly. After the week I've had, I deserve to go out and have some fun.

"Great. We'll meet you at the bar at six." The line goes dead before I can suggest a different place. Why do they always insist we meet where I work?

A fragment of me feels like I'm betraying Andrew, but another part feels betrayed *by* him—he obviously doesn't want to mend our friendship as much as I do. If he did, Chance wouldn't have hesitated to make an excuse for him. I was willing to put my feelings aside, but he obviously doesn't want to do the same. I'm not going to let him affect my feelings anymore. If he wants to act like our friendship is disposable, so will I.

CHAPTER 24
Katt Andrew

Steal My Girl - One Direction

KAT

Chance is already occupying a seat at the bar when I arrive early to Sam's. His blue eyes perk up when he scans my casual outfit as I walk towards him.

"You look great." I know he's just being nice, because all I did was throw on my favorite blue crewneck and ripped jeans.

"Thanks, you too." He's always so clean cut and precise.

One of my coworkers, Brina is behind the bar making drinks like her life depends on it. She's been at the bar so long, she can make drinks with her eyes closed.

"The usual?" She's talking to me, but honed in on the drinks she's making.

"Duh, and my friend will have a beer." She gazes over at Chance when I gesture to him. I pretend not to notice the heated looks they exchange before she finally turns to walk away.

"Where's Hiro?" His loud personality fills any room he's in, making his absence noticeable.

"He's running late, but he'll be here soon." His fingers are tapping against the countertop nervously, but Brina comes back with our drinks before I can comment on it.

"Shirley Temple for you, beer for you. I'll be around if you need me." I smile when I notice her makeup looks touched up from just a few minutes ago, I'm sure because of Chance. I'll have to find her later to inform her he's single.

"Shirley Temple?" I can smell the judgment as he eyes my drink.

"I don't drink." I've became accustomed to the odd looks I get, and I can tell he wants to ask for an explanation, but instead, he averts his eyes. I haven't even told Andrew that part of my past, so I'm thankful he didn't pry.

"I have to ask: what do you think about Drew?"

I wish Hiro would walk through the door now so I could avoid this question. "As what? a person, a friend…" I know what he meant, but I'm trying to stall.

"Just overall. What do you think of him?" He speaks in a low voice, giving me all of his attention.

"He's a good person." I give him the same generic answer as Andrew's mom.

"Now tell me what you really think." I'm getting déjà vu— he's using my own line against me.

I sigh with defeat. "There was a brief moment where I thought I liked him, that maybe he even liked me, but then he showed me it was all in my head. I should have known better. I only blame myself." I didn't think I'd be venting to him about this, but his eyes hold no judgment.

"He wasn't always like this. He's always been a player, but as a person, he wasn't always distant. He'd be the one to pull you off the wall at a party if you were left out, or he'd come fuck with you to put a smile on your face…" Lighthearted laughter falls from his lips, as if he's retrieving an old memory. "Then Elliot died, and everything changed, but we all understood."

"He says shit that hurts sometimes, but it's only because he doesn't want people to know he's the one hurting." I take it that Andrew told him what he said to me, and that's why he's trying to vouch for him. This is a sensitive side of Chance I could get used to.

"Why are you telling me this?"

A faint smile touches his face. "Because you're the reason we've seen a little piece of the old Andrew. We didn't think we'd get him back after Elliot died, but it all shifted when you started coming around. I don't even think Drew fully notices it. You should know that before you sell him short."

I try to conceal the mixed emotions that roll through me.

Before I can say anything, a look of pure satisfaction spreads across his face as he looks towards the door, and I freeze when I see Andrew storming towards us with fire in his eyes.

ANDREW

20 Minutes Prior

I'VE BEEN COOPED UP IN THIS HOUSE FOR THE PAST WEEK, AND the one night I ask Chance and Hiro to hang out, they're both *busy*. I almost called Kat, but her dry replies to my texts lately tell me she probably doesn't want me around. I don't blame her, but if she called me, I'd pick up with no hesitation.

"You're staying home again? That's a record." My dad joins me on the couch, reminding me why I don't watch tv in here.

"Chance and Hiro are busy," I say dryly.

"What about Kat?" My jaw tenses at his pestering.

"Busy." Even if she isn't, I'm sure she doesn't want me around.

"I like her. I like what she's done to you." This is the first thing he's said in years that peaks my interest.

"What do you mean?" I can't remember the last time I was able to stand being around him longer than two minutes, but now that I'm here, I notice little details about him—like the gray hairs in his mustache that weren't there months ago, or how his hair is thinner and a lighter shade of brown. I've always despised how everyone said I look like him. I'd like to think I take after my mom.

"You always used to walk around pissed off at the world, but with her you seem different."

I stop myself from biting out the snarky comment sitting on my tongue. How could he possibly know what the old Andrew was like when he was drunk most of my childhood?

Flashbacks from *that* night try to fight their way in the my mind, but thankfully, I'm saved by the bell when Hiro calls me. "I gotta take this."

I walk upstairs, taking a breath when I'm a safe distance away from my dad. My chest feels like it's going to explode with rage any time he's near.

"What's up?" I answer.

"I just thought you'd want to know what Kat's up to tonight." The hairs on the back of my neck stand at the mention of her name.

"What?" I try not to sound too eager as I wait.

"She's with Chance." *What the fuck?* My hand instinctively curls into a fist when I picture the two of them together. I confided in Chance yesterday about what happened between me and Kat, and he takes that as an opening to go hit on her? *Seriously, what the fuck?*

I can't be mad. We weren't real, but there's still this sting of betrayal in my chest.

"Why should I care?" I ask in a cool tone.

"Cut the shit, Drew. Anyone with eyes can see you like her. You're the only one in denial about it. The only question is: are you gonna fight for her or keep pretending you don't give a fuck like you always do?"

His sharp words punch me in the gut, but I try to recover quickly, "I don't like her."

"Well, when you stop kidding yourself, they're at Sam's," he spits out before the line goes dead.

My first instinct is to race to Sam's, but is that my place? If she wants to hang out with Chance, that's her decision. Hiro's voice echoes in my ears. *Anyone with eyes can see you like her.* I think I would know if I liked Kat.

I do know that my day brightens when she's around. She's the only person I trust with every part of me. I know there's a hole the size of Texas in my chest whenever she's gone, and she's the only girl who has occupied my mind for weeks. She lit up my life like a beacon to safety, and she doesn't even know it. Kat is so genuine, she guides people without even realizing it.

There is absolutely no one like her.

When I kissed her, it all clicked into place; I was just too stupid to accept that it's been real for me for a while. I almost fall to my knees from my sudden revelation. I fucked up by not fighting for her once, I won't make the same mistake again.

I RUN EVERY RED LIGHT AS I SPEED OVER TO SAM'S. I HAVEN'T worked out what I'm going to say to either of them, but especially Chance. Him and I have never fought over a girl before. This is uncharted territory I don't want to be in.

I walk into the bar collected, but anger clouds my vision

when I see the two of them sitting together at the bar. My angry eyes are only pointed at Chance, but he looks satisfied to see me.

"Can we talk?" I yank him away, not giving him a choice before he can answer. I can't resist looking at Kat, but an aching knot forms when I see her mask of sorrow aimed at me.

"We'll be right back," he whispers to her with too much cockiness for my liking.

I pull him all the way to the back alley of the bar, which also serves at the employee parking lot. It's never occupied, apart from the kitchen staff who take cigarette breaks by the trash cans.

"What the fuck, Barrett? Me telling you what happened with Kat was your invitation to take her out?"

"What's the big deal? You guys weren't a real thing. If it's just pretend, she's fair game." My blood boils when he calls her 'fair game', like she's nothing. She's the reason I manage to get out of bed in the morning, why I know there are still good people in the world. To call her something as degrading as 'fair game' makes me want to vomit.

"You're a fucking asshole, you know that?" I spit out. I pace around the alley to avoid sucker punching him.

"I'll make you a deal: I'll back off if you tell me why you're so pissed we're hanging out." My jaw ticks at how nonchalant he's being.

"Because I…" I thought I was ready to say it out loud, but the words feel impossible to let out. I swallow down the ball that's settled in my throat. "I like her."

"It's about goddamn time." I'm stunned into silence as he laughs.

"Do you know how long we've been waiting for you to admit that to yourself? We finally got tired of waiting for you dumbasses to figure it out on your own, so we decided to give a little push."

"What do you mean, a push?" I ask, reeled with confusion.

"Do you think it was a coincidence Hiro called you? That was the plan, D—to get Kat here by making her think we're all hanging out, then Hiro would tell you it was a date to see if you cared enough to come down here, and you did."

He spreads his arms out in front of him like he's revealing a trick. I can't believe this shit. I usually catch onto these things. I feel bad for almost sucker punching him now.

"Great plan, but seeing how she just looked at me, I don't know if I should tell her how I feel. Maybe it's for the best." I try to mask the heaviness I feel from admitting the truth. I slump down on the fire escape steps in defeat.

Chance comes to join me, and we sit silently for several minutes before he speaks. "I've been your friend for a long time. I've watched you hook up with different girls like water, but Kat..." He shakes his head. "She calls you out on your shit, and whether you've noticed it or not, she's helped you cope with losing Elliot. So don't fuck it up by making excuses, or trying to convince yourself that you don't want to be with her."

Damn it, he's right. Every word. I hate when he's right.

Despite what she's been through, Kat sees the world in a light that no one else does, and over the past few months, she's made me see the world through the same looking glass. The thought of some-one else having access to that light makes my chest cave in.

"So what do I do?" I've never confessed feelings for anyone. I feel like a lost puppy.

"Tell her how you feel, dumbass!" he shouts, aggressively shoving me away.

I race away towards Kat, panic settling in now that the moment is here. What do I say? Is she still pissed at me? What do I do if she is? My stomach drops to my feet when she's not where we left her. *Fuck me.*

I search the streets anxiously, saying a silent prayer that she's not gone, but my eyes light up with hope when I see brunette hair pulled back with a sage green clip about ten feet away.

"Kat!" I shout as loud as my tired lungs will let me, but she keeps up her fast pace.

"Kat, wait up!" I shout again as I run towards her. She's so close, yet so far away from my reach. I know I look fucking crazy, but I push it to the back of my mind and focus solely on Kat. I finally grab onto her arm, and despite her rage fuming, I feel a sense of peace as I admire her delicate, flowerlike features.

"What the hell are you doing Andrew?" She tries to pry herself away, but I hold onto her just to feel her warmth for a little while longer. If she doesn't accept what I'm about say, it'll be the last time I touch her.

"I heard you were here with Chance, and I had to come down here and—"

"What? Come mark your territory like I'm your property?" she seethes with anger and hurt. I'm proud of her for telling me off, but I can't look at her while she does it, so I look at my feet instead.

"It's not like that. I just—"

"Just leave me alone, Andrew. Please." A wave of nausea crashes over me seeing how her usual perky face screws up in sad-ness.

She's able to get loose from my grip and starts to get into her car, but something snaps in me. I've let her slip through my fingers too many goddamn times, and I can't stand the thought of losing her for good.

"I didn't mean what I said!" Her damp eyes find mine. I take it as a good sign when she doesn't flinch away when I move closer. "I didn't mean it, Kat. Of course the kiss meant something to me. *You* mean something to me."

Keep going. Stop being scared.

"I broke the rule, Kat. I fell for you. Hard. We both know it hasn't been pretend for a while. I let you in, and haven't looked back. It's humiliating how much of a hold you have on me." I claw for the version inside her I know cares for me—the one that knows the real me and not the façade I put on.

"You said you don't do relationships. I want something real, Andrew. What happens when you realize that you don't?" She holds her breath waiting for my answer. I won't say the wrong thing again.

"I want *you*. I'm sorry it took me so long to realize it. I should have known when you're the first person I wanted to talk to when I opened my eyes, or my mood solely depending on whether I see your smile that day. You're my exception, Kat, and I'm ready to jump. Just please tell me you'll jump with me."

I reach to swipe away the tears flooding down her flushed cheeks. Her hair tries clinging to her face, but I tuck it behind her ear. She closes the gap between us to bring her soft lips to touch mine, and I almost think I'm daydreaming until I cup her cheek and feel her warmth under my fingertips. How could I miss lips I've only touched once? But I did. I feel her struggling to grasp onto my neck from our height difference, so I lift her off the ground.

Having her in my arms just feels right. It's exactly where she belongs, and now, I know I belong anywhere she is.

Because I'm hers.

CHAPTER 25

Andrew

Here With Me - d4vd

WHEN I'M HAVING A BAD DREAM, I CAN FEEL THE WEIGHT ON MY chest pinning me to my bed, but this isn't one of those dreams. No, I'm in my driveway, just like the last time.

"Took you long enough. Grab me a wrench." Elliot perks his head up with a warm, welcoming smile, as though he was waiting for me. His t-shirt has grease stains peppering the fabric.

I focus on staying here as long as I can. I know I'm dreaming, but somehow, I can still feel the cold metal of the wrench when I pick it up and hand it to him.

"So, you and Kat?" he asks from under the hood of his truck. Even in my dreams, I can't hold back a smile when I talk about her.

"She's great. She's really helped me since—" I stop myself. Does he know he's gone in my dreams?

"I knew you'd get together eventually."

"How could you possibly know that?" I ask, moving to stand beside him under the truck's hood.

"Even before you guys were close, you looked at her like she was the most interesting thing you've ever laid your eyes on." He scoffs as he comes to rest a hand on my shoulder. Everything, all the sounds, the scenery, and his touch, feel so real, despite it being just a dream. I shouldn't be surprised he noticed. He noticed everything.

"Just don't do anything stupid, we both know Emory will kick your ass if you hurt her." He always had one type of smile reserved for Emory. If any two people deserved more time together, it was them.

"I'll try, but this is all new to me. Any advice?" He was the younger one, but he was ten times better than me in every aspect, *especially* relationships. Emory hated everyone, but by some miracle, he got her to fall in love with him.

His dark eyebrows arch deep in thought. "Treat every day as if it's your last. Don't leave anything unsaid, when you feel like doing something, do it. Don't let her feel like an afterthought."

My body gets lighter, and I know I'm waking up, but I fight. I don't want to leave this moment. "How'd you end up with all the advice like you're the big brother?" I ruffle his dark wavy hair. Before he died, he had a buzz cut because his hair started to thin from the chemo, but he has a full head of hair in my dreams.

"What can I say? I got the beauty *and* the brains." His laugh rings out deeply, and fuck, I miss it. "Time to wake up, big brother." He slams down the hood of his truck, and I don't hesitate to hug him tightly.

"I miss you, E." I never called him by his full name, always E. Those are the last words I get out before I'm forcibly shaken awake.

"Wake up, D." My eyes bulge at the sight of Chance and Hiro hovering over me.

"What the fuck? Who let you guys in?" My words come out as a grumble as I bury my head under my pillow.

"It's not rocket science—you've left your key under the fake plant since high school, but your mom let us upstairs." Hiro drops down on the mattress, barely missing my legs as Chance snatches away my pillow. "We didn't race over here for nothing. What happened with you and Kat?"

I never took them for gossipers, but they sure love to be in the know. Yesterday feels like a magnificent blur. Kat is my *real* girl-friend. I try to hide my satisfied grin, but I know they both notice it when they glance at each other.

"We kissed again, and we're, um, dating." I finally let out two words I thought would *never* leave my lips.

Chance stretches his hand out to Hiro with a cocky grin. "Pay up."

I watch their exchange as Hiro unhappily lays a twenty-dollar bill in Chance's hand. "You guys bet on this shit?" Why am I not surprised?

"Hell yeah. I said you guys would get together this month, but he said next month." He mocks Hiro as he puts the money in his wallet and flips him the middle finger.

"You guys woke me up just to settle your fucking bet?" I can't even be pissed—it's kind of funny. It's ten o'clock, so I should be up anyway, but I hate being woken up.

Chance smacks me on the head playfully. "We also came to see what you had to eat."

They used to come and raid our fridge religiously, but they stopped when Elliot got sick again. I don't want to leave my warm bed, but I know they won't leave me alone until I do. They follow on my heels as we head to the kitchen, where my mom is at the stove.

She eyes us skeptically. "How'd I know you guys would coming running as soon as I started cooking?"

"Because we'll eat anything you cook, Emily." Hiro says, glancing over her shoulder to see what's she's cooking.

"Well, I'm making Huevos Rancheros, you know the rules." She points to the cupboard where the dishes are. They know the rule: that they have to help set the table any time they eat here.

"I take it you were with Kat last night since you didn't get in 'til late." She acknowledges me now. I stayed out longer than I'd planned. I didn't want to leave Kat's side. We went back to her house, and I pretended to like the tea her grandma served while I flipped through more photo albums.

"Sorry, Ma." I say.

"Don't be sorry. It must be getting serious if you're spending all your time with her." Technically, we just started, but to her, we've been together for a while.

Even with everything going on in the kitchen, my mind lingers on Kat and ways I could make her smile so hard, her dimple shows. It's comical how everything I used to be so scared of seems easy when it comes to her. She was the exception all along.

※※※

I'VE BEEN TO KAT'S HOUSE PLENTY OF TIMES, BUT THIS IS THE first time I'm nervous. I feel like a teenager as I wait for her to come out. I was going to plan our first official date, but she beat me to it.

I'm in awe of her all over again when she swings her door open. When we were just friends, I would keep it to myself when I liked something she wore or the way she did her hair or makeup, but now, I can voice it freely.

"You look amazing."

She rolls her eyes and smiles shyly. "I'm in jeans and a hoodie."

"You are wearing the hell out of that hoodie." I kiss her gently on the forehead before grabbing her hand to pull her towards my truck. I'm surprised when she doesn't get in as I open the passenger door.

"Actually, can I drive? I want where we're going to be a

surprise." She cranes her neck to look up at me, her green eyes hypn-otizing me.

I want the color of her eyes etched on a canvas forever.

I only hesitate because Elliot and I are the only people to ever drive this truck. A part of me feels ridden with guilt, like I'm ruining something that only he and I share, but I don't want to take away the excitement oozing from her. I hold out the keys. I know Elliot would approve if he were here.

She squeals as she snatches them from my hands. I'll do anything she wants if that means I get to see her like this more often.

"Can I have a hint as to where we're going?" I ask, buckling myself in.

"No—just trust me." A dimple appears on her cheek from smiling so hard at the roar of the loud engine. "Gramps had a truck like this, but he sold it to buy a guitar signed by his favorite singer." She runs her hands over the leather steering wheel before putting the truck in reverse.

She rarely talks about her past, and the only subject she doesn't budge on is her parents. I don't take it personally, though. I can only imagine how she feels about her parents being gone.

I'm the one keeping her in the dark about my past. I trust her with my whole being, but I'm terrified of digging up my buried baggage.

"You okay over there?" Her angelic voice brings me back to the moment.

"I'm just terrified for my life with you in the driver's seat," I joke.

"Shut up." I rolls my eyes with a smile when she flips me the middle finger.

I was afraid we'd lose our friendship when we crossed the line into a relationship, but it actually made it stronger.

We drive for about thirty minutes until we reach a baseball stadium parking lot.

"We're watching a baseball game?" I ask. My confusion grows when she drives to a deserted part of the parking lot instead of where dozens of cars sit.

"Not exactly." She climbs out of the truck with a wide grin. It's pitch black aside from the flickering lamp post, and if I didn't trust her, I'd think I was being led to my death.

"C'mon, Cortes. We got some climbing to do." She yanks me by my hand up a steep incline. If she wasn't grasping onto my hand, I'd easily fall back, but she treads on like she's done it a hundred times.

I was expecting to find bleachers at the top, but instead, it's just an isolated bench that faces the field. I use the concrete seat to catch my breath while Kat takes in the view.

"My grandpa was the groundskeeper for this field for twenty years. He used to bring me every Friday night around this time." She sits next to me but doesn't take her eyes off the sky.

"Why around this time?" My hand inches towards hers, and I can't believe I went this long not being able to hold her hand.

"Just wait." She lays her head on my shoulder, and I ignore that some of her wavy hair is in my face, because she seems comfor-table.

Minutes go by before the whole sky lights up with loud fireworks that blend together to form different colors and shapes. I've seen fireworks before, but never ones like this.

"I've never brought anyone here—it's my favorite place in the whole world." She squeezes my hand tighter. My heart swells at the idea that she trusts me enough to bring me somewhere so special to her. She's giving me the key to her whole heart, and I don't take that lightly.

"Thanks for bringing me," I whisper before kissing the top of her head. We don't say anything else, but we don't need to. We just soak up this special moment.

Kat finds the littlest things in life the most beautiful, which makes me find them beautiful too. She's the first breath of fresh air you take after being trapped somewhere, or the first flowers that bloom after a gloomy winter.

I was never one to believe in fate, but if that's what brought her to me when I didn't deserve her, then I'll thank fate every day.

December

CHAPTER 26

Kat

Video Games - Lana Del Rey

I'VE NEVER BEEN ONE TO MAKE A BIG DEAL OUT OF CHRISTMAS, but since I have a boyfriend who loves it, I guess there's a first time for every-thing. Grams and I just get each other pajama sets and end the day drinking hot cocoa, but this year, Andrew's family invited us over for a big dinner and gift exchange. Andrew insisted that I didn't get him anything, but thankfully, Chance and Hiro had a brilliant idea that I couldn't pass up.

I'm able to drive to his house, my car finally finished a couple of weeks ago. It was done weeks before that, but Andrew wanted to keep taking me to work. He still comes by the bar when I get off late, just to make sure I get to my car safely. I thought for sure it would have been a rough transition from friends to a relationship, but he's adjusted a lot better than I expected.

"They sure have a big house," Grams says, admiring the extravagant home we're parked in front of. I walk over to her side to guide her out of the car and up the steep driveway. They must really love Christmas, because the décor looks like someone puked up the holidays.

"Merry Christmas," Emily chimes when she opens the door to let us in. I greet her with a tight hug and introduce her to Grams.

Emily and I have gotten a lot closer since Andrew and I became official. Once a week, I come and get a lesson on cooking a Mexican dish while she and Andrew teach me Spanish. I like feeling connected to his culture, and I love when he speaks Spanish—even though half of the time I don't know what he's saying.

Chance and Hiro are watching a football game on the couch when I walk in.

"Merry Christmas." I sit between them on the couch and pretend to know what's happening. I grew up watching more baseball than football, but I get the gist of it.

"Your boyfriend is upstairs, struggling to wrap gifts," Chance laughs, and I rush upstairs—I can already picture Andrew cursing and chucking the gifts across the room out of frustration. His patience with me doesn't translate to everything else.

I already hear his grunts from the hallway, but I stay back and watch as he concentrates on lining up the wrapping paper. Only about two minutes pass before I start to feel bad and finally cut in.

"Need some help?" His frown disappears when I enter and sit at the foot of his bed, the presents suddenly not his priority anymore.

"Merry Christmas, freckles." He snatches me by the waist and pulls me onto his lap to kiss me softly but urgently. He always kisses

me like he's out of oxygen and I'm his air supply—desperate, but not too eager.

"Chance wasn't kidding when he said you were struggling to wrap gifts." I look around at the shredded paper that cover every inch of his floor. "I hope you like the gift I got you." I wrap my arms around his neck while he stares at me like I'm the only thing that exists. I've always dreamed of being looked at like that; honestly, I didn't think it happened outside of movies.

"You're my present," he whispers close to my lips before kissing me again.

He flips me over so he's hovered over me, my back against his bed, and traces every crevice of my face with his finger.

I shiver from the way his brown eyes rake over my body, but right before our lips touch once again, we're interrupted.

"Get a room." Hiro says, hitting Andrew with his own pillow.

"We are in a room. Mine, asshole." He lifts off of me to hit Hiro back.

"I thought you were watching football?" I ask as I adjust my shirt that Andrew lifted up with his gentle fingertips.

"We figured we'd come bother you guys during halftime." Chance says, as he finishes wrapping the gifts Andrew gave up on.

"Everyone! Get down here and set the table!" Emily shouts from downstairs.

"Last one down has to say grace." Hiro rushes out. We all squish through the doorway, fighting to get out, but Andrew pushes Chance and Hiro to the ground so I can get out first.

Hiro is the last one down, but he laughs it off.

"Boys, set the table. Kat, can you get the napkins out of that drawer, mija?" Among the Spanish words I've learned is the word mija, which means daughter. I can't help but smile every time she says it.

My stomach rumbles at the sight of a golden-brown turkey and too many side dishes to count.

"What's this?" I ask, looking at whatever delicious-smelling concoction sits in the pot on the stove.

"It's Pazole, a soup we have every Christmas." Andrew spooks me when he speaks near my ear.

Anything Emily makes is amazing, so I have no doubt that I'l love it. She made these pastries called empanadas last week, and Grams and I ate an entire plate.

Andrew's dad joins us with a pleasant smile on his face, admi-ring the spread. "Everything looks great, amor." He kisses Emily on the cheek before walking to the head of the table; Andrew thinks I don't notice his jaw subtly tick whenever his dad is around, but I do.

As we all take our seats, I notice the empty placemat, just like every time I have dinner with them, and I know that's where Elliot probably sat. My heart breaks a little bit, and I grab Andrew's hand.

"Hiro, I heard you're saying grace this year. Take it away," Emily says.

While he spouts out his own version of grace, I glance around the table. Despite their family losing Elliot, they still welcomed us in without a second thought. It's nice to feel part of something again, and I know it means a lot to Grams, since she hasn't stopped smiling since we arrived. We've created a little unit by somehow all being brought together.

You might not get to choose your family, but you sure as hell can grow up and create your own new one.

"NO YOU DIDN'T!" I EXCLAIM WHEN I UNWRAP ANDREW'S GIFT. I try to suck back in the tears gathering in my eyes.

In my hands is an identical guitar to the one my gramps used to play. He sold it before I was born to get Grams her engage-ment ring, but our photo album is filled with photos of him rocking out with it. It's a vintage guitar, so it must have cost him a fortune.

"I can't take this, it's too much." I hold it out, but he refuses it.

"Consider it my payment for all the songs I want you to play for me."

I can't stop the tears from falling down my cheeks now as I place the white acoustic guitar in my lap and tune the strings. Grams is choking up too as she admires me. I thought all her tears were dried up after seeing the gift that Andrew got her: a necklace with a locket, a picture of me on one side, Gramps on another.

I just got his mom a lousy perfume set and a sweater for his dad, but you would have thought I gave them keys to a brand-new car from their excited reactions.

"Okay Hiro, Kat, and I got Drew something, but we have to go outside for it," Chance announces as he stands amidst a mountain of shredded wrapping paper.

It's not even my gift, but I get butterflies when I release my hands from his eyes to reveal a sports motorcycle sitting in the driveway with an obnoxious red bow on it—Hiro's idea. He's too stunned to even move as he stares in disbelief.

I had no idea he even wanted a motorbike until Chance and Hiro told me it was his dream to own one. It was a bitch to track down, and it broke my bank account, but he's worth every penny, and so is the astonished look on his face. It's used, since a new one was way out of our budget, but it's in mint condition. The black paint looks unscathed, and the guy we bought it from just put new decals on it, giving it a sleek look.

Andrew's disbelief is obvious from how he's wary to touch it.

"What the fu—how did…" He can't even manage to get out a full sentence.

"You think we forgot about your dream? We finally had a

third person to pitch in for it." Chance nudges his head towards me, and Andrew's watery eyes find me seconds later. I almost choke on tears just seeing him glow with happiness. He rushes the three of us to bring us into a tight group hug.

"One more thing," Emily says, holding a box with a black bow. He unwraps it eagerly to reveal a blacked-out helmet to wear on his trips.

"Thank you. I love you guys," he says before starting up the bike. My eyes widen as the engine roars down the entire block.

"Wanna go for a ride, freckles?" I take his stretched-out hand without hesitation. I smile at the significance of this moment. Riding on the back of a guy's motorcycle is a pivotal moment in most of my favorite movies. The deep blare of the engine vibrates in my chest as we race down the street, and I let out a scream of excitement. My long hair flows in every direction as the wind blows through it, but it's so freeing, I don't even care.

CHAPTER 27

Andrew

New Year's Day - Taylor Swift

NEW YEARS EVE—A NIGHT I USED TO SPEND SURROUNDED BY booze and random girls. Now, though, all the company I want is Kat. It's baffling how fast life changes, but I really like this one. My parents throw a party every year, so I stay away from my house at all costs. This year, that means being dragged to a party by Chance and Hiro. They just want to go to find someone to kiss at midnight.

I've never had a New Year's kiss. It felt way too sacred. I didn't want to share that with anyone—until Kat. There are so many firsts I'm experiencing with her, and I feel like a teenager being coached through all of it.

Everyone's hovered around the TV, drinking as though the world is going to end at the stroke of midnight.

"Got anyone to kiss at midnight, stranger?" I see sage green fingernails tap my shoulder, and I turn around to see Kat in all her glory, a red solo cup filled with water in her hand. Her long legs are showcased in glittery silver dress that makes her look like a sexy disco ball.

Fuck, I can't believe she's mine.

"I do, actually. It's my girlfriend. She talks a lot, but she's hot, so I deal with it." I pull her in by her waist and leave a trail of wet kisses over her face and down her neck.

"Midnight kiss is officially secured." Chance joins us, wrapping his arms around us both for support.

"I love you guys. I never thought I'd see our little Drew settle down, but he caught himself a good one."

"I have two contenders for my midnight kiss. I need your help picking." Hiro comes to join us, looking more sober than Chance.

"Or you can kiss both," Chance chimes in before taking another sip of the liquid in his cup.

I find myself soaking up this moment while Kat talks to Hiro about his choices as Chance listens. Me, my two best friends, and my girlfriend, at a party we'll reminisce about over breakfast tomorrow.

"Three…two…one…Happy New Year!" everyone shouts over the loud music before either taking a shot or kissing the person next to them. Chance starts making out with a blonde while Hiro disappears to who knows where.

"Happy New Year," Kat says with her arms wrapped around my neck. Her tender smile aimed at me makes my heartbeat skip.

"Happy New Year, freckles." I pick her up off the ground and kiss her so deeply, it even leaves me dizzy afterwards.

If I knew this was the life waiting for me on the other side of the darkness, I would have welcomed it a lot sooner.

CHAPTER 28
Kat

Fall in Love with You. - Monte Fish

I MADE THE MISTAKE OF WAITING UNTIL AFTER WINTER BREAK TO grade all my papers, so now, I'm buried alive, my only saving grace Stevie Nicks playing softly in the background. Trying to understand the chicken scratch my students write on their papers unfortunately takes up most of my time. Since I don't have time to eat lunch, I'm surviving off this stray can of soda I found in my mini fridge.

The door creaks open, and I spring into teacher mode when one of my favorite students, Luke, walks in, his cheeks wet with tears.

"What happened?" I ask, guiding him to a nearby desk to sit. I grab tissues to wipe his red face, which seems to calm him down, but he still seems too embarrassed to answer my question. I hate seeing anyone cry, but especially a kid.

He finally sniffles his nose one last time and cries out, "Joey and his friends called me names and then tripped me in front of everyone."

I try to keep my face emotionless, but inside I'm fuming.

Joey's a good kid in class, but he's a bully outside of it. He's targeted poor Luke since the first week of school. I've sent home notes, emailed parents, held meetings with the principal, and each time, I'm met with *boys will be boys.* If I had a dime for every time I heard that one, I could retire.

Consequences be damned. "Go up to the office and ask to see the nurse. I'll figure the rest out."

He nods, still whimpering as he walks out. I've always felt compelled to watch over him more than the other kids, and maybe it's because I was bullied too—middle school was pure hell. It got better in high school when I stopped caring about fitting in, found my own sense of style, and kept to myself. I wasn't popular, but I was me, and that was enough.

Before I can think it through, I answer my ringing phone.

"What?" I usually don't greet people rudely, but my mind is preoccupied. "Ouch, what did I do?" Andrew's deep voice manages to make me smile.

"Sorry, it's not you; just something going on at school, and I don't know what to do."

"What can I do to help?" he asks quickly.

He's a very hands-on boyfriend. I could mention something as tedious as needing to go buy pens for work, and he'd have them for me the next time I saw him. He's brought me a bouquet of white roses every week since we've officially started dating, and he's even started attaching handwritten notes.

"Nothing. It's just this kid, Joey, picks on this other kid, Luke, who's so sweet. I've done everything by the book, but nothing works. I don't know how to help." I let everything out in one breath.

"I'll be in your class in twenty minutes." The line cuts out before my confusion wears off. Why do I feel like this will definitely get me fired?

I'M AT THE WHITEBOARD, TALKING THROUGH A MATH PROBLEM, when Andrew comes striding through the door with a visitor's badge and a big white box. The kids' attention leaves me and fixates on whatever is in his hands. They all squeal with excitement as he places the box on my desk and walks to the front of the class.

"Kiddos, you remember Andrew, right?" You'd think he was famous by the way they all cheer when he waves.

"What are you doing?" I turn and whisper to him.

"Relax. I got this." I'm slightly panicked, but I really want to see what he's up to, so I give him the figurative floor while I sit at my desk to watch.

"You guys see that box over there? My friend Luke told me to bring donuts for all his friends today." They all shout with more enthusiasm than they've given me the entire year.

"Luke, can you come up here, please?" He freezes from all the eyes darting to him, but he walks up to the front anyway. I guess Andrew realized how intimidating he may seem, because he gets on his knees to Luke's eye level.

"Do you want me to hand out donuts to your friends, or do you want to?"

Luke nods and points to himself, and I think this is the first time I've seen him genuinely smile this year.

"He's nice enough to share, but the donuts are only for the people who are following Miss Harrison's rules by being nice to each other." Everyone is excited except Joey and his group of friends.

"Okay then, come get a donut from Luke and say thank you." I didn't even know Andrew could speak so softly; it's endearing.

Everyone starts to tackle each other to get to the front, quickly turning into chaos.

While everyone is enjoying their treat, Andrew approaches Joey and his friends, who are obviously pissed.

"It doesn't feel good to be singled out, right? You guys can have one if you promise to be nice to my friend Luke. Miss Harrison and I are friends, so she'll tell me if you're not."

Is he subtly trying to threaten a child? *Shit, there goes my job.* Before I can interrupt the moment, the kids nod in agreement with wide eyes, as if they're afraid what'll happen if they don't.

"Don't forget to tell Luke thank you and invite him to play tomorrow for me, alright?" He fist bumps the boys and throws a victorious smile towards me.

Seeing him interact with the kids this way makes my ovaries explode. It's a new side of him that I haven't seen, and I wouldn't mind seeing more of it.

There's more to him that meets the eye—he's caring, gentle but rough when he needs to be. He's selfless, and protective. There's no way he's real. He's everything I've ever wanted, made just for me. I find it harder and harder to not fall in love with him, and I think it's already happening.

CHAPTER 29

Andrew

Labyrinth - Taylor Swift

My parents went to a couples retreat in Tucson for the weekend, so I invited Kat over. I almost regretted my decision when she insisted on bringing some of her favorite 80s movies.

I'm kind of freaking out. This is the first time a girl is sleeping over at my house. I keep fluffing the goddamn couch pillows, as if she actually cares about how they look, and I must have dusted my entire room a dozen times. Kat makes me nervous by just existing, but in a good way. I take one last look in the mirror and ruffle my hair just the way she likes it when the doorbell rings.

"Hey, freckles." I lift her off of the ground and over the entry-way before kissing her like I haven't seen her in weeks.

"I brought the classics: *The Breakfast Club*, *Sixteen Candles*, *Stand by Me*, and my personal favorite, *Say Anything*."

I lean against the doorway, just watching her enthusiasm. I could watch her peel paint and still be in awe of her. She pulls out all of the movies and snacks she packed in her tote bag, and slicks her wavy hair into a bun with the sage green scrunchie she always has on her wrist.

"Why are you looking at me like that?" Her silky voice brings me out of the trance she unintentionally put me under.

"No reason. What should we watch first?" I ask, sorting through the movies I've never seen. I've never been much of a movie person. If I watch tv, it's a sports game, or Spanish novellas with my mom when I was younger. She said it was so I could hear the language and not forget it, as if she didn't engrave it into mine and Elliot's brains as kids.

"Considering you didn't know who John Bender was, we're starting with *The Breakfast Club*. I can't believe I'm dating someone who hasn't watched the classics." She shakes her head as she starts it up.

"You knew what you were getting into. Now you're stuck with me." An subconscious smile tips at the corners of my lips. She drops into my lap like a piece of heaven falling from the sky and kisses me. When she tries to move off, I hold her in place—I want her close enough that her crystal necklace dangles in my face and her citrusy scent fills my nostrils. My hand glides from her waist to her upper thigh, but she stops me.

"We're never watching the movie if you do that," she teases while smiling against my lips.

"Fuck the movie." I let out in a groan as I pull her back to me.

✦

MY EYES ARE DRY FROM BEING FORCED TO SIT THROUGH THREE long movies, and hearing Kat gush about her childhood crushes. They were good, but not life changing as Kat says, but I can never tell her that. We're close to finishing the last movie, Say

Anything, which happens to be her favorite, when Mom's name comes across my phone screen.

"Hey, Ma." I greet.

"Hey, mijo. Just checking in. Todo bien?"

"Yeah, I'm just watching movies." My mom doesn't hold me to a lot of rules, but if I told her Kat and I were alone, she'd have a heart attack.

"Are you alone?" I swear, I can hear her smile through the phone. "Yeah, why wouldn't I be?" I ask.

"Because I left my twenty-three-year-old home alone, so of course you have your girlfriend there." She sounds more amused than pissed, but I don't confirm or deny anything until she laughs.

"Relax, mijo. I trust you; just remember that I'm not ready to be a grandma just yet, okay?"

"Mom!" Thankfully, she's not on speaker, but from Kat's pink cheeks, I think she heard anyway.

"I just had to mess with you. Your dad says hi, by the way."

I stay silent for several seconds, contemplating whether to say anything back. "Tell him I say hi," I say distantly.

"We're going wine tasting in a bit, so I'll call later. We love you." Her words make my muscles tense, because I can't remember the last time my dad said those words to me, though, I'm sure he said it occasionally after I brought him a beer as a kid or some shit.

Kat is seemingly interested in a particular scene of the movie as I hang up the phone. "Grams showed me this movie when I was a kid, I remember the moment when I decided I wanted the *boombox over the head to serenade me* moment. Iconic."

I'm only half-listening while my mind replays old memories of me and my dad from the earlier, shitty years. I hate how three simple words can send me spiraling back to square one when I fought like hell to get to where I am now.

Kat must notice my turmoil, because she pauses the movie and focuses her attention on me.

"Are you okay?" Her voice sounds muffled and far away as I focus on pushing the memories away.

"Hey, look at me. What's wrong? You can tell me." She grabs my face to force me to look at her green eyes and freckled cheeks.

I've hesitated letting her fully in out of embarrassment for my past, but she deserves to have every piece of me, even the bad. "You want to know why I hate my dad so much?"

Her mouth gapes open in shock at the words. I never thought this would be shared with anyone outside of my family. That night haunted all of us for years, but I'm the lucky one it's followed even until this day.

"Only if you want to tell me." If I wasn't already convinced that I could trust her, that would have done it. Her aura is unlike anything I've ever witnessed—to be with her is to feel brave enough to share anything. I cover both of her hands with my own trembling ones.

"I had to walk on eggshells with my dad my entire childhood. He was a really shitty person. He used to call me useless if I didn't want to bring him a beer, but as long as it was me and not Elliot being treated that way, I was okay with it." My breath hitches as my throat grows tight, but I gain the strength to continue when Kat tightens her grip on my hands.

"One night six years ago, I heard my parents arguing, which was normal for them, but this argument was different. I went to see if my mom was okay..." I wince as the memories start to come back. "I watched from a distance, but when I saw my dad's hand move up to her face, I just snapped. All I remember is charging at him. I was seventeen, so I had been in boxing for awhile, and I just started hitting him and hitting him..." My body rejects the words as I try to fight back tears.

"You were protecting your mom."

I'm sure she'll change her mind about my character when she hears the rest of the story. "I didn't stop, though; my anger made me black out. When I finally snapped out of it, all I saw was my dad on the ground with a bloody face, my mom was screaming, and Elliot cowering like he was afraid of me."

She wipes away the slow rolling tear before I can.

"My dad swears he wouldn't have hit my mom, that he was just pointing in her face, but I still didn't feel guilty. He was shitty for years. He wanted us to to pretend like none of it happened after just because he got sober. I still have nightmares about my mom's screams. She forgave me, and my dad's been trying to get on my good side ever since, but every time I look at him, I remember all those years of being scared of him. Then I think about how it got us to that night." I finally look up at Kat, panicking when I see her red eyes.

"Why are you crying?" I drag my thumb across her wet cheek to catch the tears.

"You didn't deserve that—none of you did." I didn't know that I needed to hear that from someone until it came from her perfect lips.

"Can I ask you something?" she asks, and I nod my head, pushing the hair out of her face.

"Is that why you never wanted a relationship? Because you didn't want to end up like your parents?" She reads me like a damn book without me having to explain myself.

"I figured if I never settled down, I wouldn't risk being like them. They're better now, but it doesn't erase the past." She brushes careful fingers through my hair in pleasant silence.

"We won't be like them, Andrew." she says matter-of-factly. Those words unlatch the last lock to my heart, the last part of me I was harboring for dear life. Now that she has it, I don't want to get it back—it's hers forever, no matter what happens between us.

"I know," I say with all the confidence in my soul before

kissing her as if the world is crumbling and this is our last moment. She pulls back to caress my cheek before she uses her fingertips to lift her shirt and throw it to the ground. I can't peel my eyes away from the black lacy bra that barely covers her breasts. She's so perfect, I'm afraid to touch her.

"You sure?" I ask, trailing my fingers slowly along her arm.

"I'm sure." She crawls onto my lap and slowly trails kisses down my neck while grabbing handfuls of my hair. How am I the one who's fucking nervous right now? She's so confident, but I can't even touch her without fucking hyperventilating. We've been a real couple for three months, and we haven't slept together yet, due to me being scared shitless. I've never slept with a girl with feelings involved—it was always just sex—but I want it to be more with her.

She's different. *Everything* is different with her. The world is brighter with her in it. *Existing* is better with her. I don't know how I got so lucky, but I'll thank whoever's responsible forever.

She lifts the bottom of my shirt to pull it over my head but stops when she feels me tense. *I'm acting like a damn virgin.* I have the most mesmerizing woman sitting on my lap, and I'm hesitating.

"Am I doing something wrong?" She blushes with embarrass-ment.

"No, it's nothing you're doing. It's me. I just can't believe I'm yours." I finally say my intrusive thoughts out loud. I didn't want to say she's mine, because Kat is too strong of a woman to be owned, but I'll happily be owned by her.

Her laughter makes my heart ache as I feel it rumble in my chest. I just want to bottle up her laughter and drink it every day for the rest of my life. She looks pleased with what she sees after throwing my shirt on the ground to join hers, and I thank all those hours in the gym.

When our lips finally meet again, I'm a goner. She slips her tongue into my mouth, and I get a taste of the strawberry candy she was sucking on earlier. I flip her over so I can crawl on top of her, but our lips don't stop, and I pull back only to get one more look at her.

"Te amo," I whisper, tracing my finger from her freckles all the way down to the button of her jeans. I shock myself that the words slipped so freely from my mouth, but I don't want to take them back.

"What does that mean?" Her breaths are staggered, but I make her wait. I want to tell her, but is it too soon? I don't want to ruin the moment by scaring her off with *I love you*.

"It means...you're beautiful." The lie feels like acid, but I let my fear get the best of me.

She reaches for the button on my pants, and we both laugh when she has trouble getting my belt off. I help her, then undo her zipper and bra with my free hand. Our movements are rushed, like we can't get to each other fast enough. My hand travels recklessly to her neck while I use the other to slide off her matching lace underwear. I thought she was perfect with her clothes on, but *fuck*. I take a mental photograph of her in her most intimate state—bare body glistening with sweat already, messy hair, jagged breaths.

"Why are you so good at doing that with one hand?" she asks, smiling in between our rushed kisses.

"Just shut up and kiss me, freckles." I mutter before effortlessly sweeping her into my arms and throwing her over my shoulder. I refuse to have sex with her for the first time on my mom's couch. Our lips don't leave each other's until I drop her down onto my bed and admire her beautiful canvas of a body.

Just before I crawl on top of her again, I say gently, "By the way, I get tested frequently, and I'm clean."

"I trust you," she whispers.

If I'm certain about anything after tonight, it's that Kat Harrison has my entire heart in the palms of her hands, and she doesn't even know it.

CHAPTER 30

Kat

Adore You - Miley Cyrus

It's been two days since Andrew and I slept together for the first time, every moment is still etched into my mind. I had only been with one guy before, but I can't see it getting *any* better than that. He was so greedy to learn every inch of my body, yet he still took the time to make sure I was pleased.

The next morning, we just admired each other for what felt like hours. He looked at me with a look in his eyes that he didn't have before.

The only real-life example I have about being in love is my grandparents, but that night, it clicked for me. It was before we even slept together, when he told me about his dad. I saw the real Andrew, the one he hides from the world, and I wanted nothing more than to protect him. He was vulnerable with me, and it was *attractive*.

Realizing I was in love with him wasn't a big moment like it's depicted in movies. It was way more peaceful, like the feeling had been there for a while, just waiting to be woken from its slumber.

"Kat, before you leave, can you stock the beer?" Sam's voice brings me back from my erotic flashbacks.

Time flew at the bar today. I asked Sam for an early shift so I could hang out with Grams tonight. I love when Andrew comes over to hang out with us, but I miss it just being us.

My phone blares in my back pocket, and I'm surprised to see Emory's name. We text frequently, but it's mainly just checking in. Long distance friendships are hard. I remind myself to call her once I clock out, because I do miss hearing her voice, even it it's usually a smart-ass remark.

"How's that boyfriend of yours?" Sam pries.

"Why? Are you deciding whether to threaten him?" I ask, swiping my employee card to clock out.

"I already did." His mustache moves frantically as he lets out husky laughter.

"Yeah, he said that you told him something along the lines of hurt her, and you answer to me."

"Sounds about right. He knows I mean well. I have to look out for you." I give him a pat on the back as I walk past him.

"Thanks, papa bear. See you tomorrow." I jolt out of the door and dial Emory on the walk back to my car. A sprinkle of rain starts to fall, so I'm glad I'm getting home before the storm starts.

"No way is this Kat Harrison, the girl who never calls me."

"You know the phone works both ways, Emory Jewel Diaz." I know she hates it when I call her by her full name.

"You're right; let me shut up. So what's new?" I contemplate whether I should start off small or just drop the bomb—I might as well rip off the band-aid.

"Well, for starters, I slept with Andrew."

I hear her gagging on the other end. "Kat, never tell me that again. He's like my big brother—I don't want to know who he's fucking, especially if it's my best friend."

"Well you asked what was new, and that's new." I can't contain my laughter as I start my car.

"Gross...but I won't rag on you too much. You both deserve to be happy."

"You wanna know something crazy? I think I'm in love with him." It feels real now that I've admitted it out loud instead of it stay-ing a thought inside my head. The only sound I hear is her hitched breaths.

"Holy shit, did you tell him yet?"

"No. I guess I'm just waiting for the right moment." Another moment of silence passes.

"Promise me you'll *make* a moment the right moment, please? After losing..." She chokes on Elliot's name, "I learned that you have to make every moment count. When you feel something, say it. When you wanna do something, do it."

I take her words to heart, because she knows all to well about that. She spent weeks pissed at Elliot last summer when she wasn't aware he was dying. By the time they finally admitted their feelings for each other, she found out he only had weeks left. She's never admitted it to me, but I know she hates herself for that.

I've never said the L word to a guy before, and I don't want to mess it up. What if he doesn't say it back? Could we both move past that rejection?

"I'm scared, Em. You know Andrew—he's unpredictable. What if he doesn't say it back, and I look stupid?"

She scoffs before answering in a cool tone. "You're right—I do know Andrew, which is why I know he probably fell in love with you the second he met you but was too stupid to know it."

I'm stunned into silence. There's no way she's right. "What do you mean?"

"Remember when you told me you wished someone looked at you the way Elliot looked at me? Well, while you were noticing him looking at me, I was noticing Andrew looking at you. Something was there from the beginning; it just took some time for you both to notice it."

Butterflies explode in my stomach, and I can't stop the wide grin from forming on my face. "Who knew you were so sentimental," I tease. I have to use my windshield wipers to see the road clearly now that the rain is starting to pick up. All I think about is Andrew— he's hated driving in the rain since he was a kid.

"Don't remind me. I wasn't this cheesy until I fell in love." We share more laughs, talking about how she's doing in school and making new friends who aren't as talkative as me.

Who would have guessed known that the moody girl I had to train on her first day would become so important to me?

Life is full of coincidences, but this one is my favorite.

CHAPTER 31
Andrew

You Are In Love - Taylor Swift

I can't take it anymore. I've been tossing and turning, unable to sleep for two nights, because all I can think about is what I really want to tell Kat—what I should have told her on the night we slept together.

I want to tell her that I didn't say she was beautiful—even though I think she's the most beautiful woman I've ever laid my eyes on. I want to tell her that I said I love her. Because I do. I feel like a fucking idiot that it took telling her about my dad for me to realize it, but if I have to go another day with her not knowing, I'm going to go insane. I don't care if she rejects me. I don't care if she tells me to my face that she's not ready to say it back; I'll say it every day until she is. I'd rather get my heart shattered by her than have it whole with anyone else.

My nerves rattle at the sound of strong winds and rain hitting the pavement outside. I couldn't tell you why I hate driving in the rain. Of course the one night we have a goddamn rainstorm is the night I have to tell my girlfriend I love her.

I WENT UNDER THE SPEED LIMIT THE THE ENTIRE WAY TO HER house, taking me double the time to get here. It's a little after one in the morning, so I know she's asleep, but I'll have to pull out tricks from her favorite movies.

The rain is coming down even harder now, and the winds making the trees threaten to fall, but I exhale a big breath before sprinting over her grass and stopping at her window. I can barely see, but I carefully step over the small pebbles that outline the garden of flowers. My fingers are so cold, even the gentlest tap on her window makes them feel like they're being cut by glass. I keep tapping on her window, hoping she'll hear. I know I look stupid right now, but I'll look stupid for her any time.

To my relief, it only takes a couple of minutes until I see her pull back her green curtains with half-open eyes. When it registers that I'm standing in the rain, her eyes bulge out of her head as she panics to unlock her window and pull it above her head.

"What the hell are you doing, Cortes?" she shouts over the loud patter of rain.

"I love you!" I'm completely unfazed by water falling over me as her face goes white.

"Say it again," she demands with a smile. *Anything for you.*

"I love you, Kat. I never want to go back to living a life without you. You make existing worth it. I always thought I hated the idea of being in a relationship, but maybe I knew you'd show up one day, so I was just waiting. You're it for me. It's always going to be you, freckles."

I can't tell if it's the rain or her tears making her eyes swollen, but she grabs me by my shirt and pulls our lips together. I can taste the saltiness from her tears mixed with her flavored lip balm. She's unprotected from the water now, so we're just two crazy people kissing in the rain like in a cheesy rom-com. I'm sure she wouldn't want it any other way.

"You have my heart forever, Andrew Cortes," she says, smiling against my lips between tender kisses. As soon as I hear those words, everything is right in the world. There's no past or future—just me and he, right now. I used to think I got dealt a shitty hand in life because it was karma for something I did, but if someone like her can love someone like me, I'm the luckiest person to ever live.

Being in love with her feels like a Sunday morning—peaceful and renewing. I want to keep that feeling for as long as she'll let me. I pick her up to lead her back into the safety of her room, and she pulls me into her bed, where we stay all night.

Wherever she is, that's where I want to be. Home isn't a place to me: it's her body. It's her soul. It's her smile. It's her.

CHAPTER 32
Kat

Angeleyes - ABBA

TODAY IS THE DAY. I'VE BEEN PSYCHING MYSELF OUT OF IT FOR months, but I can't anymore. Waking up to Andrew, peacefully asleep in my bed this morning, gave me the push I needed. He's slept over for the past week, and now my bed feels empty when his warm body doesn't occupy it.

The night he came to tell me that he loves me replays in my head as I run my fingers along his prominent jaw line. It was the most romantic thing I've ever experienced. I didn't get much sleep that night, I just watched him, in awe at how fast I fell in love with him. Andrew thought it was impossible for someone to love him, but I found it as easy as breathing.

My touch must have woken him, because his eyes start to open slowly. I'll never get tired of being greeted by his lazy smile in the morning.

"Morning, freckles." His whole body takes up my queen-sized mattress when he stretches.

"Can I show you something today?" He must pick up on the

nervousness in my tone by the way his brown eyes narrow on me.

"Of course. Let me just shower first—I'm sweaty from last night." I roll my eyes when he winks and flashes a smug grin at me. His cockiness is *sometimes* a turn-on.

I use his absence to dress and get a head start on something I've been avoiding for almost a year. I dig into my top drawer and feel around for the round key to my grandpa's music room. It's been in the same place since the day of his funeral when I received it: out of sight, but definitely not out of mind. I pass by that room every day, but I was never able to bring myself to go inside until Andrew. He got me to play, which invited that piece of Gramps back into my heart again. Turns out, he was the *real* key to opening that door all along.

My hand lingers over the lock as my mind tries to convince me to leave it alone, but I hear the water running in the shower, reminding me that Andrew will be joining me inside soon.

A wave of nostalgia hits me when I swing the door open and look around at the dust-filled room. You could always find him sorting out his vinyls. He spent years collecting milk crates because he was obsessed with the room looking like an old record store where he and Grams met. She was working as a cashier, he was the guy obsessed with music. He'd collect all his change to buy a record so he'd have an excuse to see her every week.

They blamed me being a hopeless romantic on the movies I watched growing up, but it was really their love story.

In the corner of the room is a collection of instruments that were all shown plenty of attention when he was alive, and I can't hold back the tears.

"So this is the famous Billie Harrison I've heard about." I dry my tears before turning around to face Andrew, who's holding a picture of Gramps in his early touring with his band days. "Does he have a mullet?" he asks, bringing the picture closer to his eyes.

"Believe it or not, he got my grandma to fall in love with him with that haircut." I manage to muster up a laugh despite the heavi-ness in my chest.

Andrew scopes around the room while I stay frozen in place, afraid to touch anything.

"What's your favorite vinyl in here?" he asks, browsing through the collection. My fingers are itching to do the same, but I can't bring myself to move. He must notice, because he walks over to where I am and cups my face with his hand.

"You okay?" I lean into his touch and let his thumb caressing my cheek soothe me. "I just haven't been in here since he died. This was his favorite place to be."

"Just take it slow. Start with playing a vinyl." His deep voice rattles in my chest, almost making my anxiety dissipate. My legs finally gain the strength to walk over to the milk crate that harbors my favorite vinyl of all time. "I love you, but really?" Andrew asks, trying to mask his distaste as soon as the music starts to play.

I try to suppress a giggle as the ABBA vinyl plays *Angeleyes*. I point at Andrew's eyes as I mouth the words, and then, as if the song summoned her to us, Grams creeps in with the biggest smile I've seen on her face in a long time.

Her movements are a lot more stiff than they used to be, but we still manage to dance around like we used to. This house hasn't been filled with music in so long—it suddenly seems more colorful, as though it missed the sound. Andrew stays back, arms folded across his chest, but it's Grams who forces him into our circle. He's never been able to say no to her, but I know he wants to in this moment. I never thought I'd smile again in this room, but just like a lot of things, Andrew changed everything.

"Oh, c'mon, Grams—I'm twenty-three now. Can I have at least one of your cookie recipes?" I plead. Andrew and I are huddled in the kitchen while we watch her make her famous persimmon cookies.

"You're not ready for that responsibility yet, lovey." She throws flour on my nose, which gets rich laughter to erupt from Andrew.

"C'mon, Muscles, I need your help putting the trays into the oven." She hands off trays full of raw cookie dough to him. Seeing them bond like this fills me with a joy I didn't know was attainable.

When the doorbell rings, I decide to get it while they're distracted, but I wish I hadn't when my past is on the other side of the door.

She's different, but the same. Her blonde hair is healthier, more golden than it was the last I saw it. She no longer has a sunken face or bruises all over her body, her eyes still the dark green shade that she unfortunately passed down to me.

"There's my little girl." Her eyes rake over me with judgment.

"Grace." I have to swallow down vomit just from her name. I remember when calling her mom used to fly off my tongue.

"Fair enough. Can we talk?" Her heeled boots tap impatiently against the cement as she waits.

"No."

She laughs with amusement at my harshness. "Either you come out here and talk, or I go in there, and I don't think you want that, considering you have a guest." She nudges to Andrew's sports bike parked in the driveway. I look back at the kitchen one last time before stepping outside to confront the baggage I've been trying for years to leave behind.

"What do you want?" Just breathing the same air as her makes me stiffen.

"You changed your hair."

"Anything to not look like you." The hatred rolls off my tongue with ease. I dyed my hair years ago because I couldn't stand to look in the mirror every day knowing we shared so many similarities. I couldn't do anything about the color of my eyes, but I could change my hair. I've been brunette ever since.

"Ouch. Is that all I get after all these years?" Her devilish smirk makes my blood boil. I haven't seen her in eight years, and she comes ringing my doorbell like she's selling cookies.

"What. Do. You. Want?" I reiterate with gritted teeth. The sooner I figure out why she's here, the sooner she leaves.

"This was the only way to get a hold of you, considering you haven't written me back. I'm glad you changed your last name—your dad's was shitty."

As soon as I turned eighteen, I changed my last name so I would share it with my grandparents.

"I had nothing to say to you," I say bluntly. Usually a mother is supposed to bring out the good in you, but she summons the ugliest part of me I don't want to harbor.

"Lucky for you, I have plenty to say for the both of us." She hands me a folded piece of paper, and I snatch it from her hands.

"What is this?" I scan the paper, but none of it make any sense to me.

"It's the money I was forced to pay your grandparents in back child support for you years ago. You're an adult, I figured you were in a position to pay it all back to me now."

Is she fucking serious?

This is the first time in my entire life I have no words. I'm shaking with rage as I look at the five-thousand-dollar balance.

"So this is what you were writing me for? Money? Not to see

how your only goddamn kid is doing after you abandoned her?" I rip the paper into tiny shreds and let them fall across my lawn.

"Lucky for you, Kat, you're not my only kid anymore. I moved to New Jersey, got married, and you have two little brothers."

I can't fight the way my insides twist at her admission. I loved my life with my grandparents, and I wouldn't change anything, but I also hate that her sons experienced the sober Grace I dreamed of.

"Well, you can go back to New Jersey, because I'm not paying you a fucking penny. It's the least you could have done for me after leaving me with Dad."

For six months, I had to endure my dad's wrath alone. For six months, I locked myself in my room, only coming out to go to school. My grandparents went as fast as they could to get full custody of me, but it wasn't fast enough.

"That wasn't my proudest moment, but I knew my parents would save the day, so am I really the villain here? They did better than I ever could." I can't believe someone like her came from my favorite people in the entire world.

"Gee, thanks." I roll my eyes at her with disgust. I always imagined what I would say or do if I ever seen her again. My answer always changed, but I never anticipated I'd have this much resent-ment and hatred. The way she has no remorse for what she did proves she never had any intention on coming back for me, and that fills me with sorrow for little Kat who waited on her.

"I'm in a bind, so I'm not leaving town without my money Kat."

Her emerald eyes darken, but I don't relent. "Then I guess you won't be seeing your new kids for a while, Grace."

"You ungrateful little shit I raised you for—" Her shouting is cut off when Andrew walks out with cold, relentless eyes directed at her.

"Hey, you were gone for a while, I wanted to check on you." A protective hand lays on my lower back, and for the first time since I walked outside, I feel safe. His body is faced towards her.

"Can we help you?" I've never heard his voice so raw and harsh.

"You sure know how to pick 'em, Kat." She eyes Andrew with a seductive smirk. If he wasn't shielding me, I'd smack it right off her face. "I'm Grace, Kat's—"

"She's someone who was just leaving," I cut in. He can't find out who she is. I told him she was dead. At the time, it was the easier route than explaining that *this* is what I come from.

She puts her hands up in surrender, but not before throwing me a threatening smirk. "I can see I'm not welcome, but I'll see you soon." I feel like I'm going to vomit all over the perfectly-cut grass as I watch her back out of the driveway.

"Are you okay? Who was that?"

I snap myself out of my trance when I hear Andrew's distant voice.

"No one important." I try to push Grace as far out of my mind as I can, but the ripped up letter flying all over the grass taunts me.

"I leave you alone for two minutes..." He says as he tucks a strand of my hair behind my ear. Just looking at him makes every-thing else disappear.

"So don't leave me again."

I get up on my toes to kiss him quickly on the cheek. I wish I could forget what just happened, but I know I can't.

Grace showing up today was just a wakeup call that no matter how fast you try to run away from your past, it always has a way of catching up with you.

CHAPTER 33
Andrew

Iris - The Goo Goo Dolls

I'LL NEVER GET TIRED OF WAKING UP TO BROWN HAIR DANGLING over my face and the overwhelming scent of peach shampoo filling my nostrils. Kat is incapable of staying in one place while she sleeps, but somehow, she always ends up cradled in my neck. I thank my lucky stars every time I wake up to her freckled, angelic face. I've recently discovered she has seventeen freckles spread across her cheeks. I've counted them over twice while she's slept.

Even in my wildest dreams, I never imagined getting as lucky as I did with Kat.

She's usually awake before me, but she's been working herself to death at the bar all week, plus volunteering extra hours at school. I hate seeing her exhausted, but she won't tell me why the sudden need for extra cash. I press my lips to her neck and cover her back up with the blanket before slipping out of the room. Today is her only day off this week, the least she deserves is breakfast in bed. Vera prefers oatmeal, so I boil water to make her breakfast too. While Kat's been gone, I've been bonding a lot with her grandma. The more time I spend with her, the more similarities I find between them.

I pull eggs and bacon out of the fridge and lay them out on the counter before I find a pan. I used to only manage to make toast, but since Kat is a shitty cook, I've learned to perfect some dishes. I'll have to get her some cooking lessons.

I smirk to myself at the man she's made me—making breakfast in bed for her, while I make future plans in my head. If you would have told me a year ago that this would be my life, I would have laughed in your face. As I flip the bacon in the pan, I feel hands smooth up and down my chest and stop at my waist.

"Morning." she greets before leaving a soft kiss on my back. Even her groggy morning voice is music to my ears. I turn my body so I can get a good look at her bare face before trailing kisses.

"You were supposed to stay in bed."

"I missed you." She pulls at the drawstrings of my shorts with a tempting grin.

"I'm really tired of being a sex object to you." I try to keep a straight face, but I fail when her full-hearted laughter fills the kitchen.

I lift her onto the countertop and kiss her deep enough to make up for the hours I didn't get to while we both slept. I know I have to stop, but I can't. She does this thing where she tugs on my hair, and it gets a fire going inside me every time.

"We're going to have problems if you burn that bacon." As hard as it is, Vera's fragile voice is what makes me pull away.

"Sorry, Grams."

"Hey, I was young once. You should have seen how your grandpa and I—"

"Please, for the love of God, don't finish that sentence," Kat shouts as she hunches over the kitchen sink and imitates throwing up.

Instead of serving breakfast in bed like my original plan, we decide to eat breakfast together and laugh our asses off at some of Vera's stories from the 70s and Kat's childhood. I never knew a house could be filled with so much laughter, until theirs.

KAT'S LIKE A MERMAID WHEN IT COMES TO SHOWERING. SHE'LL stay in there all day if you let her, so I know I have time to put on a movie. I stick some popcorn in the microwave and wait to hear the water stop.

When the doorbell rings, I assume it's Vera coming back from the store with Kayla, but I'm surprised when I see the woman who Kat seemed bothered by the other day. All I needed to hear was her raising her voice at my girl to know I don't like her.

"Can I help you?" I ask rudely.

"Is Kat here?" She tries to look over me and inside the house, but I block her view.

"Why do you want to know?" I mentally beg for Kat to stay in the shower until I can shoo this woman away.

"I'm sorry, who are you?" I dismiss her hand that's reached out to me as I meet her eyes in a challenge. It's hard to ignore how much she and Kat resemble each other—the rich green eyes, long wavy hair, and they even sound similar.

"Andrew, her overprotective boyfriend," I answer with a threatening tone.

A glimpse of humor washes over her face. "She tried so hard not to be like me, but I guess she inherited my taste in men." I squint my eyes with confusion as I try to make sense of what she said.

"Don't look so confused. I'm sure she's told you all the ways I've fucked her up." I'm stunned into silence when it clicks.

"Are you her mom?" *Am I hallucinating?* Kat told me her parents were dead.

"The one and only."

"You're lying. Her parents are dead," I say confidently.

"I can't say much about her dad, but I can assure you I'm *not* dead, pretty boy." Her scornful, dark chuckle makes me nauseous.

"What do you want with her?" My mind is spiraling with questions for Kat, but I want to know why this is the second time *her mom* has appeared.

"I've made it easy: I get the five thousand dollars she owes me, and I'll disappear for good."

It disgusts me how she doesn't hold an ounce of sympathy or remorse. I freeze up when I hear the bathroom door open and see Kat come out, her hair wrapped in a towel.

"You read my mind with the popcorn." She blanches at the sight of who's on the other side of the door.

"I knew you hated me, but isn't telling people I'm dead a little low, even for you, Katlyn?" her mom scoffs.

"I told you not to come by the house again." She storms towards us, anger flashing. "And I told you I'll leave you alone once I get my money. It's an even trade, sweetheart."

"I don't owe you shit," she spits out. I didn't even know she had a mean bone in her body. I'm upset with her that she lied, but I still stand protectively in front of her, in case this woman tries any-thing.

"Here's the address of where I'm staying if you change your mind. I have nothing but time." She hands a piece of paper to Kat before turning to walk away.

As soon as her car peels out of the driveway, my anger starts to bubble to the surface. *She lied.*

My mind spirals, remembering all the lies my dad told when I was a kid. He'd say he'd quit drinking, and the next day, he'd be drunk off his ass. My mom would lie to people about his addiction so we would seem like this picture-perfect goddamn family, but in reality, we were far from it.

I've been surrounded by lies my entire life, even my own, but I never expected any from Kat. Suddenly, it feels like I'm being suffocated by them, and I can't breathe.

"You lied." I break the deafening silence, and she's pale as a ghost as she chokes on the words. "It was better than the alternative of telling you the truth."

Before this moment, I thought it was impossible to ever be mad at her. "So you go with both your parents are dead? Who lies about that? How can I ever trust anything you say after this?" My voice gets louder as anger starts to cloud my judgment.

"Andrew, you know me. Everything else I've ever told you was real, why shut me out over this?" Her watery eyes plead to me—the same ones that have brought me comfort, but looking at them now, it's the opposite.

"It's not like you lied about your favorite fucking color, Kat. You said your parents were dead! That's not a little white lie to me, but if it is to you, then maybe I don't know you the way I thought I did." The anger I have feels reckless. I have to get away from her.

"I know. I'm sorry. I love you. Can we just talk about this?"

It feels shitty seeing her sob. I know she loves me, and I love her with every fiber of my being, but my distrust in her is overcoming every other emotion right now.

"I can't right now. I need some time to think." There's a crippling ache in my chest as I leave her with broken sobs, and my hands tremble all the way to my truck as I fight the urge to turn around and comfort her.

I know we have to talk about this soon, I just can't right now while my judgment is fogged with anger.

Seeing her in my rearview mirror, standing in the middle of the road, crushes all the good parts of my heart, but I keep going —a crumbled piece of paper with an address in my hand.

CHAPTER 34
Kat

Fix You - Coldplay

I FINALLY GAINED CONTROL OF MYSELF ABOUT TWENTY MINUTES after watching Andrew drive away. I've spent the last hour pacing my living room, waiting for him to walk through the door and tell me he's changed his mind, that he'll let me explain everything. There's a knot of guilt the size of Texas in my stomach. I wish he would have just heard me out, let me explain that since my parents acted as if I didn't exist my entire childhood, it was nice to pretend *they* didn't in my adulthood.

He's never looked at me the way he did before he left, and I've never looked at him and seen someone so unfamiliar. His sharp words echo in my head, and I keep telling myself he didn't mean them.

He's just upset. Once I give him the space he asked for, he'll hear me out, and everything will go back to the way it was. *He just needs space.*

I knew nothing good would come from Grace being back. She's a tornado who ruins everything in her path, and of course she just had to fuck up the little piece of my life left unscathed by her. I'm on a seesaw of emotions, going from regret and sadness thinking of Andrew, and pure rage when I think of Grace.

My car keys hanging on the shelf tempt me. She gave me the address of where she's staying, and while I'm not giving her a dime,

she's going to leave town anyway after she hears what I've had pent up for eight years. She can't leave a trail of destruction and skip out of town like nothing happened. I look around frantically for the paper she gave me, but it's nowhere to be found. Luckily, I have perfect memory, so I know exactly which motel she's staying at.

My car starts up with ease, just as it has since the day Andrew gave it back, and I speed to confront the last ghost of my past.

I NEARLY DRIFT INTO THE PARKING LOT OF THE SHITTY MOTEL and find room thirteen while rage is still fresh in my bones.

I ignore the men who whistle at me like I'm a dog as they smoke cigarettes in the hall. I don't even want to think about what Andrew would do to them if he were here.

My heart pounds in my ears as I wait on the other side of the door that desperately needs a new paint job. I know she's here—she wouldn't miss an opportunity of getting her money.

"Oh look, it's my daughter who told people I was dead. Come to apologize?" She opens the door with a smug grin on her face, a cigarette between her lips.

"I'll apologize when you admit you can't pull off this outfit anymore." I scan her full leather outfit that's at least twenty years out of style and definitely doesn't fit her body.

"I forgot how witty you are. Maybe we're not so different

after all." She smiles boldly, as if she's proud of my insult before taking another hit of her cigarette. I nudge past her into her room with the full intention of telling her off, but instead, I go stiff when I see the half-packed bags sitting on her twin bed.

"You're leaving town?" Just as I think she finally decided to give up and leave us alone, a cynical smile covers her face, sending chills down my spine.

"You can thank that boyfriend of yours."

My brows furrow as I dissect her words. "What do you mean?"

"He came about half an hour ago threatening me to leave you alone, and throwing money at me. I'm sticking to what I said and leaving town now that I have what I want."

The air in the room suddenly feels thicker, making it hard to breathe. There's no way. She's lying; she lies like it's second nature.

"I call bullshit," I say, folding my arms defensively across my chest as she puts her cigarette out on an ashtray. The hairs on the back of my neck stand up when pulls out a wad of hundred-dollar bills from a duffle bag full of clothes.

"He's good looking and has money. Nice work pulling that one, kid."

I can feel the bile burning my throat. I can't believe I roped the man I love into my mess. It wasn't his to clean up, but he did it anyways, because that's who he is. He looks out for the people he loves.

Despite the shitty circumstances, my heart leaps just thinking that there's hope for us after all. He wouldn't have come to get rid of my mom if there wasn't. I'll work overtime to pay back every cent.

I came here to tell Grace off, but now, all I want is to be with Andrew.

"Well you got what you wanted, so...have a nice life." I

bump her shoulder on my way out, not sparing her another glance, even though younger Kat pleads for it from inside.

"Kat..." Her voice stops me just as I grip the doorknob, but I keep my back turned. "I wanted to come back for you, but I knew I wasn't good, so I let my parents take you in. You're still my daughter, and I hope we can at least be friends someday."

I fight the tears that threaten to fall for the girl who wanted nothing more than her mom to love her. I don't believe a word she's saying. She's just trying to leave on a good note so she doesn't have a guilty conscious, but I won't give her the satisfaction.

"I have enough friends, Grace. I guess I owe you a thank you, though, because your parents loved me enough to last my whole life, so I don't need you."

I shut the door on my past once and for all, desperately holding in the sob that wants to erupt from my chest until I'm alone in my car. The only thing that halts the hot tears falling down my cheeks is Andrew's face clouding out everything else.

AN IMMEDIATE SENSE OF RELIEF WASHES OVER ME WHEN I SEE his truck in the driveway, but a wave of panic follows. I don't exactly want to unpack my entire childhood so soon after confronting my mom, but if it'll get him to trust me again then that's what I'll do.

The front door is unlocked, so I walk into the eerily silent house and go upstairs to find him staring blankly at the TV on his wall.

"Andrew," I say warily. It takes several seconds for him to acknowledge me, but when he finally does, I startle at his blood shot eyes.

"What are you doing here?" he asks, gripping something in one of his hands for dear life.

"I'm here to tell you what I should have back at my house." I kneel on the floor to meet his gaze, but he won't even look at me.

"Why would I believe you?" His voice is cold and edged.

Before I can speak again, my body goes numb when I finally see what's in his hands.

"I thought you threw them all out?" He assured me months ago he flushed all his pills down the toilet, but from where I'm sitting, it looks like he's holding onto a handful.

"I found some at the bottom of my drawer." He still doesn't meet my eyes as I reach for them.

"Andrew, give me the pills." He shakes his head, but I don't relent. "Give them to me before you do something stupid." His grip tightens when I use all my strength to pry them from him. I fought so hard to never end up in this position, and yet here I am, in it anyway.

"Kat, stop," His broken voice calls out. "I'll stop when you give me the goddamn pills!" He continues resisting as I wrestle with his hand until the tablets finally go flying. I feel nauseous as I watch his watery eyes desperately search the floor. "Andrew, be honest with me: if I didn't just walk through that door, would you have taken those pills?" There's at least seven scattered across his floor.

He hesitates, but then nods his head in defeat, and I can't bear to see it.

"Everything just started coming back in my mind—my dad, Elliot, you. I didn't want to take the pills, but they make everything just go away." He sinks to the floor and hugs his legs to his chest as he rocks back and forth. Seeing the person you love like this and not knowing how to help is something I wouldn't even wish on my worst enemy.

"Talk to me Andrew, please." I don't hold back my tears as I see the man I'm in love with in broken pieces on the floor.

The only words to slip from his lips are, "Why did you lie?"

I fall to the floor next to him and take a big breath of courage before I let it all out into the world.

"My parents cared more about drugs than they ever did about me. My lovely mom, who you met, walked out, leaving me with a dad who never stopped reminding me he didn't want me. If you lived even a day in my childhood home, you'd want to pretend it didn't exist too. I'm not sorry I wanted to pretend they were gone forever." I look around at the pills scattered on the floor, then back at Andrew, his face tense in thought. "This can't…this won't be my life, Andrew. Not again."

He finally meets my eyes, but they're not the same ones that feel like home. "I know," he whispers.

"We can get you some help, though. Maybe therapy…"

He cuts me off mid-sentence. "No. *We* aren't going to do something. *I* am." A pit of emptiness settles in my stomach as the energy shifts.

"What are you saying?" I ask, afraid to hear the answer.

"I'm saying look around you, Kat. You just wrestled pills out of my hand. That's not the life you want, but it's all I have for you right now. I gave myself too much fucking credit. As soon as shit hit the fan, I spiraled back to square one. I can't promise this won't happen again, and that makes me feel like shit." He doesn't have to tell me he's hanging on by a thread: I can see it in his lost, dead eyes.

I don't say a word. He turns to fully face me, covering my hands with his own cold, trembling ones. "I love you too much to drag you down with me, freckles. I have to do this on my own." He leaves a trail of kisses across my hand and down my arm. I memorize the feel of his lips on my skin just in case I never feel them again.

"What if we don't come back to each other?" I whisper through the sea of tears. This isn't what was supposed to happen.

"There will never be anyone but you, Katlyn Rose Harrison, but promise you won't wait around for me. The world deserves to experience you." I know I can't do that. He's etched himself in my soul, that I can't imagine my life without him. "I love you." They're the only words I manage to choke out as I take in his red, swollen eyes filled with tears.

"I love you more, mi vida."

I know vida means life in Spanish, so I choke up even more —he just called me his life when we're about to part.

"So what now?" I ask between shaky breaths. He looks at me longingly, and I sink into the hand that's gently caressing my cheek.

"You're going to walk out, and not look back. You're going to cry for a couple of days, but then you'll get right back up, because you're Kat."

I rush to press my lips to his in a deep, memorable kiss. It pains me to think this might be the last time my lips will feel the warmth of his, and from the way he holds on to me, I know he feels the same.

My heart shatters when he leads me out of the room. I follow through on my promise not to glance back at him as I walk away, even though all my instincts are screaming for me to take one last look.

I wish I could say my love for him faded away after closing the door, but it's never that easy, is it? I can still feel the part of my soul that longs for him, and I fear that no matter how hard I try to ignore it, that feeling will never go away.

CHAPTER 35

Andrew

Words - Skylar Grey

I LAY STILL IN BED, JUST AS I HAVE FOR THE PAST THREE DAYS, wallowing in my own misery for letting go of the only person who actually loved every bit of me, even the broken parts. I replay our breakup over and over again, and I vomit when I remember Kat's tears as I led her out of my room.

I had every intention of taking those pills, and that's a version of me I want nowhere near Kat, not after what she's been through. I can never be selfish with her, so as my heart shattered into a million pieces, I let her go.

My fingers grasp onto the single-stemmed white rose in my hand. I was going to give it to Kat, along with the other eleven that came in the bouquet, but instead they'll stay here, wilting away.

I must be going crazy, because I started thinking of Kat as the rose—metaphorically speaking. Letting her leave felt like death by a thousand cuts, but if I didn't, she'd end up getting burned by all my demons.

If living without her means protecting her, then I'll go the rest of my life with a hole where my heart used to be.

June

THREE MONTHS LATER

CHAPTER 36
Kat

Right Where you Left Me - Taylor Swift

"You want chicken or pasta for dinner?" Emory shouts while I flip through channels on her TV. I've gotten used to her cooking the last few weeks I've been staying with her. She invited me to San Diego for summer break, and while it was a hard decision to leave Grams, I felt like I had to come. It's been a shitty three months, and I wanted to be around a friend.

I talk to Grams everyday. I miss her so much, but thankfully, she's not alone since Kayla offered to spend most days with her. Sam also calls once a week to fill me in on all the juicy details I've been missing at the bar.

I've been taking advantage of the ocean so close by, and it always excites me to see the locals here so full of life. It's peaceful here, but I'm surprised how much I miss Phoenix. I thought once I left, I'd see how much I was missing, but it actually makes me appre-ciate home more.

"Why not both?" I shout back to her.

"This is why we're friends."

I settle into the decorative pillows on the couch, and Sage

comes to cuddle with me. We're joined quickly by Emory's emotional support dog, Winston, a gift from Elliot before he died. Some nights, I can hear her crying when she thinks I'm asleep, but it stops as soon as Winston goes to console her.

Emory invited me here to help with the breakup, but I think I ended up helping her too. I've been able to convince her to have fun once in awhile.

"By the way, Seth asked for your number again." She drops down on the couch next to me to watch the animated movie playing on the screen.

"Gag," I say with distaste.

Seth works with her at the nearby restaurant. I went to visit her one day at work, and now he hits on me every time I'm in the vicinity. He's not bad looking, but Andrew is still in the forefront of my mind.

It's been three months since I've heard from him, but the soul crushing feeling of his absence is still there. My heart almost pounded out of my chest after seeing a truck that looked identical to his just last week, and don't even get me started on how long I cried when I realized I accidentally packed one of his shirts.

I promised I wouldn't wait around for him, but every time my phone rings, I wish it was him. I'm not sure that hope will ever fade. No one talks about how a mutual breakup hurts so much more than a one-sided one. Even though I know we needed to be apart, the love I have for Andrew is still imprinted on me.

"Remember when you told me that in order to get over someone, you have to get under someone else? What happened to that Kat?"

I ponder her words: it's still relevant advice, but I can't even look at anyone else without seeing Andrew's brown eyes or dark messy hair. "She fell in love," I say back.

She rolls her eyes and hits me in the face with one of the pillows. "Get over him." She and Andrew are nearly family, but that doesn't stop her from trying to knock some sense into me when she notices I miss him. I didn't tell her the real reason we broke up, only that we both decided it was better this way.

"You know what it's like to date a Cortes brother: they sink their claws into you," I whine.

"Yeah, and I got the better brother, thankfully." She throws her head back with laughter, and I watch with a smile at how she didn't freeze up like she usually does when she talks about Elliot. I'd like to think I had something to do with that.

"I'm gonna take a shower." I say, heading to the guest room.

"Dinner will be ready when you get back, your highness." she shouts back.

I brush out the knots in my hair before gathering my clothes for my shower. I cut it up to my shoulders—I wasn't ballsy enough to commit to a full chop.

They say hair holds memories, and those included all the mornings Andrew would run his gentle fingers through my strands when he thought I was sleeping, or how he looked up videos on braiding hair when I said I had never styled it that way.

Breakups look a lot less painful in the movies: none of them could have prepared me for this kind of hurt. I shut the dresser drawer a little too hard, and the mirror shakes, sending a picture flying directly in front of me. *Thanks, Universe.*

I should have left this back home. It's a memory from our second date as an official couple, but it was the first one he planned. We went to this arcade and stumbled on a photo booth, so I forced Andrew to go in with me. The first photo is of me goofing around while Andrew looks annoyed, the one under of him after I finally convinced him to make a funny face with me. The last two are candids the camera caught of us making out.

I hold it with a shaking hand, tempted to crumple it up and pretend it never existed, but a love like ours isn't erasable.

I feel as though I'm waiting alone at a restaurant, constantly being asked to give up the table, but I stay, collecting dust as I keep looking at the door for Andrew to enter.

Promise you won't wait around for me. Those words have echoed in my head for ninety days straight. I'm usually one to keep my promises, but there's a first time for everything.

CHAPTER 37

Andrew

SuperCut - Lorde

"So, this is our fifth session and we've made some progress, but I want to dig a little deeper." My therapist, Julie sits across from me with a notebook in her lap. I was always resistant about seeing a shrink, but losing Kat was a harsh wake up call.

I don't want to be mad at anyone anymore. I don't want to use pills as a crutch. I don't want to backtrack ten steps after an inconven-ience. That's how I've ended up in this chair twice a month for the past three months.

"What do you want to know?" I ask anxiously.

"Considering how you tense up any time we mention your dad or your childhood, let's start with that." My first sessions touched on the topics I was comfortable talking about—my relationship with my mom, my friends, Kat, and occasionally, how I've been coping with Elliot's death. Never about my dad.

My leg starts to shake vigorously in the chair, making the flowerpot on the coffee table threaten to fall. "Like I said Andrew, you've made progress, but unless you want to go back to square one when something pisses you off, you have to confront *everything* from your past."

Fuck. I shift nervously before I speak, "My dad was a raging alcoholic, and even though he's sober now, I'm still pissed at him for what he put us through." She nods while writing things down but still listens intently as the word vomit starts. "I mostly got the brunt of it to protect my brother. He never hit us. It was always verbal, but some-times, I think that was worse." Sweat starts to gather on my palms at the memories of shoving Elliot into his room every time my dad was in one of his moods—which was often.

"Sometimes verbal abuse leaves bigger scars than physical."

"As soon as he got sober, everyone cleaned the slate, but I remember everything."

"Do you ever think that was their way of coping? Your way was anger while theirs was forgetting it happened."

No, I had never thought of that. I shake my head, not wanting to speak.

"Andrew, the way you handle this isn't wrong. Your reaction to him is a result of the environment he put you in as a child. You can't unlearn your coping mechanism in a day, but the cycle is just going to continue unless you confront him on how he's hurt you."

Just thinking of confronting him fills me with agitation and uneasiness. "I can't even look at him without getting pissed off," I blurt out in a distant daze.

"If you don't forgive him, that anger will consume you even more than it already has. You said you lost the girl you love because you didn't want to drag her into your mess. This is a start on cleaning it up."

The last thing I want to do is have a heart to heart with Dad, but I meant it when I said that I don't want to be mad anymore. It hasn't gotten me anywhere—instead, it cost me everything.

The timer goes off, meaning our hour is thankfully up.

"I want details of how it went at our next session."

She guides me out of her office, and my mind spins on the walk back to the parking lot. There's years of pent-up anger settled inside me, and I'm afraid what'll happen once I let it out.

Kat's face suddenly comes to mind as I start up my bike. She used to beg me to pick her up in it just so she could wear the helmet I had custom made, *Andrew's Passenger Princess* printed on it.

The image of her hair blowing and bright smile as she held onto me plays in my head. When I let her go three months ago, I had hope that one day I'd be the kind of person who deserves her. If confronting my dad gets me closer to that, then the thread of hope feels like it's getting closer and closer to snapping.

I ENTER THE GYM, AND THANKFULLY, IT'S NEARLY EMPTY. I WAS on my way home, and suddenly I ended up here—just as I always did when my mind was spiraling.

I walk over to the corner where all the punching bags dangle from the walls, and something just comes over me when I start to hit one with bare knuckles and all the force in my body. I keep hitting as flashbacks roam through my mind at full speed.

Mom and Dad fighting.

Dad passed out drunk while he was watching me and Elliot.

Elliot in his last moments.

Kat's tears streaming down her face when I ended us.

I let everything out with grunts of anger as I keep hitting the bag until my knuckles are red.

"Don't break my equipment now, Cortes." Ralphie comes to hold the bag on the other side, his eyes find the tears that managed to stream down my face.

"You ready to talk now?" He asks somberly.

I wasn't pleased when Ralphie advised me to talk to my dad, but on some level, I knew that's what he would say. I hate to admit it, but I feel lighter after dumping everything out on him.

I really hope that's the last time I'll ever cry in front of him.

My dad is sitting on the couch watching a movie when I walk into the living room. He's usually not home this early, so I wasn't expecting to see him so soon after my heavy sessions.

I'm not ready to unload everything with him, but if I'm being honest, I don't think I'll ever be.

"How was therapy?" He's seemingly excited to ask the question.

I had to tell my parents about the sessions because they got suspicious when I was gone for an hour the same days every other week. They didn't shy away from being ecstatic. They've been trying to convince me for years.

"Fine. We talked about you." Might as well rip off the Band-Aid. *This is me trying to clean up my mess.*

"Me? What about me?" His shoulders tense, but he tries to play it off by repositioning on the couch. I take a seat across from him, avoiding eye contact.

"How pissed I am at you for treating us like shit when you drank. I wish it was all rooted in that one night, but I was pissed way before that—I just decided that night was when I'd had enough."

He scoots closer to me with hesitation, but I don't try to move away. "I think about how I treated you every goddamn day of my life. I know you had it worse because you were protecting Elliot. You were always better at it than I ever was…" His face turns red as tears fall into his mustache. "That night changed everything for me. I knew I had to change. I haven't picked up a drink since then, so I guess you could say you beat the alcoholism out of me." I try to fight it, but laughter erupts from me as a smile breaks across his lips.

"We've been so avoidant, we weren't there for each other when we needed to be the most. Losing your brother is...hell on Earth." A sudden cold chill runs up my back at his mention of Elliot.

"You and Mom seemed fine after we lost him," I finally admit out loud, with more edge than I intended.

"Trust me, we are *not* fine. We put on brave faces because the alternative is staying in bed wasting away, but Elliot wouldn't want that. There isn't a day where we don't think about him." He continues before I can cut in, "I think about the night he died a lot too. He told me to watch out for you because you took care of him his entire life, and no one ever looked out for you. I'm sorry I didn't keep my word, mijo."

I wipe away the water gathering in my burning eyes and fold my arms across my chest. "I don't wanna be mad anymore, Dad." I let out on an exhausted breath. I'm tired of being weighed down by my unhealed trauma. It's getting too heavy to carry.

For the first time ever, I let him bring me into his big arms and hug me tightly. An immense load lifts from my shoulders as I sink into him, and it's not long before I feel my mom's fragile hands wrap around the both of us.

"We love you," she whispers through her sniffles.

The only thing missing here is Elliot, but younger Andrew craved this moment, even though he never admitted it to anyone.

July

CHAPTER 38

Andrew

I Miss You, I'm Sorry - Gracie Abrams

EVERY MORNING FOR THE PAST FEW MONTHS, I'VE BEEN TRYING to make coffee that tastes like Kat's, but I can never get it right. I've been searching for anything I can to remind myself that she was real—that *we* were real. Even if we never met, I fear my soul would still long for her the way it does now.

Mom comes into the kitchen with a fresh face of makeup, dressed sharp in jeans and heels.

"Where are you going?" I ask, taking a sip of coffee and spitting it back into the mug. I guess I can only tolerate Kat's shitty coffee.

"A job interview. I want something that doesn't keep me away much, now that our house isn't a war zone." She ruffles her hands through my hair.

It's been an adjustment since me and my dad made amends. The memories will never go away, but I don't let them hold power over me the way I used to.

She sits across from me as she bites into her banana muffin.

"Have you talked to Kat lately?" It's been almost two months since she's asked about her.

"No, and I don't know if I ever will again." I haven't told her all the details of what happened—just that we broke up, and it was my fault. The longer we go without speaking, the more I feel her slipping away. She's probably happier without me, and I'm trying to make peace with that.

"Me and your dad separated for a time, but we came back to each other. You and Kat will too. The moment you brought her over, I knew she was special. You guys just…fit."

"It was fake when you saw us together, Ma." I have nothing to lose from telling the truth now, and she looks puzzled when the words slip from my mouth.

"What do you mean?"

"We weren't actually dating in the beginning. She agreed to help me out by being my fake girlfriend so you would stop pestering me about settling down."

Her eyes blink rapidly as she stares at me, clearly bewildered.

"So when she came over for dinner…"

"It was fake. We didn't date for real until November." She shakes her head in disbelief, but instead of saying something judg-mental, she surprises me.

"I would have never guessed from the way you two just glow around each other. It doesn't matter how it started, though, it matters what you feel for her now. If you love her, then she's worth fighting for. You don't want to look back in ten years and wish you went after her."

"You don't get it, Ma. I broke up with her because she's better off without me. I can't be someone who deserves her. I'm broken."

The wound re-opens. Every time I think I'm making progress, I remember the day we parted ways. I've thrown out every single pill in my room, and I've spent weeks talking it over in therapy, but how can I be sure that part of me is gone for good? What if he's just waiting to reappear when I least expect it? It'd be selfish of me to risk putting Kat through that again just because it feels like I can't breathe without her.

"Oh, Andrew, you're not broken. Maybe you used to be, but I can see you starting to put the pieces back together. If you think you haven't changed for the better, then you're not paying close enough attention. The Andrew you were last year and the Andrew sitting in front of me are two different people. Acknowledging that you needed to be better for her is the exact reason you deserve her." She must sense that I'm not fully convinced, because she adds to her lecture.

"No one will ever be perfect, mijo, but if you're willing to wake up every day and try to be better than the one before, you're already worthy of someone like Kat."

The words slam into me like I ran into a brick wall, and every moment I've shared with Kat races through my mind. The first time I held her hand—she always ran cold, so I clung onto it for as long as I could to warm her up. The first time she made me dance with her, and I realized she was the only one I wanted to be forced to dance with. Every morning we woke up next to each other, and I knew that she was my little piece of heaven on Earth.

I convinced myself I could never give Kat the kind of life she deserves, but maybe I can, because everyone deserves to be loved the way I love her.

Besides, to me, she's the sun, and you need the sun to survive.

※※※

I couldn't stand another day not seeing her face, so I rush to the bar with no plan except falling to my knees and hoping she still reserves a piece of her heart for me, even after four long months.

I double park my truck as I swing into the parking lot of Sam's. I use my reflection in the window to check my appearance and mess up my hair the way she likes it before walking in.

The place is packed, but if I even saw a glimpse of the back of her head, I'd know it was her. Sam is at the bar pouring drinks, but I can already sense his irritation as I approach.

"I knew you'd come begging for her one of these days." I wonder if Kat told him the whole truth about the breakup, or the shortened version I've been telling people.

"Is that such a bad thing?" I ask.

His mustache thins with criticism. "It's a bad thing since you were dumb enough to let her go in the first place."

"I know I fucked up, okay? I couldn't be who she wanted four months ago, and I don't know if I ever will be, but even though I know she's too fucking good for me, I still want her. I can't function without her, so please, just tell me where is."

If I know Kat, she's probably hiding in the back somewhere, avoiding waiting on tables. He sets the beer bottles in his hands down on the bar top and scrutinizes me, like I'm someone taking out his daughter for the first time.

"She's gone. She left months ago."

Words scramble in my brain as I try to find them again, "What do you mean *gone*?"

"She's with Emory in San Diego for the summer to get some much-needed space." He's lying. He'd say anything to keep me away if he thought he was protecting her.

"Seriously, Sam, where is she?" I can't hold back the panic in my voice.

"She's gone, man." His words brand me, leaving a stinging sensation around my heart.

He looks at me like I'm an injured puppy before leaning in closer. "Look, Andrew. For some reason, Kat loved you, and after your corny ass monologue, I can see that you really love her, so…" He scribbles something out on his notepad before passing it to me.

"That's Emory's address. If you manage to get her back, and break her heart again, you'll answer to me," he threatens before getting called to do something in the back.

I hold on to the paper like it's my first sight of water after wandering around in the desert. It's close to a six-hour trip from here to San Diego, so I better get driving.

CHAPTER 39

Kat

OUR DAY CONSISTS OF WHAT IS USUALLY DOES ON EMORY'S DAY off. We went down to the beach and walked along the waves with Winston before eating at a local restaurant with an ocean view. Then, she watched as I overloaded our cart at the grocery store. We're back at the house, prepping snacks for our movie night now.

It's a weekend, and she lives close to a university, so there are plenty of parties going on in her building. We even got invited to a few, but thankfully, Emory declined for us both.

"Don't even think about choosing a movie from the 80s," she threatens as I look through my collection. When I first arrived, I made her sit through all the classics, but she still prefers the modern take on romance.

"How about the 2005 version of Pride and Prejudice?"

"Now you're talking."

A beat up copy of the book sits on my nightstand back home, full of annotations. It's every girl's dream to be loved the way Mr. Darcy loves Elizabeth. I thought Andrew and I had a love like theirs—the kind that consumes every part of your soul—and maybe we did, but obviously, we don't have the same ending.

CHAPTER 40

Andrew

How You Get The Girl - Taylor Swift

My eyes are nearly shutting from driving non-stop for the past five and a half hours. I listened to Kat's playlist she made just for me the entire way, thinking of what to say, and I still came up blank. Not because I don't have the words, there's just too much that I can't hone in on everything. I do have a plan that I think she'll appreciate.

The paper with Emory's address is secured safely on my dash as my phone directs. I thought about giving them a heads up, but I didn't want to entertain the idea that Kat would tell me not to bother.

As I drive, the ocean on my left, all I can think of is Elliot. I remember how he wished he could move here with Emory before they diagnosed him with weeks to live. He wanted to go down to the beach every morning to see the sun rise, just like he did from our garage every morning.

I'm tempted by a sign coming up, OCEAN BEACH spelled out in bold letters. I'm eager to see Kat, but there's something I have to do first.

After paying twenty dollars to park and hiking through the heavy sand, I reach the edge of the waves. The long, concrete pier goes for what seems like miles into the peaceful ocean. There's people around me reading, walking their dogs, laughing and smiling, and here I am, trying to hold back tears as I process that I made it here before Elliot. He would have loved this life, and I wanted it for him.

Therapy helped me cope with his death—as much as I can.

The pain of him being gone will always be there, but I'll see him in every sunset, in every old truck I see, and the brightest star in the sky.

I look up to the clouds and whisper to wherever he is, "Help me out one last time, little brother."

EMORY'S APARTMENT COMPLEX IS BIGGER THAN I EXPECTED. I don't have the code to get in the building, but I guess that works out perfectly for my plan—I'll just have to guess which window is hers.

My fingers struggle to hold the old radio I had to scrounge for in our garage as I lug it over to the grass outside of the apartment windows. I didn't grasp how embarrassing this is going to be if people hear me, but fuck it. Anything for her.

I dial Emory's number and hope she doesn't decline the call. The last time we spoke was when Kat and I were still together. We've known each other since we were kids, but I've been too embarrassed to talk to her lately.

"What's up?" I feel immense relief when I hear her voice, it means I'm one second closer to seeing Kat's face.

"Look out your window," I say before hanging up and pressing play on the giant boombox. I struggle to lift it over my head and wait patiently, nerves traveling through every inch of my body. I don't know how the guy did it with such ease in the movie.

She could never peel her eyes away any time this scene came on in *Say Anything* when Lloyd did this to serenade the girl. I figured it was the perfect time to use that move in real life, and hopefully, she thinks the same, because there is no girl after her. It's her or no one.

I'm starting to lose hope when I don't see any windows open-ing as the music continues to play. Is she listening? Does she still love me? Even if she doesn't, I'll still love her for the rest of my life.

Suddenly, Emory's black hair comes into view as she peeks out of a window at least three stories up.

She leans over and shouts, "Boombox over the head? Smooth move, Cortes."

I take it as a good sign that she approves of the gesture. "It's good to see you too, Diaz," I shout over the music blaring in my ear. It really is nice to see her. Emory was special to me even before she fell in love with Elliot, like the little sister I never had.

"You're family and all, Andrew, but you know I can't let you up here until she says I can."

"I know." I almost give up, but my eyes catch sight of brown hair blowing in the wind behind Emory, her mouth open in shock at the sight of me.

"Andrew, what the hell are you doing?" she shouts.

My neck is killing me from craning to look up at her, but I don't care. "I took some notes from Lloyd to get the girl."

"Andrew…"

I don't like her hesitance, so I interrupt her. If I'm too late, I'll accept that, but she needs to hear this. "I don't care about your past—I just want your future, if you'll have mine too. I fucked up thinking you'd be better off without me, but I underes-timated how lost I am without you."

Before I can continue, she disappears from sight, crushing my soul. Of course this didn't work. It's been four months. At least I can't say I didn't try.

That's when I see her coming out of the building, her hair shining in the sunlight like she's an angel. My chest aches as I look at her wildly beautiful face for the first time in months, soaking in every crevice.

"Hi," she says shyly.

"Hi." My voice cracks from being too consumed with her.

"You drove six hours with a boombox for me?"

"I would have drove even farther if I needed to." I reach to touch her face, and I'm relieved when she lets me feel her warmth. There's so much to say, and I want to make sure she hears it all, just in case it's the last thing I say to her.

"The person I am only with you is the person I wanna be, Kat. I wanna wake up to your face every morning and drink your shitty coffee while I make you breakfast because you burn everything you touch in the kitchen." The sound of her laughter is like finally coming home.

"I can't live without you, not after you made me believe there was a life worth living again. You're my light, Freckles. It's almost impossible to make you as happy as you make me, but I wanna try every day of my life."

Her mascara is smeared from sobbing, but she's still glowing with beauty.

"Can you speak up? I can't hear you guys!" Emory's voice echoes from her window. I finally look up to see that we have an audience of almost everyone in the apartment complex.

"Took you long enough," she cries out before grabbing my neck and pulling me in for a kiss that defeats all other kisses. I never want to touch any other lips ever again.

She's like a reward after all the bad shit I've endured, but I'd do it all over again if it meant I got her.

"Gross, get a room—preferably not one of mine," Emory shouts with disgust as she creepily watches down on us.

"You're stuck with me now," she whispers softly as our foreheads meet.

"That's the plan, Harrison."

CHAPTER 41
Kat

Paper Rings - Taylor Swift

2 YEARS LATER

"Babe, what are we doing?" Andrew's lucky I trust him with my life, because he's guiding me blindfolded in an unknown area.

"You'll see in just a couple more steps."

After two years together, I thought he couldn't surprise me anymore, but I have no idea what's going on. I usually hate surprises, but I have butterflies in my stomach as his protective hand leads me.

When he finally lets me take the blindfold off, I see the baseball field I've brought him to a hundred times. "We come here all the time. You didn't need to blindfold me," I laugh.

He has a cocky grin on his face, like he's up to something. I'm always one step ahead of him, but not this time. He kisses me softly on the forehead and wraps his arm around my waist as we wait for the firework show they do every Friday night to appear.

We used to come every week, but it's been less frequent now that we're both busy with work. I'm a full-time teacher now, and Andrew used money from his trust fund to open a mechanic shop called *Elliot's*. He wanted to honor his brother by fixing cars and not ripping people off, and I think it's perfect.

I'm still in awe by all the colors in the sky, even though I've seen this firework show thousands of times. This show is different, though—the fireworks are spelling out words instead of shapes.

Will you marry me? fills the sky, and my eyes immediately well up. I'm so in shock, I didn't even notice that Andrew got down on one knee.

"You're it for me, Katlyn Rose Harrison. I could be with you forever and it still wouldn't feel long enough, but I'll settle for it. Will you marry me?" He opens up a velvet box to reveal the most beautiful emerald colored diamond I've ever seen. Even if he unveiled a paper ring, my reaction would be the same.

"Yes!" I don't even have to think twice as I shout it loud enough for the world to hear.

Of course I want him forever. I've never felt like I belonged anywhere, but I know my place in this world is wherever he is.

Epilogue
ANDREW

Till Forever Falls Apart - Ashe, Finneas

10 YEARS LATER

"Whose turn is it to open their gift?" My dad, or should I say "Santa", shouts over the hectic atmosphere in my parent's living room.

The kids jump like they're hyped up on sugar as they wait to be handed their gifts. They shredded through the mountain of gifts under the tree this morning and immediately wanted more. Luckily, they're spoiled rotten, so of course there's more.

"Can you open your gift from me and Jacob, Daddy?" Our youngest daughter, Amorina, asks with a mesmerizing smile.

She's three, while our oldest son, Jacob is six. We gave him Elliot's middle name, and he ended up resembling him so much. I can feel him around us on days like this, and I know he's looking down on us with a smile.

"Of course I will." I grab their chaotically wrapped gift from her tiny hands—they must take after me with their gift wrapping skills.

I was expecting to unwrap a school project, but my heart explodes when I unwrap a framed picture of the four of us when we visited Yosemite last year. I'm smiling hard in the picture, because how could I not? I have everything I could ever need.

I gather them both into my arms and squeeze tightly. My life can't get any better than this, but somehow, it does every time I lay eyes on my wife—the girl who saved me in every way, making this life possible. She's even more beautiful today at thirty-five than she was at twenty-three when I met her. I never believed in love at first sight—I still don't, because the love Kat and I have is the kind that was built, and got stronger over time.

She comes to sit on my lap, which I happily accept. "It took them three days to pick out which photo to frame, I think it's perfect," she says, pecking me on the lips.

"I love it. Thank you. Now, go open some presents with your cousi—" I can't even get all the words out before they scurry off with Emory's kids.

Emory married her college sweetheart, Easton, and they have two kids. Daisy is two—she's named after an inside thing between Emory and Elliot. One day, I'll find out what it is. Their youngest, Diego, just turned one.

Chance ended up marrying someone he went to school with in Boston. They have a two-year-old named Mia, who takes after her mom in the looks department, thankfully. Hiro isn't married, but he's working on proposing to his girlfriend, with the plan to have an entire fleet of children someday.

Even though none of the kids are blood related, we've taught them to treat each other like family. My parents love having all the grandkids over; it was their calling to have a house full of children.

Kat and I live in her grandparent's house with Vera, who loves being a Great Grandma. Emory and Easton live five minutes from us, while Chance and Hiro both live two blocks away. We're a close knit, blended family, and it feels right.

"I want another one," Kat whispers in my ear as we admire the kids running around with their new toys.

"My parents still have my old room set up, we could go make a baby right now," I say, grabbing the back of her neck to pull her lips to mine. I've been in love with her for over ten years, and I still can't get enough of her.

"We've got plenty of time to make a baby, Mr. Cortes." She runs her gentle fingers through my hair, admiring me like I'm the only one in the world.

"Forever, Mrs. Cortes." I used to think there was no way I would ever have a life like this, but it was all her. She pulled me out of my darkness as if it wasn't even an obstacle, and together, we've built a home filled with love, laughter, and of course, music.

Long story short—we survived.

I used to think those 80s movies Kat likes so much were all bullshit, but not so much anymore.

Sometimes, the guy really does get the girl in the end.

THE END

Grandma's Secret Recipe

Grandma's Secret Recipe
Persimmon Cookies

Ingredients

1 1/2 Cups Sugar
    1/2 Cup Shortening
    1 Cup Persimmon Pulp
    1 egg
    2 Cups Flour
    1 Teaspoon Baking Soda
    1/2 teaspoon salt
    1/2 teaspoon Cinnamon
    1/2 teaspoon Nutmeg
    1/4 teaspoon Nutmeg
    1/4 teaspoon Clove
    1 Cup Raisins (optional)
    1 Cup Walmuts

Directions

GRANDMA'S SECRET RECIPE

Cream together the sugar and shortening in a large mixing bowl. Add the persimmon pulp and egg. Set aside.

Mix all the dry ingredients together then combine with the persimmon mixture and blend.

Drop them on a cookie sheet in teaspoonfuls. Bake at 375 for 15 minutes or until their golden brown at the top.

Also By Lana Vargas

Summer in Phoenix

Author's Note

This book wouldn't exist if it weren't for you, the readers. Thank you for loving Kat and Andrew enough for me to give them their own happily ever after.

Resources

If you, or anyone you know struggles with addiction, or with a mental health disorder, please call the SAMHSA Hotline at, 1-800-662-4357.

Acknowledgments

I can't believe I'm writing acknowledgments for another book. AHH!

First, thank you to the readers. I never imagined Summer in Phoenix turning out the way it did, and because of you making my lifelong dream come true, I got to write another book.

My family—Dad, Kayla, and Grandma. I wouldn't be able to do this without you guys in my corner. Thank you for being my rock and voice of reason. I love you guys more than words can describe.

Alexa Thomas, my editor. Thank you for taking my story and making it what it is. I can't imagine what this book would be without you.

Silver, at Ever After Cover Design. Thank you for taking what was in my mind for the cover and making it a hundred times better.

Grace Elena, my formatter. You took this book that was already so special to me and made it look beautiful. Thank you, thank you, thank you.

Nicole, I don't know what I would do without you. Thank you for giving me a pep talk anytime I get lost.

Kaley, I'm so glad I have your friendship in my life. Thank you for being my voice when I feel stuck. I love you so so much.

My greatest friends—Janelle, Yoselin, and Bri. Thank you for being supportive of my dreams, always. I love you guys.

My beta readers—this story would not be what it is without

your input and advice. Every single one of you holds a special place in my heart for showing so much love for these characters and their story.

    I can't wait to bring you guys another book. I'll see you then <3

About the Author

Lana Vargas is a Mexican-American Romance author who was raised, and still resides in California. Her debut novel, Summer in Phoenix is a story she thought of at 13 years old, and would later land her in the top 40 on Amazon at 25. She plans to bring more Latinx representation in her future books, and show women that we all deserve great love stories.

TikTok & Instagram - authorlanavargas